I0729280

Elaine MacLeod, the most feared and revered Mistress of Rowan House, is frustrated. Overworked, still hurt and angry over the departure of her long-term lover, she refuses to admit Rowan House needs another Mistress to accommodate their guests. Unconvinced anyone will be able to meet her high standards, Elaine grudgingly agrees to audition the sole applicant, Petra Grendhal.

Robin Broadacre would do anything for the woman who rescued her from certain death at the hands of her previous employers. When she volunteers to assist Petra with her audition, Elaine is forced to reckon with her desire for Robin. Drawn to Petra's fiery strength and icy demeanor as well Robin's devotion, Elaine finds herself torn between her passion for both women. When Petra disappears on a trip to Oslo, Elaine and Robin's search leads them to menaces from Robin's past and a fight for their lives.

Double Six

Rowan House, Book Five

Brenda Murphy

A NineStar Press Publication

Published by NineStar Press
P.O. Box 91792,
Albuquerque, New Mexico, 87199 USA.
www.ninestarpress.com

Double Six

Copyright © 2019 by Brenda Murphy
Cover Art by Natasha Snow Copyright © 2019

This is a work of fiction. Names, characters, places, and incidents are either the product of the author's imagination or are used fictitiously. Any resemblance to actual persons living or dead, business establishments, events, or locales is entirely coincidental.

All rights reserved. No part of this publication may be reproduced in any material form, whether by printing, photocopying, scanning or otherwise without the written permission of the publisher. To request permission and all other inquiries, contact NineStar Press at the physical or web addresses above or at Contact@ninestarpress.com.

Printed in the USA
First Edition
November, 2019

Print ISBN: 978-1-951057-84-8

Also available in eBook, ISBN: 978-1-951057-83-1

Warning: This book contains sexually explicit content, which may only be suitable for mature readers, knife and edge play, kidnapping/abduction, homophobic slurs, and scenes of graphic violence and death. This book is part of a series but can be read as a standalone story.

To C, Always. And Elizabeth, thank you for your patience and guidance over the course of the Rowan House series.

Chapter One

"ARE YOU SURE this is what we need?" Elaine lowered the hairbrush and shifted her gaze to Martha's face, reflected in the dressing table mirror.

Martha quirked her mouth. "We've been over this. Just give her a chance. You can't keep up with our client requests."

Elaine tossed the brush on the top of the dressing table. "Because you and Lucia don't help." She swept her titian hair back and up into a high ponytail.

Martha handed her an elastic. "We're not having this argument again. Lucia and I are finished with that side of the business. We can't keep putting people off or they'll find other houses to visit.

Elaine knotted a hunter-green ribbon in her hair. "Oh please. Like they could find anyone like me. Or what we offer here." She shoved away from the vanity and turned to face her sister. "Fine. We'll see how she handles herself. But the timing sucks."

Martha placed her hands on her sister's shoulders. "We had to work with the dates she gave us. Lucia thinks she'd be a good fit. We've had our trip planned for a long time. We trust you to make a good decision.

Alone. Again. "I'm not worried about making a wrong decision. Who'll sub for her? Benita and Fallon are on holiday. No one else likes heavy pain play."

Martha grinned wickedly at Elaine. "Maybe you could give it a go?"

Elaine rolled her eyes at her sister. "The switch gene is not in me. Go on, go on your holiday. I'll figure it out." *Somehow. Damn, I miss Roxy.*

LUCIA AND MYFANWY stood next to the car, their breath visible as they chatted in the frosty gray morning. Millie loaded the last of their luggage into the trunk and closed the lid gently. Martha placed her hand on Elaine's forearm. "You have our itinerary. We can return if it's an emergency"—she straightened to her full height and squared her shoulders—"but we are not to be disturbed unless it is."

Elaine rolled her eyes at her sister. "Yes, sister dear, goddess forbid I interrupt your honeymoon. Like you haven't already had one. I won't bother you." She let the devil show in her eyes. "I expect you'll be tied up."

Martha settled her fedora on her head. "I'm not going to waste my time replying to that, and please for the love of all that's good, try to get along with Petra. We don't have any other candidates."

"So we should settle?" Elaine placed her hand on her hip.

"No one is saying settle. What I am saying is do not make a snap judgment. Or piss her off so much she leaves."

Elaine shrugged. "If she can't stand the heat..."

"Martha, we need to leave now." Lucia spoke over Elaine, her voice a soft command. "I'm sure Elaine and Petra will sort things."

"See, even your Miss agrees." Elaine smirked at Martha.

Martha smiled at Elaine, not giving her the argument she craved. "Try it some time. You might find you like it."

"Ha. A cold day in hell. Go now or you'll miss the ferry."

Martha gave Elaine a quick hard hug before she hurried down the steps to the car.

THE LIMOUSINE STOPPED squarely at the foot of the walk leading to Rowan House. Elaine stood on the steps, her hands planted on her hips, dressed in a form-fitting pair of tan riding pants, black riding boots, and her favorite thick blue sweater to greet the new arrival. *No use getting dressed up. Don't want to give her the wrong impression.* A stiff wind blew across the porch. Elaine shivered and shoved her hands in her pockets to warm them. She winced when the thick raised scar on the back of her hand scraped on her pocket seam. *Ridiculous time of year for an audition with half the staff on holiday. Catering to her dates. She should have been willing to take whatever dates we set.*

Millie exited the car and opened the rear door. A pair of shapely legs covered in black hose, wearing burgundy Manolo pumps appeared. Elaine blinked. *Good taste in shoes, that's a plus. Must be doing well to afford those. Fantastic legs.* The woman wearing the shoes emerged from the car and pulled her navy-blue wool coat tighter around her body. Her jet-black bob brushed the top of her shoulders and a large pair of sunglasses shielded her eyes. Millie offered her arm and the woman placed her black-gloved hand on her forearm and allowed Millie to escort her to the steps.

"Petra Grendahl, Elaine McLeod." A mischievous grin settled over Millie's face. Elaine stepped down off the porch, her gaze fixed on the new arrival's face.

Petra removed her sunglasses. Her eyes were brown, so dark they appeared black. She met Elaine's direct gaze with one of her own. A smattering of freckles was scattered across the bridge of her nose and wide cheekbones. Her elegant mouth pulled into an insolent smile. *Fuck. I should've reviewed her application. Those eyes. Bewitching. Get it together. She's here for an interview not for playtime. Pity that.*

Petra tilted her head to the side and peeled her glove off slowly before she extended her hand.

Mesmerized by her deliberate motions, Elaine stared at her perfectly manicured hand with blood-red nails. *Say something.*

Elaine thrust her hand out and clasped Petra's hand. "So pleased you're here."

"Really?" She lifted her chin in challenge and squeezed Elaine's hand with a firm grip before releasing it.

Elaine's face burned. "Yes." *Oh hell, does she think she's going to be in charge? Hell no.*

"You seem surprised. You were expecting someone taller maybe? Younger? Whiter?" Her tone was mocking.

Elaine pursed her lips. "No."

Petra crossed her arms over her chest and rocked back on her heels. "If you make an offer, and we come to an agreement, would your clients be annoyed when I walk into their room instead of a white blonde-haired goddess?

Elaine frowned at her. "We're not that kind of establishment. We do not tolerate racists and we would never allow our clients or staff to engage in such appalling behavior. Why would you expect we would?"

"With my name"—Petra uncrossed her arms—"I like to get it out of the way. Saves time." Her expression remained guarded.

Where has she worked that her race has been an issue? Elaine studied Petra's face. Beneath the carefully applied makeup and hard expression she noticed her soul-deep weariness and simmering anger. *Saves time. Not the first time she's had this conversation. There's more there. Later. After she's rested.* "Millie will place your bags in your suite. Would you like tea? Or coffee? Something to eat?"

"Coffee." A gust of wind blew the hem of Petra's coat open and she shivered.

"Forgive me for keeping you in the cold. It's warmer inside." Elaine held Petra's gaze, unable to look away from her dark eyes. She took a step back and opened the door. She held it open and stepped to the side to allow Petra to enter the house. Her pumps clicked loudly on the hardwood floor as she strode into the hallway. She removed her other glove and handed the pair to Elaine. After she shrugged out of her coat she tossed it toward Elaine. *What the hell? I'm not her sub.* She caught the coat in spite of herself.

Elaine straightened her shoulders and dropped the gloves and the coat on the sideboard. "Millie will show you to your room. I'll send someone to attend you."

Petra tilted her head to the side and fixed her gaze on Elaine. "Not you?"

Oh hell no. Time to let her know who is in charge. Elaine stepped closer to Petra, pressing her height advantage. Even in four-inch heels Petra was a head shorter than her, and Elaine used every inch of her six-two frame to make her point. "Perhaps it was unclear from our introduction but I am one of the Mistresses of this house."

Petra's lips pulled into a taunting smile. "Not unclear at all."

A hint of gardenia perfume rose from Petra. The challenge in her eyes stoked Elaine's interest and made her mouth water. Elaine stepped closer and drew in a breath, indulging her need to assert her power. "Whatever decision you have arrived at concerning me, I will not tolerate disrespect."

"Understood." Petra held her ground, their bodies a breath apart, her dark gaze locked onto Elaine's face. "Just know it goes both ways."

Her mouth. Goddess I want to kiss that smirk off her face. Maybe flog it off. Maybe flog then kiss. Trouble. She is so much trouble. Get it together. Interview. She's here for an interview. Don't screw this up. Elaine stepped back. "Wait here. I'll send someone to attend you." She turned her back on Petra and the raging fire of want burning low in her belly.

Chapter Two

"ROBIN, WHERE DID Myfanwy leave the order for the grocer? I've let you run the kitchen without me and now I don't know where anything is." *Too busy with clients.*

Robin handed Elaine the order sheet. "Are you sure you don't want me to go? I'm not afraid."

Elaine tilted her head at Robin. "Not until we know you'll be safe." *Wouldn't want to lose her. Where did that come from? Since when am I so invested?*

Robin bit her lower lip. "Thank you. I would go if I could, Mistress. You shouldn't have to do the shopping. I hate that I can't help you." The dejection in her voice made Elaine's heart squeeze hard.

So sweet. Sub to the core. Why couldn't I be happy with someone like her instead of wasting my time with Roxy? She'd want me to be exclusive, to stop seeing clients. Elaine reached out and cupped Robin's chin before she ran her thumb over her lower lip. "You help me. In other ways you help me. Never doubt that. We couldn't have run the kitchen nearly as well without you. You are an integral part of Rowan House." She pressed a chaste kiss to Robin's cheek and reveled in the way Robin trembled under her touch and the way her eyes shone with Elaine's praise. *Enough. Stop now before she thinks it's more. Before I want more.*

She stepped back and shifted into her bitchiest command tone. "While I'm gone, I want you to pull all of the menus for the last year. Our last round of guests complained the food was 'too predictable,' whatever the hell that means. Everyone is a food critic these days. I want to make some changes and I expect the menus on my desk when I get back. Do not disappoint me."

Robin's hungry expression at being given an assignment and the unspoken threat of punishment should the task not be completed stirred the embers of Elaine's desire. *Maybe I should see if she's open to sceneing again? She's delectable, the perfect morsel. It was so easy with her. What a sublime submissive. No. She'd want more. No clingy subs for me.*

PETRA SAT ACROSS from Elaine in the small dining room set aside for the Mistresses of the house. Elaine leaned back in her chair and studied her. Petra wore a cable-knit sweater set and a black pencil skirt with knee-high boots. After their initial exchange of banal pleasantries, their conversation had dried up. The silence between them stretched out. Not one for idle chatter, and dismissive of individuals compelled to fill every second with words, Elaine observed the way Petra reclined in her chair, secure in her power, comfortable with the silence between them as she continued to eat without distress.

A good sign in a Domme. She knows who she is. Elaine folded her napkin before she placed it next to her plate. "I trust Tessa was acceptable this afternoon?"

Petra raised her wineglass, swirled the contents, and took a sip of the deep red wine. She placed the wineglass precisely on the tablecloth and pursed her lips before she answered. "Adequate."

"Was there something you wanted she wasn't able to provide?" Elaine sat forward in her seat.

"She was, as I expected, and as I said, adequate. I didn't expect any different."

Oh fuck that, dissing our subs? "Adequate"—what the hell does she mean? "If there was a problem you need to tell me specifically what it was so I can address it." Elaine glared at Petra. "Our subs are selected for their skills, pledged to the house, and expected to meet our standards at all times."

"Don't worry. I addressed it."

"What?" Elaine leaned forward. "You are not in charge here." She rapped her knuckles on the table. "You are a job candidate and not to 'address' anything with any of the subs unless it is cleared through me."

Petra glanced at the door leading from the dining room. "When is the official tour of the house?"

Elaine placed both hands flat on the table. *Ignoring me? Oh hell no.* "Did you hear what I said?"

"Oh, I heard. I chose not to respond." Petra smiled at Elaine, a predatory smile, and her eyes gleamed. "If I am auditioning for a place here wouldn't you want to know I'm capable and willing to address anything less than perfect in a submissive's behavior? Why else did you send me a submissive with an attitude that needed adjusting? Although from the expression on her face when she left my room, I think she quite enjoyed the tune-up."

Petra's raging self-confidence and direct defiance enraged and roused Elaine. *What would it be like to break her? To have her under me? Her mouth. To make her beg me. No. Focus. She's testing you. Let it go.*

"As soon as you've finished your lunch I'll show you the house." Elaine knotted her fingers together under the table.

Petra dabbed at her mouth with her napkin. "I'm finished. Lead on."

PETRA'S FLAT EXPRESSION remained firmly in place as they toured Rowan House's playrooms. Their last stop was the dungeon. Elaine opened the door and turned on the lights before leading the way into the cavernous space.

"Mmm." A wolfish grin spread across Petra's face. "How marvelous. This stonework is fantastic. It is a real dungeon. The idea alone makes me wet."

Elaine blinked rapidly to clear the images flooding her mind. Petra at her feet, wet and willing. Petra's eyes gleamed as she walked around the room. Her smile widened as she surveyed the polished rows of bondage equipment and various discipline devices.

Elaine mounted the dais and sat in the midnight-blue velvet-covered chair. Enjoying the feeling of her position of power, she studied Petra as she examined the pieces of equipment.

Petra stopped in front of Elaine's second favorite device and turned to her. "Good lord, you have a rack?"

The impressed sound of her voice sent a tingle of pleasure through Elaine. "It's a simulated one. It provides the sensation and headspace for subs without the risk of dislocating joints."

Elaine noted the way Petra gave the brazier with its branding irons a wide berth. *Not for her. Interesting. Wonder what that's about?*

Petra trailed her fingers over the stocks set into the floor. She paused beside the newest addition to the dungeon. A large polished wine cask mounted on its side, it was adorned with cuffs and chains to secure submissives over its wide curved surface. She drummed her fingers on the cask. "Victor's Vineyard. I know this winery. I had no idea they offered anything besides wine."

"They don't. It's a gift from a former client and her submissives. They commissioned it." Elaine shifted in her chair and crossed her legs.

"She must have been very grateful." Petra stopped next to an iron and wooden device resting against the wall. She side-eyed the antique torture cabinet. "An iron maiden?" Petra rested her hand on her hip and quirked her mouth at Elaine. "Really?"

"Just for the head fuck aspect. It's not functional. I've considered having it modified so I could use it for seclusion. But my sister insists it would destroy its value as an antique. Pity."

Petra sauntered to the polished wood whipping post and drew her fingers over the top of the post. "This is fantastic." She eyed the collection of various single tail whips hung on pegs on the long wall. As she walked along the rack, she tipped her fingers over the assortment of coach whips, dressage whips, camel whips, hunting whips, and quirts before she stopped and perused Elaine's personal collection of signal whips, bullwhips, and snake whips. She reached toward a black and red braided bullwhip. Stopping before she touched it, she turned to Elaine. "May I?"

The eagerness in her voice tickled Elaine's ears and she lifted her hand and waved it, giving her permission. *So excited. Fascinating. Wonder if she'll split her lip?* She'd witnessed more than one Mistress miscalculate their skill with a single tail. She lifted her hand to her mouth to hide her smirk.

Petra lifted the whip from its peg. She turned to face the whipping post set in the patterned stone floor. She shook out the whip and flipped her wrist forward, snaking the twisted strips of black and red leather along the floor to gauge the distance to the post. She took a few steps forward to adjust her stance. She extended the whip behind her and brought it forward with a graceful snap of her arm and wrist. The crack of the popper against the narrow post made Elaine's nipples hard. Petra had placed it precisely, no wrap around, the braided cracker landing exactly on top of the post. The whip arced through the air again. Elaine pressed her legs together to stem the flow of want that surged with the snap of the whip. *Fuck. She's good. Damn it. Who can I get in here for her to show me more? Robin? No, she'd never agree. None of the others like pain as much. Roxy would've loved it.* The ache in her heart, the one she had been able to ignore, returned full force. She gripped the arms of the chair, her knuckles white, the scar on her hand painfully tight. *Why did I tell her she could use the whip? Fuck me. I hate this, hate feeling like this. Focus. Focus on the now. It's over. Roxy's not coming back. Let it go.*

Petra turned to her, eyes bright. "This is utterly delightful. I haven't worked many places I could use a bullwhip. It's my favorite implement."

"Mine as well," Elaine rasped. At Petra's raised eyebrow she cleared her throat. "We don't have many clients who ask for it, but I've found most submissives can be persuaded it's worth the pain for the reward."

"Indeed." Petra turned and flicked the whip toward the post again. The crack reverberated off the stone walls and echoed off the vaulted ceiling.

Elaine swallowed hard and stood abruptly. "Let me show you the pit." She stepped off the dais, willing her legs to be steady as she made her way to the control panel. She pressed the buttons to open the pit and turned the lights on.

Petra gathered the whip and coiled it in her hand. She walked over to the opening in the floor and peered into it. "Lucia neglected to mention this. How spectacular."

Elaine frowned. "Lucia had an unfortunate experience with the pit."

Fear flashed in Petra's eyes before she backed away from the edge of the pit. "She hates small places. As do I."

She knows of Lucia's past. Was she trafficked? Is that how they know each other? Elaine tapped the screen in front of her. "It's wired for communication. After Lucia's experience, we installed emergency buttons to alert all the house phones as a safety, including a hidden one known only to house staff to end a scene and summon assistance."

Petra nodded. "A wise addition." She gestured around the room. "I'm impressed. This is special. I know of no other house possessing such a room."

Elaine preened, basking in her approval. *What the hell? Why do I care she's impressed. Why does it matter? Who cares what she thinks? I do. Damn it.*

"We have an outdoor play area as well, but it's too cold to view properly now. Is there anything else you'd like to see?"

"Not at the moment." Petra raked her gaze over Elaine's body. "Unless there's something else you'd like to show me." A soft smile played about her lips.

Elaine stared at her mouth, drawn to the taunting expression on her face and the suggestive tone of her voice. Her body, still wound up from watching Petra work with the single tail, responded with peaked nipples, and a flush of heat burned through her. She swallowed her desire. *No. She's here to apply for a job. Stop. Don't give in. Why aren't Lucia and Martha here? They should be handling this. Her energy. Like a slow moving river. I want to make her lose control, bask in her submission.* "No. No, we've covered all of the public play spaces." Elaine stepped back and away from Petra.

"Are there private play areas?" Petra took a step forward. "Where do you play?" Her smoky gaze locked onto Elaine's face.

Elaine moved back another step, and her back bumped into the door. She lifted her chin as she reached behind her for the handle and clasped it. *Stay in control. Get it together.* She lifted an eyebrow at Petra. "Anywhere I want to." She turned the knob to open the door, turned, and walked away. Elaine lifted her arm, indicating Petra should follow, not bothering to check to see if she did. "Let me show you the other areas we have for guests and staff.

ELAINE SIPPED HER tea and watched Robin as she worked the raisins, soaked in orange liquor, into the mound of dough on the pastry bench. "I adore Myfanwy's orange rye raisin bread. Thank you, Robin."

A bright red blush spread over Robin's neck, starting from her delicate collarbones before moving up to her hairline, enchanting Elaine. The delicate scent of orange rose from the warm dough, and Elaine's mouth watered.

The kitchen, normally bustling with activity and other staff, was quiet. *How long has it been since I sat like this? How long since I abdicated my role as cook? A year? Two. Myfanwy and Robin have done well. I've missed this. Missed her.* She sipped her tea and sorted through her memories of afternoons spent working hip to shoulder with Robin to create sumptuous meals. Robin possessed an uncanny ability with herbs and spices, able to add the perfect ingredients to change a good dish into the divine. Elaine shifted in her chair and stretched her legs as she indulged herself with more salacious memories. Images of Robin's blonde curls wrapped in her hands as her talented mouth worked magic between Elaine's thighs made her press her legs together against the wet ache there.

"You're welcome, Mistress." Robin finished shaping the dough and placed it into the form for the second rise. She covered it with a towel before putting it in the proofing cabinet. She wiped her hands on her side towel. "More tea, Mistress?"

"No, thank you. What do you think of Petra?" Elaine studied Robin's reaction to her question.

"Mistress Petra is"—Robin busied herself tidying up her workstation, using the dough scraper to clean the surface—"she's dangerously beautiful, she scares me."

"In a good way?" Elaine watched Robin's hands as she worked, noting the slight tremble, the way her movements quickened and her blush deepened. "Does she scare you as much as I do? Or used to?" *When you wanted to be mine?*

Robin peered into Elaine's eyes, her expression wary. "I haven't been afraid of you for a long time, Mistress, and even when I feared you, I always trusted you. I don't know Mistress Petra."

Elaine raised her eyebrow. *Not afraid of me. Not anymore. Maybe that's a good thing?* "I'm happy you trust me, Robin. Would you like to know Mistress Petra better? I've seen the way you look at her."

Robin dropped her gaze. "I'm sorry, Mistress, if I was inappropriate." Her voice trembled. "It's hard not to."

Elaine drummed her fingers on the table. "It's been a long time for you, hasn't it? Since you've been with anyone? Do you miss it?" *Miss me?*

Robin turned away and turned the taps on, and water splashed into the sink. "I keep busy, Mistress."

Elaine stood and walked to Robin. She reached around her and turned the taps off. Robin stilled, her hands resting on the sink. "That is not an answer. Eyes to me." She clasped Robin's shoulders and turned her to face her.

Robin lifted her chin, eyes wide. Her breathing quickened and she trembled in Elaine's grip. "I do miss it, Mistress. But I don't want..." She lowered her chin to her chest and pressed her mouth in a thin line.

Elaine gripped Robin's chin, forcing her to meet her gaze. "What is it you don't want? You can speak freely, Robin."

"I don't want to go back to working with clients. I like my work in the kitchen."

Fear. She's afraid I'll ask her to accept clients again. And she'd do it to please me. So much fear. "I would never ask you to do that. No clients ever, unless you ask me to go back to working with guests. It is our agreement. And my promise." She released Robin's chin but did not back up.

"Oh, I wasn't suggesting—forgive me, Mistress. I know I can trust you. But if you wanted, or needed me to..."

"Needed what?" Elaine studied Robin's face, the way her eyes glittered.

"If you needed someone to work with Mistress Petra, I would." Robin's gaze burned as she met Elaine's. "I'd do it. Tessa hates heavy pain."

"You would?" Elaine clasped Robin's shoulders and rubbed her thumbs over the top of her arms. Robin's hands were knotted together in front of her waist. "Why?"

Robin's voice was steady, her expression resolute, and a rueful smile crossed her face. "Pain is not an issue for me. And I'd do anything to help you. Anything you asked of me."

Elaine's mind stuttered over Robin's confession. "I wouldn't ask, Robin. It would go against our agreement."

"Then I volunteer, if you agree. I'll take Tessa's place." Robin's voice was steady, a breathy edge to her voice. She shifted her gaze down and away from Elaine's face.

"And why would you do it? Truth this time." Elaine brushed the back of her knuckles over Robin's cheek. "For Tessa?" Elaine stifled the jealous flame sparking low in her chest.

Robin turned her face to Elaine like a drowning woman seeking the shore. "For you, Mistress. To pay you back."

Not because she cares. Because she feels like she owes me. It's not for me. Not for me. She sees it as a debt to be paid. "You don't owe me anything, Robin. We've been over this. Tell me why you want to do this." Elaine cupped Robin's cheek.

"Because it's something I can give you. A way to help you. Please let me." She trembled under Elaine's hand and closed her eyes before she lowered her chin to her chest. "Will you be there, Mistress? To watch?"

Robin's submission, the desperate desire in her voice to give Elaine everything, to surrender herself to another Mistress's control sent a fierce wave of want rolling through Elaine. *So brave. Kiss her. Strip her, take her, right here, right now, make her scream with pleasure. Take everything she wants to give. No. She wants to pay me back. Feels obligated. Don't confuse indebtedness with caring.*

"I would observe. It's part of the audition." Elaine released her grip.

Robin shivered. She sank to her knees and spread them wide, her short black skirt pulled taut. Back straight, she rested her hands on her thighs palms up in the required submissive position of the house. "I volunteer Mistress. Please, please let me take Tessa's place."

Elaine reached out to rest her palm on the top of Robin's head. *Say no. Take her to your rooms. Take her. Make her yours. No. She'd say yes because she thinks she owes you something. Not because she cares. And she'd want more. More than I can give.* The touch of Robin's forehead on the toe of her shoe ended Elaine's woolgathering. *Say yes. Give her what she wants.* "You may take her place. Finish out the day in the kitchen. Tessa will take your place here tomorrow, assisting me. You will attend Mistress Petra until such time as your services are no longer required. Eyes to me."

Robin sat back on her heels, lifted her head, and met Elaine's gaze.

"If at any time you want to return to your duties in the kitchen, you will let me know immediately." Elaine lifted her chin. "I want your word on it."

Robin bowed her head. "I promise, Mistress. Thank you, Mistress."

Elaine swept from the room. She waited until the kitchen door swung shut behind her to curse herself under her breath. *Why the hell did I say yes? Because she asked. Because I hate to tell her no. Because I want to watch them together. Because I'm an idiot.*

Chapter Three

ELAINE ROLLED OPEN the door to the indoor ring and flipped the light switches on. The overhead lights hummed to life. She tugged some cavalettis into a figure eight pattern. Satisfied with her arrangement, she walked back to the barn with her hands deep in her coat pockets against the cold. She shoved the wide barn door open enough to enter and waited until her eyes adjusted to the dim light.

Most of the horses dozed, but a few lifted their heads as she walked by. She stopped in front of Luna's stall door. She picked up the lead shank before she rolled the stall door open and stepped inside. Luna's ears flicked forward and she snorted, nuzzling Elaine's hand roughly. "Easy, girl. Let's go get some exercise." She clipped the lead line to her halter and left the bulk of it curled in her hand as she led Luna out of the door and along the covered walkway leading to the indoor ring.

Once inside, she clipped the mesh gate in place and rolled the door closed, shutting out the cold. After entering the ring, she unclipped the lead and clucked to Luna. "Let's go, girl." Luna lifted her head once and walked away from Elaine. When the horse was clear, she closed the gate.

She let the horse wander around the ring for a few minutes before she clapped her hands to draw her attention. "Luna!"

Luna raised her head and flicked her ears forward before she trotted in Elaine's direction. When she was a few feet away, Elaine held up both hands at chest level, palms out. "Stop." Luna took two steps closer and then stopped. "Good girl." Luna turned her head to the side to look at Elaine and snorted once.

"Go! Play." Elaine moved her hands in a pushing motion away from herself and spread her arms wide. Luna turned her body away from Elaine, took a few steps, picked up her pace to trot, and then broke into a gallop. She charged around the ring in a wide circle, bucking occasionally. Elaine smiled to herself as she watched her mare enjoy her time. Luna's mane fluttered as she passed by Elaine. The muscles in her lean body bunched and flexed as she ran.

What if I just did this? Filled my days with the kitchen and Luna. No worries about clients. No worries about appearances. Would it be so bad? I could make do with one of the subs, maybe Benita or Tessa. Make do. What is wrong with me? Finest subs in the world and I'm not satisfied. Because they're not Roxy. Robin. So delectable. So complicated. Does she care for me? Or is it Stockholm syndrome?

She jogged to the center of the ring. "Luna! Come!" The mare ignored her command and continued trotting as she circled the ring. Elaine lifted her fingers to her mouth and whistled sharply. "Luna! Come!" Luna slowed and turned toward Elaine. She trotted over and stopped a few steps away from Elaine. Elaine stood still. Luna walked forward slowly until she was close. She extended her neck and rubbed her head against the front of Elaine's coat, nearly knocking her off balance. Elaine pressed on Luna's chest to move her back a step, and then rubbed her neck and behind her ears. "Good girl."

"Impressive." Petra's voice from behind her made Elaine start.

Luna wheeled in Petra's direction, placing her body between Elaine and Petra, ears back flat against her head. She pawed at the ring flooring, extended her neck, and bared her teeth.

"Luna. No." Elaine took a quick step, caught Luna's halter, and hauled her back. "Easy, girl." Luna stilled with Elaine's sharp command.

Petra backed away. "Sorry. I didn't mean to frighten you."

Elaine rested her hand on Luna's shoulder. "I'm fine, but don't ever sneak up on a horse, particularly this one."

Petra eyed the white mare. "I haven't much experience with horses. I've not had the opportunity. I apologize."

"I can't speak for Luna, but I accept. It's too cold today, or I'd ask if you wanted to go for a ride." Elaine filled her voice with innuendo, watching Petra's face for her reaction.

Petra raised an eyebrow. "And when the weather clears? What if I did?"

Elaine met her gaze. "Do you?" She was fully aware and pressing the subtext of their conversation.

"Does that work?"

Elaine frowned. "Does what work?"

"Asking? I was under the impression you were a woman of action, not much for talking." Petra rested a hand on her hip. A ghost of a smile played about her lips.

What the hell? Flirting? Or not? Is she into rape play? Elaine pressed her lips together in a thin line. "Consent is not up for debate here. And it's strictly enforced."

"Has it always been?" Petra met Elaine's hard glare with a cool expression.

"We may have allowed play without safe words in the past, but play without consent has never been allowed. No matter what gossip you've heard." Stung by Petra's accusation, she considered releasing Luna just to watch Petra's reaction. "Do you think I'm a rapist?"

Petra pursed her lips. "My apologies. I didn't mean to imply anything."

Elaine lifted her chin. "Didn't you? Why say it? Trying to unsettle me? See if I'm as much a hothead as my reputation? What are you trying to accomplish here? Make me mad enough I want to fuck you whether you wanted me to or not? I don't play that way." Her stomach roiled. *What did she hear to think I disregard consent?* "What do you want?" Elaine stroked Luna's neck. "You didn't just wander in here."

Petra clasped her hands in front of her, and her expression morphed into one of stone. "I wanted to ask if you would like to discuss the particulars of my audition. A moot point now. Sorry I disturbed you." She turned and stalked away from Elaine. When she arrived at the door she turned to face Elaine across the ring and stared at her a moment before she turned away and pushed out the door.

A gust of icy wind blew through the door as she left. Elaine cursed softly under her breath. *Fuck. I did exactly what I promised I wouldn't do. Damn it. How to fix this? Fuck me, Martha's going to kill me.* She walked Luna over to the post where the lead shank was draped and clipped it to her harness. Her thoughts tumbled in her head like a line of dominos. *What the hell am I going to do to fix this? Talk to her. I can't believe she thinks we'd allow non-consensual play.*

Elaine walked Luna around the ring to cool her down before she took her back to the barn. She replayed their conversation and how it had gone sideways. *Maybe she didn't mean anything? Maybe I misread her. Maybe. What if she does want to play? Would it be okay? Ethical? Right? I'm not part of the package. How would it work? A Domme but pledged to the house? What would Martha and Lucia say? Damn it, why did they leave me alone with this? Veronica. She's sensible.*

Chapter Four

ELAINE FLICKED THE brush over Luna's shoulder. A puff of hair and dirt she had loosened with the curry comb floated through the air. "They're going to be so disappointed. Fuck." She moved along Luna's body, brushing her back and rump. "What the hell, Luna? One conversation and I blow this whole thing up." Luna shuffled in the cross-ties, and Elaine dropped the brush in the grooming box. She picked up the soft finishing brush and moved to Luna's head. "What am I going to do?"

"The first thing you might want to do is to stop asking your horse for advice and talk to a person." Veronica yelled from the office.

"Oh, if only there was someone around to shower me with their wisdom."

On cue, Veronica strode into view.

Elaine rolled her eyes. "Where were you? And how long have you been eavesdropping?"

"Having coffee with Millie. And long enough to know you fucked up with Petra."

Elaine rolled her eyes. "I did not 'fuck up.' She's too sensitive. I mean really, what kind of Domme is she if she gets her feelings bent so easily?"

"A Domme trying to find a place she'll be accepted as a person, and not as an exotic caricature, or Asian stereotype. She's searching for some place or someone real." Veronica crossed her arms across her chest. "And if you don't stop glaring at me you're going to sprain something. Not my fault if truth hurts."

"I liked it better when you were afraid of me."

Veronica guffawed. "You must be high. I've never been afraid of you. Millie said to tell you…"

Elaine tuned out the rest of Veronica's words as she methodically brushed Luna. *That's the problem. I want people to be afraid. Easier than feeling the feels. I felt for Roxy, and where did that get me? No. Never again. Not going there again. I can't. I can't do that again.*

"Earth to Elaine." Veronica touched Elaine's shoulder. "Did you hear what I said?"

"About me being high? Yes."

"No, the rest of it. Petra asked Millie to make arrangements for her to leave."

"What? She can't. Oh, hell." Elaine shoved the brush toward Veronica. "Take this. Why didn't you tell me?"

She pushed past Veronica and ran from the barn.

ELAINE SMOOTHED HER hair down with both hands and blew out a breath before she raised her hand to knock on Petra's door. She hesitated and lowered it. *Damn it. What the hell am I going to say? I hate this. Why the hell couldn't Martha and Lucia handle this? Fuck. Be nice. Say you're sorry. You can do this. Talk her into staying.*

Elaine knocked on the door.

Petra opened the door. "Yes? Oh, it's you." She turned her back on Elaine and left her standing in the hall. She turned away and walked back over to the desk. Dominos were scattered over the surface. Petra picked one up and placed it in an ornate wooden chest.

Elaine started forward. She stopped at the threshold. "May I come in?"

"Can I stop you?" Petra's voice was sharp, her tone ice. She tucked another domino into the teak box.

"Yes. I came to talk, but if you don't want to, it's your choice. Millie told me you plan to leave. Would you reconsider?"

A weighted silence stretched between them. Petra kept her back to Elaine, her shoulders rigid under her black satin dressing gown. She continued to pack the dominos into their case.

"I see. I'll tell Millie to proceed with the arrangements." Elaine clasped the frame of the door.

Petra turned to her. "Why? Why ask me to stay? You don't want me here. You've gone out of your way to indicate how much you don't think I belong here." She strode across the room and into Elaine's space. She jutted her chin. "Are you so insecure you need to be the only Domme in this house? So afraid my presence somehow diminishes yours?"

"No. And I'm sorry if you think I've behaved badly."

"If I 'think you've behaved badly?' What kind of half-assed apology is that?"

"The only one you're going to get. I can't do any more." Elaine gripped the doorframe, her knuckles white.

"Really?" Petra's smirk was back, and she closed the distance between them. "But you want to, don't you? And that's the rub. I've noticed how you watch me. Have I misread your signals? Have I imagined you might have an interest in me beyond being a potential employer?" She reached up, stretched out her hand, and dared to trail a finger over Elaine's lips. "You want me. Don't you?"

Elaine jerked her head back and away from Petra's touch, cursing her body as her nipples hardened with Petra's taunt. She lowered her hands and shoved them in her pockets to keep from grabbing Petra's shoulders and showing her exactly what she wanted to do to her. *Not without permission. Not without consent.* "If you're still interested in the position, I'll have Millie cancel your reservations." She hardened her voice. "However, I'm not part of your audition. I'll be there to observe. Not participate."

"Pity." Petra took another step toward her.

Elaine held her ground.

Petra leaned in, and her mouth pulled into a sly smile. "I'd like to see if your reputation is deserved."

"What?" Elaine failed to keep the surprise out of her voice as evidenced by Petra's arched eyebrow.

"Is it so hard for you to accept? That another Domme might want to play with you? Do you only play with subs?"

Heat rose in Elaine's face. "I play with anyone I choose to play with if they want to play with me, as long as they follow my rules. I don't sub for anyone."

Petra pressed her body against Elaine. "And what are your rules?" Her nipples were stiff, the hard tips tenting the fabric of her satin gown. "Specifically?"

Elaine's body betrayed her. Being so close to Petra hardened her clit and desire soaked her briefs. *She's testing me. Not this way. Not goaded into it. Make her wait. Remember who is in charge here.* She brought her hand up and placed it squarely between Petra's breasts, enjoying how her breath quickened when she flicked her thumb over Petra's nipple. "First, no touching without permission. Second, I'm in charge. Third, I'm in charge." She pushed Petra away and smiled at the moue of disappointment that crossed her features before a flash of anger colored her cheeks. "My rules. My time. My way." *Angry. And thirsty. Mmm. What would it be like making her submit?*

Petra rested her hands on her hips. "And what happens if someone doesn't play by your rules?"

"Stick around and find out." Elaine stepped back into the hall away from Petra and her too tempting body. "Shall I cancel those reservations? So we can discuss this more?" She did nothing to hide her amusement at Petra's frustration over being denied.

"Do so." Petra closed the door in Elaine's face with a sharp click.

IT HAD STARTED as a small flare of jealousy during breakfast. A lingering glance, an unnecessary touch on Petra's part, and then a full-on smile bestowed by Robin, and Elaine's mood had rapidly gone south. She watched the dance of interest between Robin and Petra, and her stomach churned. They chatted quietly. Petra's fingers manacled Robin's wrist, a claim, a statement, and it was all too much for Elaine this morning.

"Robin." Elaine tapped her finger on the table.

Robin tilted her head to the side and frowned. "Yes, Mistress?"

"I understand you're anxious to begin your service to Mistress Petra, but I need you to assist Tessa with breakfast cleanup."

Petra's fingers remained wrapped around Robin's wrist. "I had planned to spend some time talking with Robin this morning. Isn't there someone else who can help Tessa?"

Elaine fixed her glare on Petra's hand. "If you want to discuss this, release Robin, and we will discuss it. There is no one else at the moment."

Robin stood there, trapped between Petra's grasp and Elaine's glare, the fine tremor of her free hand the only signal of her distress. Petra pursed her lips and released her. Robin lowered her head and fled the dining room.

Elaine leaned back in her chair. "I'll arrange for her to spend time with you after lunch. Unless you have other pressing business?"

Petra met Elaine's gaze and tilted her head. "I don't know. Do I?" Her throaty voice slid under Elaine's skin.

Elaine dabbed her mouth with her napkin. "Perhaps."

Petra sipped her coffee and replaced the cup. She held Elaine's gaze as she placed both hands on the table, palms up. "I am at your disposal."

If she had kneeled in front of Elaine, it could not have been a clearer signal. *How would it be? To sample her? To see what she's made of? She's not a switch; I don't feel that from her. What is she seeking? What does she want? Besides me?*

Elaine rose from her seat and walked to the end of the table. She stopped next to Petra. With one finger she traced the lines of her palm. "So fearless. So earnest. Are you asking to play with me?"

Petra stared at Elaine. "Yes."

Elaine traced her fingers over Petra's cheek. "Why?"

"Why?" Petra frowned. "Why does anyone want to play with anyone else? Can't you feel it? Feel the energy between us?"

Elaine rubbed her thumb over Petra's lower lip and gripped her chin hard, Petra's skin blanching pleasantly under her fingers. "Oh, yes. I feel it. The question is, what do you want to do about it? Ready to play a double six?"

Petra raised her eyebrow. "What?"

"I noticed your domino set when we had our discussion about your wanting to leave. To start the game you have to have a double six tile." Elaine lifted Petra's hand to her mouth and kissed the back of her knuckles.

Petra shifted in her seat, a lazy smile on her face as she relaxed in Elaine's grip. "Such a player. You are aware"—she rested her pump on top of Elaine's boot—"that when you lay a double six down, you can play from either end."

"You know what I like, you've obviously talked to people." Elaine hardened her gaze. "Don't expect mercy."

"I don't want it." Petra licked the end of Elaine's thumb and sucked it deeply into her mouth. She raked her teeth over the sensitive scar tissue at the base of her thumb. Elaine groaned at the sensation. She pulled her thumb from Petra's mouth, leaned down, and braced both arms on either side of her chair. "Strip. Now."

"Here?" Petra waved her hand to indicate the dining room, a fine tremor in her voice.

The dining room was open to the rest of the house. Whatever occurred would be visible to anyone who walked by. Elaine closed her eyes and inhaled the enticing scent of fear and uncertainty laced with desire rising from Petra's skin. She nuzzled her neck before she gave her the edge of her teeth. A faint groan reached her ears and she licked a line from Petra's jaw to below her ear.

Elaine straightened and arched an eyebrow. "Was there some part of strip you did not understand? Or is this too much?"

"No, Mistress."

"No."

Petra started at Elaine's sharp tone.

"No. I'm not your Mistress, you are not pledged to me, or this house." *Not yet. Maybe not ever.* "You may call me Ma'am."

"Yes, Ma'am." Petra pressed her mouth together in a thin line, and her brow drew down. She stood and shoved her chair back. Elaine crossed her arms over her chest. Petra's fingers flew over the buttons of her shirt. She peeled it off and dropped it to the floor with a Domme's indifference. Her gaze fixed on Elaine's face, she unzipped her skirt, let it fall to the floor, and stepped out of it. She leaned forward, unfastened her bra, and shimmied her breasts free before she added it to the pile of clothes. A lacy red thong was her only remaining garment, a dark stain on the strip of fabric between her legs evidence of her desire.

She turned from Elaine and bent at the waist. Petra unbuckled her ankle-strap pumps and removed them. With one smooth move she hooked her thumbs into the waistband of her thong and drew it down her legs, giving Elaine a view of the slick between her legs.

Once she was naked, she turned back and stood with her hands behind her back, clasping her forearms. Head high, chin raised, she met Elaine's gaze. Her breasts were large, topped with light-brown nipples, larger than Elaine had imagined. Her waist was narrow and her hips wide, her thighs thick and muscular. A sparse thatch of dark hair between her thighs glistened in the light of the dining room. Elaine stepped close to her and gripped her chin, smiling as the skin blanched beneath her touch. She pinched one of her nipples hard. Petra's eyes were dark, her pupils blown wide. "Safe word?"

"Red to stop, yellow to slow down." A shiver shook Petra as she trembled in Elaine's grip.

"Red to stop, yellow to slow down," Elaine repeated before she released Petra and pointed to the table. "Bend over, hands flat on the table."

Petra complied, and Elaine stepped forward and placed her hand in the middle of Petra's back. She traced her fingertips between Petra's thighs and collected the liquid silk on her fingers. Petra trembled under her touch. "You like this. Exposing yourself to me. Teasing me." Elaine swept her fingers over Petra's swollen clit. She pinched it, jacked it quickly, and Petra cried out. She shuddered and a surge of wetness flowed from her over Elaine's hand.

"Coming without permission." Elaine tsk-tsked loudly. "Now, I'll have to punish you."

"Lucky me," Petra drawled.

Pushback. Delicious. Missed this. So much. Time to make a believer out of her.

Elaine wrapped her hand in Petra's black silky hair and yanked her head up. She brought her lips close to her ear and traced the edge of the delicate shell with the tip of her tongue. Petra shivered beneath her. "We'll see if you feel that way afterwards." She released her hair, drew her hand away, and slapped Petra's ass, leaving a dull red mark on her skin. "Down."

Petra lowered herself to her knees, head high. Her eyes glittered, her expression somewhere between love and hate, and Elaine was more than ready to find out which.

Elaine sat in her chair. "Come here." Petra rose and came forward. Elaine met her gaze. "Over my knees."

Petra tossed her head and shook her hair back before she draped herself over Elaine's lap. Elaine sighed at the press of Petra's body against her thighs. She fondled the curves of Petra's generous ass. "Ready?"

"Yes. Mistress."

Elaine pinched Petra's ass sharply.

Petra squirmed over her lap. "Yow. What was that for?"

"I'm not your Mistress." She pinched Petra again. "Understand?"

"Yes. Ma'am." She wiggled her ass. "Whatever you say, Ma'am."

Petra's sassy tone made Elaine pause a moment to savor her bratty behavior before she drew her hand back and brought it down in a sweeping arc, lifting the weight of Petra's ass cheek as she struck. Petra whimpered under her, and Elaine throbbed between her legs. "Count for me."

"Yes, Ma'am." Petra's voice was thick.

Elaine swatted her again.

"One, Ma'am."

Elaine smoothed her hand over the heated skin of Petra's ass before she spanked her again.

"Two, Ma'am."

The quaver in her voice and the tension in her body signaled her uncertainty. Elaine bent and kissed the handprints on Petra's ass, soothing them with her tongue. "Not used to being on this end of things, are you?" she murmured against her hot skin.

"No, Ma'am."

Elaine massaged her ass. "Two more. Ready?"

"Yes, Ma'am."

Elaine delivered two more blows in quick succession, lighter than the first two. Petra's voice was thready as she counted. Elaine rubbed her fingers over her reddened ass. "Not going to come again without permission, are you?"

"No, Ma'am." A sob escaped from Petra before she mumbled her words, and she clutched Elaine's leg with her hands and rubbed her face over the calf of her knee-high boots. "Thank you, Ma'am."

Tears already? Relief? Or is it more? "Clear the rest of the table, place the dishes on the sideboard. Then lie there. Face up. Legs spread, hands over your head, and wait for me."

Petra rose and kept her eyes averted as she set about clearing the table.

Chapter Five

ELAINE ENTERED THE kitchen and pulled her keys from her skirt pocket. She flipped through them until she found the small brass key marked with red nail polish. The lock to the drawer was sticky and stiff. After she unlocked the drawer she rooted through it until she located the purple cloth bag of sex toys she kept hidden there. She tucked the bag under her arm and relocked the drawer while she ignored Robin and Tessa's curious expressions. With a silent wave, she left them working at the sink.

PETRA LAY ON the table, eyes closed, with her hands over her head. Her chest rose and fell with her breathing. Elaine stood off to the side of the table and reveled in the sight of Petra stretched out before her. *Someone new to explore. This. Tabula rasa. I could not give up this. The new. The challenge.* She pulled out a chair and placed her bag on it before she slipped her briefs off and laid them over the back of the chair. Her excitement slicked her thighs and she gave her clit a soothing stroke as she contemplated Petra's stunning physique. "Eyes to me."

Petra turned her head and met Elaine's gaze.

"What are your hard limits?"

"No scat, no watersports, no race play, no anal penetration, Ma'am."

"No other limits?" Elaine's body tingled at the prospect of the blank canvas before her.

"None, Ma'am."

She tilted her head to study Petra's face, keying into the physical signs of her submission. "Is your ass sore?'

"Yes, Ma'am."

"Remember your pleasure is mine to command at this moment."

"Yes, Ma'am."

She plays the sub well. Maybe she's not playing? A switch? Goddess, she's built. Hiding all that muscle under soft clothes.

"Do you like being displayed? You are a sumptuous feast for the eyes. Do you like knowing anyone could walk through and see you?"

Elaine passed her hands over Petra's body, pressing and squeezing her firm flesh. She paused and rubbed the hard curve of her bicep. "Maybe I'll invite them to pass by the table and give them permission to touch you as they willed? Let them do what they wanted to you? Or should I chain you naked to my chair, keep you as my pet?"

Petra's breathing quickened, and her nipples peaked. Elaine traced her fingers over her skin, following her curves, and the shallow space below her hipbone. "What if I let them see what a slut you really are? Let them see how hard your clit gets thinking about all of the things I might do to you."

Petra bit her lip but not before a soft groan escaped her. "Oh, no. Please, Ma'am, not that."

"What if I made you touch yourself?" Elaine drew her finger down the dark line below Petra's navel leading to the thin patch of neatly trimmed hair between her legs. "Made you put on a show for them?"

"Oh, please, no." Her tone was earnest, but the gleam of desire pooling under her on the table betrayed her words. "Please, Ma'am, not that. I'll do anything you want."

Elaine chuckled. "You will anyway. You're not even bound, yet you lie here for me, offering yourself." She set the bag of clothes pegs on the table between Petra's legs. "Do you know about the Gates of Heaven? Have you heard of it?" She pinched the soft skin on the inside of her thigh, letting the back of her knuckles brush against the silky heat between Petra's legs. Petra moaned and Elaine squeezed the ends of the clothes peg together, placed it over the skin she held between her thumb and forefinger, and released it gently, the wooden ends closing softly on Petra's flesh.

Petra whimpered and shifted on the table. Elaine slapped her thigh, gratified by her sharp intake of breath, and the way her hips lifted from the table, seeking more of Elaine's touch. She moved to the other thigh and repeated the soft brush of Petra's hard clit with the back of her knuckles before she pinched her flesh and applied another peg. She moved down the inside of her legs until each one bristled with clothes pegs.

With each stroke of Elaine's knuckles against her clit Petra's groans deepened. Elaine moved from between her legs and pinched the flesh on the outside of her breast. She leaned down and licked the tip of Petra's nipple before she applied the clothes peg. A tremor shook Petra's body. And so it went, Elaine giving her a brief touch of pleasure, and then the sharp pinch of the pegs. She continued, the quiet punctuated only by Petra's heavy breathing, her deep groans, and the sharp hiss of pain after each clip was applied. Elaine held up the last four clothes pegs. "Ready?"

Petra's eyes were glazed with pleasure and the haze of endorphins. "Yes."

Elaine leaned down and sucked hard, pulling Petra's nipple into a tight point.

"Oh god, Misstre—Ma'am. Please, I'm going to come." Petra panted.

Elaine applied the clothes peg to her nipple and Petra howled. Her scream of pain sent a white-hot wave of desire through Elaine. "Not yet." She kissed Petra, sipping her pain, drawing it into herself, savoring it. She broke their kiss and gazed into Petra's eyes as she waited for Petra to get herself under control.

Elaine bent over her and drew her other nipple deep into her mouth.

"Oh, oh please. Oh. Please let me. I'm going to, I can't..."

Elaine released her nipple, applied the second clothes peg, and clamped her nipple. Petra's wail was louder this time, her breath ragged. The chest-rattling groan she finished with made Elaine press her legs together to stem the tide of her desire.

She moved down the table and lowered her head to lick and suck Petra's clit, edging her. She used her fingers to spread her wider. She eased back the hood covering her clit to tease the proud tip with the flat of her tongue.

Petra wailed. "Oh, Ma'am, please let me come, please, please let me. Oh, Ma'am, please. Please."

Elaine licked her clit while she pinched her labia and slowly released the ends of the clothes peg over her slick skin.

Petra screamed, her hips arching into Elaine's mouth, before she collapsed back on to the table panting, pupils blown wide. Elaine kissed her, savoring the desperation of

Petra's silent plea for release. Anxious for her own release, she bent her head to Petra's clit, giving her just enough but not enough to come before she applied the last clamp.

No scream this time, but a low keening started in Petra's chest, and she panted. She rolled her head from side to side on the table, eyes unfocused. Elaine leaned over, cupped her face to still her movement, and studied her face. *So beautiful. So tough. She's exquisite.* She wiped away the tears pouring from Petra's eyes, lifted her fingertips to her mouth, and tasted the bitter salt. "Such a good girl. Now, we take them off."

Elaine flicked the first peg off her nipple. Petra's sharp squeal made her close her eyes as she savored her pain. She leaned down and kissed her as she flicked the second one off her other nipple. She swallowed Petra's scream in a deep kiss. Elaine reached down between her thighs and released the first labial clamp gently. Petra groaned. "Oh, god, 's so good."

Elaine released the second labial clamp, and Petra trembled. Elaine leaned down and licked her clit and flicked a clothes peg off her thigh. A squeal and a groan, and so she went, taking her time, alternating legs, licking Petra's clit and soothing her between each removal. Petra's begging turned into incoherent babble. Elaine climbed onto the table and straddled Petra. She reached between them and opened herself. She closed her eyes against the pleasure of the slick slide of Petra's clit as she rocked her hips and rode out her pleasure. Elaine came hard, and with both hands she flicked the remaining clothes pegs off as she swept her hands up under her breasts. Petra's long scream filled her ears and Elaine came again with the sound. She kissed Petra, savored her desperation for release, and shifted her hips to reach between them. Pushing her fingers deep, pressing the heel of her palm against Petra's clit as she fucked her hard and fast, and Petra raised her hips to meet her strokes.

Elaine broke their kiss to look into her eyes. "Come for me." Eyes wide open, her mouth a perfect O, Petra came without a sound, her body arching up to meet Elaine's thrusts as she clenched around Elaine's fingers.

The harsh sounds of their rough breathing filled the room as they held tight to each other. Petra lifted a shaky hand and reached for Elaine's cheek. Elaine drew back. Petra let her hand fall back to her chest. Elaine turned away from the hurt in her dark eyes and pushed herself to sitting before she slid off the table. She reached into the bag and pulled out a soft fleece throw and covered Petra with it. Petra curled her fingers over the edge of the blanket and drew it up to her neck.

"I'll get you some water." Elaine fled the room, running from the wave of emotion threatening to pull her under.

In the kitchen she poured a glass of water with trembling hands. *So responsive. So perfect. She took everything. Only Robin's been able to tolerate that before. What have I done?*

She hurried back to Petra who lay with her eyes closed, curled on her side. Elaine touched her shoulder and she started. "Drink this." Elaine waited while she pushed herself to sitting. She took the glass from her and kept her eyes averted from Elaine's face as she sipped her water.

Robin pushed through the door and swept her eyes over the scene, her gaze briefly connecting with Elaine's before she backed out of the room. The swish of the kitchen door closing was loud in the silence between them.

Petra cleared her throat. "Well, I can see why they talk about you." She took another sip of water.

Elaine traced her finger over the pattern on the tablecloth. "I'm not going to ask if that's a compliment." She stared into Petra's dark eyes. *What would it be like if I swept her up and carried her back to my room? Kept her there and tested her limits for the rest of the afternoon?* She lifted her hand, aching to touch Petra's hair. *No. She's not yours. She's only here to see if she wants to stay. Let it go. This was a one-off to sample the wares.* She dropped her hand to her side.

She swept Petra's pile of clothes off the floor. Arms stiff, she held them out to her. Petra held her gaze, waited a beat, set her water glass aside, and plucked the clothes from Elaine's hand. Her fingers brushed Elaine's as she took them. Elaine shied from her touch and stuffed her hands in the pockets of her skirt. *Leave now. Now, before you do anything stupid. More stupid. Or make this more awkward.* "I've got some business to attend to. I'll send Robin to you after lunch."

She left Petra there amid the debris of their scene.

"MISTRESS?" ROBIN STOOD at the entry to Elaine's office.

Elaine glanced at Robin over her laptop screen. "Come."

Robin's face was a mask, her eyes flat. "I've finished with Tessa. She should be able to keep up now."

Elaine frowned at the resignation in Robin's voice. She closed her laptop. "Are you regretting your decision? You can always change your mind." *Please change your mind.* "You don't have to do this."

Robin's head snapped up. "I want to. Why should you be the only one to enjoy her talents?"

Elaine drummed her fingers on the desk. "What I do or do not do as Mistress of this house is no concern of yours. You are a free agent, Robin, but do not forget your place."

Robin snorted. "I haven't had a place here since you snipped off my collar and released me from my contract. I'm tolerated. A liability. A pair of hands and an obligation until you feel safe enough to release me into the world."

Elaine studied her expression and her eyes. *Hurt. Angry. At me? She's jealous.* She placed both her hands flat on the desk. "You have never been merely an employee." *Tell her. Tell her how you feel. Say it.* "I care for you."

Robin's eyes blazed with anger. "You've an odd way of showing it." She lowered her chin to her chest.

Elaine stood up and crossed the room. Robin stood with her hands knotted together in front of her. Elaine lifted her hand to touch her, to bridge the frozen air between them. *It's for the best. She wants too much. More than I can give.* "I can't promise anything or ask for more with you right now, do you understand?"

"I understand you're not interested in me that way. You've made it clear." Robin lifted her head and met Elaine's gaze, teeth clamped on her lower lip.

Elaine returned her gaze a brief moment before she turned her back on Robin and went to sit behind her desk. *Keep it professional. Keep the desk between you. Don't think. It's business. Don't feel. Let it go. Let her go.*

"When do you want me to report to Mistress Petra?"

Elaine's breath caught, her heart clenching as she thought of the two of them together. Under the desk she balled her hands into fists. She took a breath and exhaled it, squared her shoulders, and relaxed her hands. "Report to her room this afternoon. The first audition will be at eight tonight. I trust it will be enough time for you to explore your mutual interests and plan the scene."

Robin held her gaze. "See you then, Elaine." She turned and stalked from the room.

Elaine lowered her forehead to her desk and fought her desire to go after Robin. It had been purposeful, Robin's use of her name instead of Mistress, she had no doubt of that. Elaine opened the bottom desk drawer and stared at the bottle of Edradour whisky and the two glasses tucked beside Martha's Webley revolver and box of cartridges. She stared at the bottle, her mouth watering as she imagined the warm burn and soothing effect of the whisky. *No. Not now. Not before a scene. Later. Maybe.*

She slammed the drawer shut. The wind rattled the window and small bits of ice ticked against the glass. *Damn it. Too miserable to go for a ride. Why did I scene with Petra? All it did was make it worse. I need to get rid of this energy. Robin. Petra. I need to get it together before tonight. It's going to be hard. But why? Because I want what I can't have. And because I want both of them. Damn it.*

Chapter Six

THE GASLIGHTS WERE lit in the ballroom. The wine cask with its bondage gear in place had been brought from the dungeon and was centered in the room. Two large mirrors were positioned around the cask, one to Elaine's side and one behind the cask, angled to allow Elaine to view what occurred on the opposite side of the barrel. A low table was placed off to the side of the barrel. Elaine had her favorite leather club chair brought to the room and a fainting couch placed next to it. A thick blue blanket was draped over the back of the couch. Elaine assessed the layout and shifted her chair closer to the play area. Close enough to watch the scene, but far enough away to give the illusion of privacy.

In spite of an hour in the gym beating the hell out of the heavy bag, an hour practicing her Krav Maga skills and sparring with Millie, she was still keyed up and restless. Elaine lounged with one leg over the arm of her chair and studied the toe of her favorite pair of black riding boots. *Need a shine.* She brushed a bit of lint off her long black skirt. The tickle of wet between her legs made her question her decision to wear a thong. She was braless and the silk of the shirt kept her nipples half-hard, and she shifted in the chair, relishing the sensation.

The clock struck eight, and the doors opened. Robin walked through, naked but for two red silk scarves draped over her body. Tied in an X, they covered her nipples and the space between her legs. Another scarf was wrapped around her throat in a makeshift collar. She marched in with her hands clasped behind her back, grasping opposite elbows. The position arched her back and forced her breasts forward. Elaine sat up and placed both of her feet on the floor. The red scarves set off Robin's pale skin, and the curves of her breasts were accented by the way the sheer fabric was tied. *A collar. What the ever-living hell?* Robin held her head high and stared straight ahead.

Petra followed her into the room. She wore thigh-high black boots with block heels, and tight black pants hugged the curves of her ass. A slight bulge between her legs made Elaine smile as she imagined what lay in store for Robin. Petra wore a loose-fitted emerald-green short-sleeve hunter's top and her tightly muscled arms were displayed to perfection. She turned to adjust Robin's stance, and the unlaced blouse billowed out and offered an unfettered view of her breasts.

Elaine's mouth watered as she recalled the way Petra's nipples had reacted to her attentions. Petra wore short black gloves on her hands. Elaine's clit hardened as she remembered having her submit, the way she had screamed into her mouth as she came. *Focus, idiot. Focus. This is her audition. Pay attention.*

Petra inclined her head in greeting to Elaine. Petra moved quietly as she untied the scarves and pulled them free of Robin's body. The slow reveal of flesh she had seen many times ratcheted up Elaine's excitement. Petra snapped her fingers, and Robin left her side and moved to the wine cask. She stepped up on a low stool to lay over the wide barrel. The gentle curve of the wooden staves supported her body. Her arms hung down on either side of her head. She pressed herself against the barrel, and her chin rested on the dark polished wood. The position put her face directly in Elaine's line of vision. Robin lifted her eyes and held Elaine's gaze. The defiance in her expression made Elaine shift in her seat. *That look. Why did I agree to this? What was I thinking?*

Petra pulled Robin's legs wide and secured them with leather cuffs around her ankles. As she turned to the side and moved to secure her arms, Elaine noticed the flogger laid out on the side table and the coiled whip attached to Petra's belt. Her heart raced, and she licked her lower lip. Petra turned to face Elaine. "With your permission, I'll begin."

Elaine fixed her gaze on Robin's face. "Robin, do you submit to this willingly? Have you established a safe word?"

"Yes." Robin's voice was steady, her gaze bright and full of fire.

Elaine pursed her lips at Robin's failure to use her honorific in a scene. She opened her mouth to chastise Robin and closed it quickly as the sharp crack of leather meeting skin sounded in the dungeon.

Petra had applied her hand to the seat of Robin's defiance, and now she gripped Robin's hair in her fist, the blonde strands peeking out from between the fingers of her gloved hand. "You will answer a Mistress properly. Now. Or do I need to correct you again?" She yanked her hair hard to make her point.

"Sorry, Mistress Petra. Yes, Mistress Elaine." She dropped her gaze.

Petra released her hair. Elaine raised an eyebrow and nodded her approval at her instant correction of Robin's behavior.

Elaine raised her hand, palm up, and shifted back in her chair and crossed her legs. "By all means, proceed."

Petra unclipped the casters on the barrel, rotated it and fixed it in place so it was at an angle. Robin's face was visible and Petra's actions on display.

Petra moved the stool from between Robin's legs, spread wide by her bonds. She brought her gloved hand up and between her legs. "Mmm, seems my little correction made an impression." She lifted her gloved hand. Evidence of Robin's excitement glistened on the fingertips. She pulled her hand back and swatted Robin's ass again. Robin lifted her eyelids and focused on Elaine's face. Her defiance was gone, replaced by longing so sharp it made Elaine catch her breath.

Petra raised her hand and spanked the other cheek of Robin's ass. In the mirror, a red handprint bloomed over Robin's pale skin. Petra stroked between Robin's legs again, before she pulled back and spanked her again. She alternated, rubbing between Robin's legs every time before she spanked her. With each touch, followed by a sharp blow, Robin's breath came quicker. Her gaze never wavered as she opened herself to Elaine. Staring into Robin's eyes was mesmerizing. Robin sank into subspace as Elaine watched her body surrender to Petra's attention, watched as she offered all she was for Elaine's enjoyment, her gift to Elaine.

By the twentieth blow, Elaine's nipples and clit were aching. Petra stopped and smoothed her hand over Robin's ass. The deep red of her skin contrasted with the black of Petra's gloves. She leaned close and said something for Robin's ears alone. Robin closed her eyes. The loss tore Elaine's heart from her chest. *No. Let me see you. Don't hide. Please let me see you.* She bit her lip to keep from begging Robin to look at her.

Petra stepped back from the barrel and raised the flogger. In a smooth sweep, she brought it down over Robin's back. Robin groaned. With a sweeping rhythm, alternating strokes, Petra flogged her. Robin panted. "Mercy, Mistress. Please."

Petra set the flogger aside. She spoke quietly to Robin. Elaine shifted in her seat, trying to hear what she was saying. Petra smoothed her hand over Robin's back and down over her ass, stopping a moment to finger her. Robin trembled under her touch. "Come as you like." Petra's words huffed out of her mouth like a breath. Robin arched into her touch and came with a low moan.

"Good girl." Petra patted her ass before she paced off her steps from the barrel. She unclipped her whip and shook it out. She popped it off to one side, the crack of the popper making Robin open her eyes wide. Elaine studied her expression, ready to intervene if Robin was not able to continue. Her ears strained to hear Robin's safe word. Robin's eyes were wide, her pupils blown open, her face a vision of subspace.

Elaine was lost in Robin's eyes as she revealed the depth of her desire. *All of this is for me. For me. Petra is a merely a tool, Robin is doing this for me.* Robin held Elaine's gaze as Petra raised her arm and the popper landed on Robin's ass cheek. She yipped with the blow.

"Ready?" Petra's husky voice broke into Elaine's thoughts.

Who is she asking? Me? Or her? Does she feel it? Does she know this is Robin's gift to me? Or is this a gift from Petra? What did Robin ask for? Robin wants to be this for me. She is exquisite. They both are. So beautiful.

Petra's arm arced and the whip came down. Robin's scream as the popper left a thin stripe across the smooth skin of her back made Elaine spread her legs to keep from coming with the sound. She gripped the arms of the chair, knuckles white, her breath coming faster. Petra threw the whip again and left a stripe next to the first one. Precise, purposeful, and deliberate.

Robin screamed again, quieter this time, followed by a deep groan. Petra applied the whip a third time and this time Robin moaned with it. Tears ran down her face. She kept her eyes locked on Elaine's face as the whip landed again. This time no sound came from her at all. The stripes on her back were a tidy row. Four even lines. Elaine glanced at Petra and watched as she adjusted her stance and laid a neat line over the four stripes. She waited, her eyes on Robin's face reflected in the mirror, gauging her reaction. Robin shifted her eyes to Petra's face. "Please," she sobbed, "oh please, Mistress. Please. Oh please. More. Don't stop, please, Mistress."

Petra moved to Robin's side. Robin closed her eyes. She stroked her hair. "Shh, now. Easy. You did well. It's enough for now."

She laid her whip on the table next to the flogger before she stepped between Robin's legs. A hiss of a zipper lowering made Elaine shift her gaze to the mirror. She panted as she watched Petra free a bright pink strap-on phallus from her pants.

Petra dipped her hand between Robin's legs, gathered the liquid silk pooling between her legs, and smeared it over the toy. She gripped the back of Robin's neck as she set the tip and pushed slowly into Robin. Petra closed her eyes and ecstasy filled her features as she took Robin.

Elaine drew up her skirt. A trickle of sweat tickled between her breasts. She tucked the skirt down on either side of her legs and spread them wide as she moved her hand between her thighs. With one finger she lifted the edge of her panties, shoved them to the side, and thrust her hand into the searing heat between her thighs. She pushed two fingers inside and stroked her clit with her thumb under the damp silk.

"Show her your eyes. Let her see you." Petra shifted her hand from Robin's neck to clasp Robin's hips.

Robin opened her glazed eyes wide. Pleasure suffused her face. Petra pulled back and sank in again. A low desperate groan escaped Robin's lips. Petra kissed the raised red lines on Robin's back before she opened her mouth and traced one of the lines with her tongue. Robin sighed as Petra slow-fucked her, pulling out almost to the tip before she sank deep, pausing to kiss and lick the marks on Robin's back each time she thrust into her. Robin's breathing shifted, her voice ragged as she begged for more, for Petra to fuck her faster, to let her come. Petra's breath came faster and she sped up her strokes, pushing herself into her own pleasure. The short sharp growl she made as she came undid Elaine.

Elaine fucked herself, strumming her clit, her hand a blur between her legs as she held Robin's gaze, matching Petra's strokes. Petra came again as she fucked Robin. The sounds of her climax threatened Elaine's control. Robin's jaw was slack, her mouth open.

"Come now," Petra ground out as she buried herself in Robin's body. Robin screamed as she came. Elaine matched her and came herself, never looking away from Robin's face.

ELAINE TUGGED HER skirt down. Petra eased herself from Robin, taking a few minutes to detach the sex toy from the harness under her pants. Moving swiftly, she unbuckled the cuffs from Robin's legs and arms and rubbed her limbs briskly. Elaine poured water into the three glasses on the table next to her chair. Petra helped Robin down from the barrel and let her lean against her as she walked her to the couch. Robin was shivering. Petra pushed her to lie down and pulled the fleece blanket from the back of the couch to cover her. She stroked Robin's hair. Robin's breathing was interrupted by her quiet sobs as she covered her eyes with her hands.

Elaine bolted from her chair when she heard her sobs. She shoved Petra out of the way, ignoring her hard expression. She lifted Robin from the couch, cradled her in her arms, and sat down with her in her lap. With impatient movements she undid the scarf around her throat and tossed it aside. She clutched Robin to her breast, rocking her until the quiet sobs slowed and then stopped. Robin's breathing evened out, and Elaine smoothed her hand over her hair and pressed a kiss to her temple.

Petra tapped Elaine on the shoulder and held out a glass of water. Elaine shifted her grip to take the glass.

"Sit up now. Drink this." Robin pushed herself to a sitting position in Elaine's lap. Her hand shook as she attempted to take the glass from Elaine.

"Let me." Elaine held on to the glass. Robin kept her gaze averted as she wrapped her trembling fingers over Elaine's and tipped the glass to drink. After two long sips, she gently pushed the glass away.

Elaine held up the glass, never taking her eye from Robin's face.

Petra took the glass from her and cleared her throat loudly. "I'll leave you to it." She reached around Elaine and gave Robin's shoulder a squeeze. "You are delightful and well-trained."

Robin leaned her cheek against Petra's hand. "Thank you."

Elaine fought her desire to knock Petra's hand off Robin's shoulder. "Enough. Good night, Petra."

Petra exited, and Elaine moved her hips back on the couch, pulling Robin with her. "We need to attend to your back."

Robin burrowed closer to her, tucking her head under Elaine's chin. Elaine's shirt pulled tight as Robin clutched Elaine with both hands. "A little longer, Mistress, please."

Elaine held her tightly. She rested her cheek against the soft curls on the top of her head. "As long as you need."

She sighed, comforted by Robin's weight against her. The room was warm and the couch comfortable. Elaine sensed the moment Robin fell asleep. Her hands relaxed where she had clung to Elaine. She gathered the blanket around Robin and scooted to the edge of the cushion. In one movement, she stood. She shifted her grip on Robin and walked toward the door.

Robin stirred in her arms. "Where're we going, Mistress?" she mumbled against Elaine's chest.

"My room."

"It's too far to carry me, Mistress."

"Shh. You don't weigh as much as a bird."

Robin lifted her arms and clasped them around Elaine's neck, pressing her face into the crook of her neck and dropping a kiss there. She nuzzled the sensitive space where Elaine's shoulder met her neck.

Elaine trembled when Robin placed another tender kiss on her heated skin. She turned and pushed her back against the door to open it. The hallway was chill compared to the warm ballroom. Robin shivered in her arms. She cursed herself for not having a heavier blanket available for her. Down the long hall and to the wide staircase they went. Elaine's heart sped up from the exertion or having Robin in her arms, she didn't know which. She walked slowly up the stairs and turned to the right, to her side of the house. She paused outside her room. "I need to put you down to open the door. Are you able to stand?"

"Yes, Mistress."

Elaine lowered her legs, and Robin stood. Elaine kept one arm around her waist to steady her as she pulled her keys from her skirt pocket and unlocked the door. She pushed it open wide. Robin took a step forward and Elaine scooped her up, strode through the door, and kicked it closed.

ELAINE PLACED ROBIN on her bed.

"Please, Mistress. I need the washroom."

Elaine helped her from the bed and walked with her to the bathroom, making sure she was steady on her feet. "I'll give you a moment to take care of your private needs."

While Robin was in the bathroom, she flipped the duvet down and fluffed up the pillows. The whisper of Robin's feet on the carpet made her turn. Robin's eyes were wary.

"Come here."

Robin approached her slowly until she stood in front of Elaine.

Elaine cupped her face and kissed her brow. "Lie down. I'm going to call for something to eat. Stay put while I draw a bath."

Robin chewed her bottom lip. "Yes, Mistress." She stepped on to the stool next to the high bed and settled herself into the pillows.

Elaine pulled the duvet over her and tucked it in tightly around her body. She crossed the room and picked up the antique phone next to her desk and rang the kitchen. Tessa picked up on the fifth ring. "Bring a selection of cheeses and fruit to my room. For two. No. No wine. Some of that non-alcoholic sparkling cider will do. And water. Thank you."

Elaine replaced the phone and went into her bathroom. She opened the taps and adjusted the water temperature. After rummaging through the cabinet alongside the tub, she extracted a blue bottle. She added eucalyptus bath salts to the claw-footed tub. From the same cabinet she located an antiseptic ointment and her favorite sesame massage oil.

She heard a knock at the door to her room and shut the taps off. On her way out, she flipped the switch for the heated towel rack.

Robin had one leg over the side of the bed. At a sharp glare from Elaine, she retreated under the covers.

Elaine opened the door wide, and Tessa pushed in a cart with a large tray of cheese, crackers, and fruit. An ice bucket held a dark-green bottle. There were two wine glasses, a water pitcher, and two plates as well. Elaine touched Tessa on the shoulder. "I'll take it from here. And next time pick up the phone by the second ring."

"Yes, Mistress." Tessa glanced at Robin, bit her lip, and left. She closed the door softly behind her. Elaine turned the deadbolt and flipped the bar lock into place.

Robin had pushed herself to sitting. "I can serve, Mistress."

Elaine raised an eyebrow. "Was I not specific in what you were to do?"

Robin lowered her head. "Yes, Mistress."

Elaine crossed to the bed. "Come on now." She extended her hand, and Robin took it. She assisted her from the bed and led her to the bathroom. Elaine pointed at the tub. "Check to see the temperature suits you, and get in."

Robin's eyes went wide. "Oh Mistress. I can't…" She encountered Elaine's hard glare. She bent and dipped her hand into the bath. "It's perfect, Mistress." She stepped in and lowered her body, hissing when the water covered her back. Elaine kneeled next to the tub. She picked up a washcloth and dipped it in to the bathwater. "Lean forward. I want to clean your back. It will sting a bit."

Robin placed her hands on the sides of the tub and bent from her waist. The marks from Petra's whip were raised; the line crossing the others had broken the skin in a few places. Elaine wrung the cloth out over Robin's skin, wetting it. Robin trembled when the water touched the stripes on her back. Elaine soaped the cloth and gently washed her. The muscles of Robin's back relaxed under her touch.

"That's done. Lean back now." Elaine took her time and washed every trace of Petra from her body. Robin closed her eyes and gave herself over to Elaine's attention. It had been years since Elaine had cared for a sub like this, took her time, and reveled in caring for her property. *No. Not my property. Not pledged to me. She's not mine. But I want her to be. Goddess, I want her to be. Would she say yes? Could I be faithful? Would I be happy?*

The drip and splash of the water as Elaine worked was the only sound in the bathroom.

"Stand." Robin stood, and the water rolled off her small breasts and trailed down her body. Elaine took the warmed towel and dried her gently. "Turn for me." Elaine kissed the back of Robin's neck. Robin lifted her hand and cupped Elaine's cheek. She stilled, Robin's touch saying more than words. Slowly, she lowered her hand, and Elaine straightened. With tender movements, she smoothed antiseptic ointment over Robin's back. The sensation of her fingers as she tended to the sacred marks on Robin's skin, her gift, made Elaine swallow around the lump in her throat.

Robin shivered, and Elaine assisted her into her own robe, before folding and rolling the sleeves back. The robe brushed the top of the floor on Robin's petite frame. Elaine led the way out of the bathroom. She pointed to the wingback chair closest to the fireplace. Robin sat and curled her legs under her, tucking the robe around her feet.

Elaine rolled the cart over next to the matching chair. She opened the sparkling cider and poured two glasses. She passed one to Robin. Robin took a sip and placed the glass on the side table. Elaine arranged a bit of cheese on a cracker and passed it to Robin before she did the same for herself.

"This cider is delicious. Better than the last batch we tried." Robin took another sip.

"I agree. This is nice and dry. The other was too sweet. I hated serving it."

"As did I. After the first two complaints from guests, I took it off the menu." Robin leaned back in the chair and turned her face to Elaine.

"What did you do with what was left?" Elaine sipped her cider.

"We still have it. Myfanwy thinks she can find a way to cook with it."

Elaine grimaced. "Remind me to not volunteer for taste testing."

Robin laughed. Her face was relaxed and happy. *I've never seen her like this.* Her heart clenched. *Have I not noticed? Did I make her happy? Or was it Petra?*

Robin's brows drew down, spoiling her happy expression. "Elaine? What's wrong?"

Elaine started at her name on Robin's lips. She missed her honorific. *Over then. End scene. Back to normal. To just Elaine and Robin. No. Not yet.*

"Are you tired?"

Robin frowned. "A little. Not too."

Elaine stood up and pointed to the bed.

Robin's frown deepened. She lifted her chin. "I don't know what you want, Mistress."

"Yes, you do." Elaine lifted an eyebrow. "There was a time when you would not have hesitated to grace my bed. Now I have to insist?"

Robin rose to her feet, eyes bright and full of fire.

Elaine stepped close to her and lifted her chin with one finger. She pressed a kiss to the corner of her mouth. "I want to talk about this evening. About your gift."

"Talk, Mistress?" She spoke against Elaine's mouth, and she raised her hands and placed them on Elaine's chest.

Elaine tensed, afraid Robin was about to push her away. Robin's fingers curled into her shirt, and she yanked Elaine closer, rose up on her toes and kissed her, teasing her with her tongue until Elaine opened to her. She kissed Elaine until she was breathless.

Elaine settled her hands on Robin's hips. "Bed, now." Robin walked to the bed, untied the robe, slid it from her body, dropped it to the floor, and climbed into the bed.

Elaine stepped into the bathroom and picked up the massage oil she had selected and a towel. She placed them on the nightstand. Robin's gaze followed her around the room as Elaine undressed. She slipped under the covers next to Robin.

They turned on their sides to face each other. Elaine pillowed her arm on her head and reached out to cup Robin's face. Robin turned her face into Elaine's broad palm and pressed a kiss to there.

Elaine slid closer and rolled them over, so she was over Robin. Robin winced.

"Sorry. Forgot." Elaine rolled them again until she was under Robin. "Is it bad?" She cursed herself for forgetting about Robin's marks and how sore they would be even with the ointment.

"Not too." Robin traced a finger over her collarbone and down to the hollow between Elaine's breasts. "Now I'm where you want me, what can I do for you, Mistress?"

The teasing tone of Robin's voice made Elaine ache.

"I want you to tell me what you told Petra. What did you say to her?"

Robin averted her eyes.

"Robin, tell me. Please." Elaine kept her voice soft. "I won't command you. Tell me."

"I told her I didn't care what she did to me, but I wanted to be able to see your face at all times."

"Is that all you told her?" Elaine carded her fingers through Robin's hair.

"No."

"No roles now, Robin, this is us."

Robin met her gaze, the love in her eyes confirmation of what she had told Petra. Elaine saw it all. She loved her. Wanted to be hers and hers alone. No matter what Petra did to her, her response would be for Elaine. All of it. Every scream, every moan, every drop of sweat, every bit of desire flowing from her was for Elaine and only Elaine.

"You love me." A statement. Elaine acknowledging everything that had passed between them during the scene.

Robin pressed her lips together and inhaled sharply. "Yes." She avoided Elaine's gaze. "But I know. I know it's not—" She brought her gaze back to Elaine's face. "—it's not news to you, nor enough to bind you to me."

Heat rose in Elaine's face. "Why?"

"Why what?" Robin's voice held the hint of tears. "Because I'm cursed to love people who don't love me back? Because I'm an idiot to think you might ever want to be exclusive with anyone, let alone me?"

"Stop." Elaine grabbed Robin's arms. "That's not what I meant. Don't talk about yourself that way. You are not 'cursed.' And I didn't know until now how you felt about me."

Robin chewed her lip. "And now you do. And so what."

The bitterness in her voice made Elaine ache. *Has anyone ever wanted me this much? This way? Roxy never did.*

Elaine stared into Robin's eyes. "You said it. And it makes a difference. Many people want to belong to someone not because they love them, but because of what they can get from them. You've never asked me for anything. You've done whatever I've asked you to even when you were no longer collared." She kissed her. "When you looked at me while Petra was marking you, I knew, I knew in an instant what I've been ignoring for the last two years. The way you responded to Petra, I sensed you, sensed your love. I cared for Roxy, but this, what I feel for you, is beyond that. It's a wild thing inside me. And after, when I realized how much I wanted you, I couldn't let you go, let her take care of you."

Elaine's heart was racing from her confession. She studied Robin's eyes, the expression on her face.

"You want me? What does that mean to you?" Robin's expression was guarded. "Until the next thing comes along?"

Elaine frowned. "I need to keep seeing clients. We would have no house if I stopped."

"I'm not talking about that. I'm talking about us. Would you be able to be mine? To only have me as yours?"

Elaine hesitated.

Robin sighed and rested her forehead on Elaine's. She closed her eyes. "I'm tired. I'm tired of this dance. I can't. I can't keep doing this." She rolled off Elaine and moved to the other side of the bed. She turned to her side, her back to Elaine, drew her arms and legs up, curling in on herself. "Should I return to my room?"

"Stay." Elaine lay on her back and folded her arms over her head. She stared at the midnight-blue cloth canopy covering her bed. Her gaze followed the familiar pattern of silver and gold stars woven into constellations. Robin's breathing evened out into the regular pattern of sleep. Elaine rolled to her side and took in her sleeping form. She ached to reach out and touch her, to curl around her, to press against her, and hold on to the only woman who had ever said she loved her and meant it.

Chapter Seven

ELAINE LEFT ROBIN sleeping, slipping out of her room into the morning dark, unwilling to continue their discussion. *Exercise, I need to get rid of this tension. Practice with the single tail. Love. Is that what I feel? Thought I was in love with Roxy. A little anyway. Fuck me.* She opened the door to the dungeon.

Petra was standing next to the whipping post with a bullwhip in her hand. "Sorry. I didn't think anyone else would be awake."

"Neither did I." Elaine pushed her hair back with both hands.

Petra studied her hands as she coiled the whip. "I'll go."

"Stay. Please." Elaine sat on the dais and rested her chin in her hands.

Petra placed the whip on its peg and sat down next to Elaine. "You want to discuss last evening, perhaps?"

Elaine turned her head and took in Petra's profile. "I do."

"Were you dissatisfied with my performance?" Petra stared straight ahead, her mouth set in a thin line.

"Not dissatisfied at all." Elaine picked at the carpet covering the dais.

"And yet you took over aftercare." Petra's tone was even.

"I did. I was—surprised. I couldn't stop myself."

"You care for her too."

"Yes."

"She loves you." Petra's voice was a whisper.

"I know." Elaine scrubbed her hands over her face. "I know now."

Petra cocked her head to the side and raised her chin. "She wanted to show you. It was her fantasy." She turned her head and smiled a smile that did not reach her eyes. "Then I suppose I did my job. Now you are aware of how she feels."

Elaine could not suppress her glare. "Yes. I'm aware, and well and truly fucked."

Petra frowned. "How? How is that?"

"Because she wants more. More than to simply be my submissive. She wants me to be exclusive."

Petra pursed her lips. "I see. And that would mean no clients?"

"No. She understands the difference between clients and relationships. She wants to be my only submissive. The only one pledged to me."

"And this is a problem because you want what? Options?" Petra sneered. "Or are you afraid of commitment? Too much for you?"

Elaine stood up. "You don't know me."

"No. But I would like to know you, Ma'am." Petra stood toe to toe with Elaine. "Or is it too much too? Too much to risk someone figuring out what goes on in your thick skull?"

Elaine sucked her teeth. "If you are trying to push me into punishing you, you are heading in the right direction."

"Am I?" Petra bumped the edge of Elaine's boot with her own. "What would it take for you to do it?

"Another word from your insolent delectable mouth and you will find out how functional the rack is." Elaine's breath came faster as she imagined Petra spread out for her.

"Word." Petra smirked.

Elaine's hand snaked out and slapped her face. Petra sighed and raised her hand to her cheek. Her fingers caressed the red mark from Elaine's hand. She licked her lower lip and smiled. Elaine gripped her shoulders and kissed her, tasting her, crushing her lips with her own. Petra relaxed in her arms. Elaine released her. Panting, she gripped the edges of Petra's blouse and ripped it open. Buttons pinged off the stone walls. She pulled it down over her shoulders, trapping Petra's arms as she kissed her way along her neck, biting and licking her skin, inhaling the faint gardenia scent of her perfume, and under it, the essence of her warm skin.

Petra moaned, and Elaine lifted her head and took her mouth again as she dragged her blouse from her body. She broke their kiss and popped the top button of Petra's pants open, unzipped the zipper, and slipped her fingers into her underwear and pushed them down her hips. Petra shifted her legs. Her pants were around her ankles. Elaine pushed her away. "Finish it. Get naked, right now." She turned and selected a quirt from the wall behind her.

When she turned back Petra was naked. Eyes sharp, she met Elaine's gaze.

Elaine held out her hand, and Petra took it. Elaine led her to the rack. "Lie down."

Petra's eyes went wide, and she hesitated.

Elaine raised a brow. "Too much?"

"I don't know." Petra pursed her lips.

Elaine reached out and cupped her cheek. She ran her thumb over Petra's lower lip. "You decide. I'll wait."

She walked back to the dais and sat in one of the chairs. She tapped the handle of the quirt against her leg. Petra walked around the room. She stopped at the whipping post briefly, shied away from the branding brazier, and ended her stroll back at the rack.

Petra raised her chin. "This."

Elaine smiled at her. "Excellent." She left her chair and walked to Petra's side. She placed the quirt aside and assisted Petra as she mounted the rack.

Petra lay down on the wide boards of the frame. Her body trembled as Elaine slipped the rope coils over her feet and tightened them around her ankles. She left her hands free.

She smoothed her hands over her skin, pausing to roll Petra's nipples into hard points before she cupped and squeezed between her legs. Petra's breathing evened out as Elaine soothed her with her touch. "You are so beautiful like this." She raised Petra's arm and slipped the rope over her wrist and tightened it. Elaine bent and brushed her lips with a kiss before she repeated her actions with the other arm.

Elaine moved to the head of the frame and clasped the wheel that would tighten the ropes holding Petra. "Ready?"

"Yes, Ma'am." Petra's voice wobbled. Elaine moved back to her head. She stroked Petra's hair and studied her expression. "I need to know you are okay with this. Are you? It's okay if you're not."

Petra's mouth firmed. "I'm okay."

Elaine kissed her. "Good girl. Red is stop, yellow is slow down?"

"Yes." Petra's tone was firm.

"Excellent." Elaine moved back to the head of the table. She clasped the wheel, palms sweaty. She turned it slowly to tighten the ropes. She focused on Petra's breathing, watching for signs of distress as the ropes pulled her legs wide and stretched her arms over her head. Elaine turned the wheel until Petra's limbs were taut.

The padded roll under her low back lifted her hips up, providing access to the sweet heat between her legs. Elaine ran her hands over her joints, checking for too much tension. Satisfied Petra was in no danger, she moved her hand between her legs and stroked the tender skin of her inner thigh.

Elaine picked up the quirt from the head of the table. She dragged the soft leather over her body. Petra's eyes followed her movements. "You taunted me. You wanted this. I was under the impression you were a Domme. Are you a switch? Or is this research?" Elaine flicked the quirt over the smooth skin of her belly in a light blow.

"I don't know what this is." Her eyes locked on Elaine's. "Not yet. I am a Domme. But don't you crave this? To be the center of someone's attention? Their only concern? To be all they think about? To be someone's inspiration? To simply feel and not have to think?"

Elaine inhaled sharply. "I don't think about such things." She snapped the quirt again, leaving a thin red mark on Petra's right breast. Petra moaned. Her nipple hardened, the tight bud begging to be sucked.

"Why not?" Petra's gaze never wavered. "Don't you think you deserve to be thought of that way?"

"That's enough." Elaine slashed the quirt down and tagged Petra's left breast. A sharp intake of breath, a soft groan, and Petra struggled to raise her hips, unable to move and held tightly by the ropes around her ankles and her wrists. Elaine focused her attention on the quirt. She brought it down again and whipped the inside of Petra's thighs. Small dull red marks appeared over Petra's skin everywhere the quirt connected. A trickle of sweat trailed between Elaine's shoulder blades. Each blow, each small sound of pain Petra made, centered Elaine. *How would it be? To trust someone so much? To give over?* She lost focus and the quirt missed its mark. An ugly welt bloomed on Petra's upper arm.

"Ow." Petra's eyes opened wide.

Elaine stopped and gazed down at Petra. The fear and uncertainty on her face shattered her heart.

She dropped the quirt and sank to her knees. "Forgive me." She knelt next to the table and kissed the welt, soothing the raised skin with her tongue. *Stupid. I hurt her. Damn it. Stop. Stop thinking about it. Stay in the zone.* She kissed her way down her arm and along the smooth column of her throat. She braced her arms on the table to either side of her head and moved to her mouth. Petra's mouth moved against hers, kissing her, sucking Elaine's lower lip between her teeth. She nipped hard. Elaine tasted her own blood on her lips, a sanguine penance for her sin of inattention. Elaine pulled back and studied the expression on Petra's face, her eyes dark and trusting.

"Forgiven." Petra's absolution washed over Elaine, a balm for her soul.

Goddess. To have her. Like this. Mine. For me. I'm lost.

Elaine straightened.

Petra's eyes were closed.

"Petra." Elaine tapped Petra's shoulder. "I need to see your eyes."

Petra opened her eyes and met Elaine's gaze. "Yes, Ma'am."

"You said no anal, correct?"

Petra's eyes widened. "Yes. Ma'am. No anal."

Elaine opened the supply cabinet under the rack and removed a bottle of lube and a pair of black nitrile gloves. "You were okay with a few fingers the other day. How do you feel about fisting?" Elaine tugged the black gloves on to her hands.

"Fine, Ma'am." The eagerness in Petra's voice betrayed her and Elaine laughed.

"You are a delightful slut." She gripped Petra's chin. "You can't wait, can you?"

"No, Ma'am." Petra's lower lip quivered, her eyes bright in the soft light of the dungeon.

"Beg me." Elaine stroked her finger over Petra's clit. "Beg me to fist you."

"Please. Please, Ma'am. Please fist me. Let me feel all of you, please, Ma'am."

Elaine pinched her clit. Petra yipped. Elaine kissed her and drew her lower lip between her teeth. She stopped short of breaking the skin and then licked and soothed the spot with her tongue, drinking in Petra's whimpers.

"Your performance yesterday was exquisite. Although next time, I'd like to fuck you while you fuck her. Take you while you take her. Arrange mirrors so I can see your face when you come for me. What do you think?"

Petra groaned and panted. "Yes. Oh, yes, Ma'am."

Elaine moved to the side of the rack.

"You like that idea?" Elaine traced her finger over her nipples and then down her body. She marked slow circles over her stomach. Petra lifted her body. Arching into Elaine's touch, she trembled. Her movements made the table creak.

"Me too." Elaine mounted the table and kneeled between Petra's legs. She held up the bottle of lube and dripped a thin stream over Petra's clit. She rubbed her glove-clad fingers over it. "I love how thick your clit is. So hard for me. For this."

Petra groaned, her legs tensed, and she struggled against her bonds.

Elaine stroked her clit while she pushed two fingers into Petra. Petra clenched around her. Elaine stilled and kept up her stimulation of Petra's clit. Petra relaxed and Elaine spread her fingers, opening her, before she added a third. Petra groaned. "Yellow, Ma'am."

Elaine stilled her fingers and watched Petra's face as she rubbed her clit. "Is this okay?"

"Yes, Ma'am."

Elaine rubbed her clit in slow circles. "Do you want to come now? Will it help?"

"Yes, Ma'am. Please let me come for you."

Elaine sped up her touches, and Petra panted, her body tightening around Elaine's fingers.

"Oh. Oh please, Ma'am. Please, now please. May I?"

"Come for me. Give me what's mine." Elaine kept her attention on Petra's clit.

Petra came with a sharp sound. Elaine added a finger and pushed deep and rubbed her sweet spot. Petra's body tensed and she came again, her body welcoming Elaine with a gush of fluid.

Elaine pushed deeper, her fingers sweeping over the spot that made Petra thrash. "Oh, Ma'am. Again. Please let me. Again for you."

Elaine rubbed Petra's clit and fucked her in time with her strokes. The rack rocked with their motions. "I'm ready, more of you, Ma'am. Please. All of you."

Elaine tucked her thumb and pushed steadily forward. Petra's shriek as she entered fully nearly made Elaine come herself.

"Oh. So good. More please. Yes. Let me. Please, Ma'am!"

Elaine rocked forward and jacked Petra's clit between her fingers. "Now. Give it to me, now."

Petra tightened around Elaine's hand in waves as she came with a tight choking sound. Elaine turned her hand, a small twisting from side to side, and Petra's body shuddered as she wailed and came again.

"Mercy, Ma'am. Please. I can't come again. No more. Please." Petra's voice was gravel on pavement.

Elaine stilled her movements. She closed her eyes, focusing her energy on Petra and the steady pulse of Petra's body around her fist, and rocked forward once. Petra gasped and undulated as she came with a quiet cry and a slow shudder.

Elaine studied Petra's face. "Are you okay?"

"Yes. I'm good, Ma'am."

Elaine resumed stroking her clit. Petra sighed and the tension in her body relaxed. Elaine eased her hand from Petra. The gush of fluid that followed made Elaine curse the gloves between them.

Elaine stood and tugged the gloves from her hands and tossed them to the floor. Petra shivered, and Elaine kicked the wheel stop and released the tension on her limbs. She reached into the cabinet under the table and pulled out a blanket. She spread it over Petra's body and gave her thigh a pat. Methodically, Elaine worked her way around the rack. She loosened the rope cuffs one by one, rubbed and chafed her hands over the red marks left by the ropes. Petra pulled the blanket around her and sat up.

A rueful smile crossed her face as she pushed her hair back with one hand. "I'm not sure why you bring this out in me, but I don't regret it."

Elaine sat down next her. "I'm not complaining. You are exquisite. Both as a Domme and a submissive. I think you would be a good fit here. Are you still interested?"

Petra cocked her head to the side. "I would be happy to work as a Domme, but not working as a submissive." She pursed her lips. "I've not submitted in years. You bring it out in me." She laughed bitterly. "Did you ever meet Madame Givernay?"

Elaine raised an eyebrow. "Yes. Once. It was enough. Not for my sister, however."

Petra snorted. "You are so much like Madame it is frightening. She had this—I don't even know what. I couldn't help myself from bending to her will. From craving her attention."

"Were you pledged to her?" Elaine tucked her hands under her thighs.

Petra snorted. "No. I was too late for that party. She already had her inner circle. Your sister, Lucia, Vivian. I was a passing fancy. Someone to keep her entertained for a brief time."

The hurt in Petra's voice made Elaine's heart ache. "I'm sorry."

"I've not submitted to anyone since." Petra's voice was a whisper.

"Until now."

"Until now." Petra stood up and wrapped the blanket around her. She turned toward Elaine, her expression devoid of emotion. "Don't worry. I don't expect it to be more." She gathered her clothes and left.

Elaine cleaned up their play space. After disposing of her gloves, she set the rack to rights and wiped it down. She cleaned the quirt and replaced it on its peg. Focused on the routine, Elaine tried and failed to ignore the churning of her gut and the ache in her heart. *Two women. Two women who want too much. Not going there again. Bridget. Rachel. Marguerite. How many others have wanted me? And I wasted my time with Roxy. What if I asked them? And then strayed? I can't ask Robin until she has a real choice. But she'd want me to be exclusive, and I couldn't have Petra. Would I ever really have Petra? Or just the part of her that craves what I can give? Fuck me.*

THE WARMTH FROM the gas fireplace spread across the room. Elaine sipped her glass of whiskey as she read over Robin's assessment of Petra's audition performance. Petra sat across from her on the wide leather couch of the library with Robin at her feet, her head resting against Petra's knee. Petra absently toyed with Robin's blonde curls and Elaine sensed her gaze on her.

Robin's expression was flat. Petra chewed her lower lip as she peered at Elaine over the edge of her glass while she took a sip of her wine. A fine tremor shook her hand when she replaced her wineglass on the side table.

Elaine set her glass of whiskey aside. "Robin, your assessment of Petra's performance aligns with mine. Do you have any additional comments? Something you would like to share with both of us?"

Robin picked at the carpet and avoided Elaine's eyes. "She was exceptional, Mistress." Her voice was hollow.

Petra frowned and stroked her hand over Robin's hair. "You may speak freely, Robin, please. I need to know if I can improve in any way. Your tone does not match your praise."

Robin shifted away from Petra's touch and turned to face her. "I'm being honest. You made my fantasy come true, at least the part you could control." Her face pulled into a bitter smile. Petra's eyes reflected her affection for Robin.

Stung by the bitterness in Robin's tone, Elaine pursed her lips as she studied the two of them together and stifled her urge to tell both of them to kneel at her feet. "Be that as it may, Robin, are you willing to move on to the second part of the audition? Or would you like Tessa to take your place?" *Please say yes. Say you are done with this. Done with her.*

Robin fixed Elaine with a hard glare. "No. I'm willing. More than willing, Mistress."

She reached out and wrapped her arm around Petra's boot, and slid closer to her, pressing herself against her calf. Petra reached out and rested her hand on the back of Robin's neck. She tilted her head at Elaine, one eyebrow raised in challenge.

Amateur. She thinks Robin will be so easily won?

"Very well. Until tomorrow night." Elaine stood, waving for both of them to remain where they were. "I need to talk to Tessa. Petra, please feel free to stay here and enjoy the rest of your wine."

Chapter Eight

ELAINE PACED THE length of her room. *What the hell was that about? Robin claiming Petra like she was her Domme. Trying to make me jealous. Fuck it, I am.* She peered out of the window at the gray day. *Damn, why am I here and not on holiday? Away from all of this. Away from her. And her love. Both of them. Dangerous. I can't get attached again. Never again. No one is worth so much pain.*

A sharp rap at her door interrupted her ruminations. She snatched open the door. "What?"

"Are you free to talk?"

Elaine stepped back from the door. "Come in." She gestured to the chairs in front of the fireplace.

The scent of Petra's gardenia perfume wove its way into her head and she inhaled sharply, her visceral reaction evidence of her growing affection for Petra.

Petra took the chair closest to the fire. Elaine closed the door. "Can I get you something to drink?"

"No, thank you. This won't take long."

Elaine sat down and crossed her legs. "Sounds ominous."

Petra's mouth pulled into a smile. "I'm not leaving if that's your concern."

"No. Not worried about that, for now."

"I want to talk about Robin."

"Okay." Elaine shifted in her seat.

"And you."

Elaine frowned. "I don't see what we have to talk about."

Petra skewered her with her gaze. "Yes, you do. I want to know, is she a free agent? Or is she pledged to the house?"

"You didn't ask her?"

"I did. She was very cagey about it and not forthcoming."

Elaine frowned. "She's a free agent."

"She refused to accompany me on an excursion off the grounds. Why?"

Is it safe to tell her? Would it put Robin at risk? Should I tell her? She was vetted by Jaya Pomroy. Jaya wouldn't send us anyone unsafe. Trust her. "Robin was forced to cooperate in an extortion scheme threatening to expose Rowan House. We confronted Robin and Rachel, the other employee who was involved. She attacked Robin, tried to use her as a human shield, and then fled the house. We were able to thwart the scheme with Robin's help. The group behind the scheme murdered Rachel. We have an operative working on securing Robin's future. Until we know the threat has been permanently eliminated, she's here under our protection."

Petra's mouth drew down. "Poor Robin. 'The caged bird sings with a fearful trill, of things unknown, but longed for still.'"

"I think of Maya Angelou and that poem every time the anniversary of Robin's contract signing rolls around. It's been two years. Based on the last communication I received from our operative, I think it will be resolved soon."

Petra drummed her fingers on the arm of the chair. "I see why she didn't want to tell me or sleep in my room."

"What?" Elaine glared at Petra. "She's not required to sleep with you."

Petra met Elaine's glare with a soft smile. "And she knew you would be annoyed if she did, and yet you claim not to want to collar her. Why are you so reluctant to admit you want her?"

"I can't ask her, not now, not when she doesn't have the freedom to leave." Elaine stood and crossed to the fireplace, her back to Petra.

"You're afraid she would only say yes because she's trapped here." Petra's voice was soft. "Now it all makes sense."

"What does? Tell me, please, because I have no idea what's going on." Elaine glanced over her shoulder at Petra.

"She's in love with you. You're afraid she only cares because she is grateful, in love with her jailor, suffering from Stockholm syndrome. A modern-day *Beauty and the Beast*, yes?"

"Something like that, yes." Elaine turned to Petra and pushed her hair back with both hands. "No matter how I feel I can't ask her until she has a true choice."

"Will you?" Petra pursed her lips. "Will you ask her then?"

Elaine scuffed her boot over the floor. "I don't know."

"Because of Roxy?"

"What the hell has she got to do with it, and how do you know about her?"

"I have my sources." Petra held Elaine's gaze. "Afraid of being rejected again?"

Elaine's face burned with her flush. "No!" She jammed her hands into her pockets. "No. I'm not. I don't think commitment is right for me."

"But you asked Roxy, why?"

"Do you have some sort of counseling degree? I feel like I'm at the therapist's office."

Petra tilted her head at Elaine. "If you'd bothered to read my application you would know I have a doctorate in psychology. I've worked as a therapist in private practice."

Elaine covered her face with both hands and groaned. "I am going to kill my sister when she gets back."

Petra rose from her seat and crossed to Elaine. She peeled her hands from her face. "Your intentions are noble, but I think misplaced. But that's for you to work out."

Elaine stared into Petra's eyes, drawn in by the tenderness in her gaze. She swallowed on a dry throat. Petra took her hands and kissed the backs of them, her lips soft, before she tugged Elaine into her arms. Elaine relaxed. *Safe. She makes me feel safe.* She pushed away the other feeling, the one she didn't want to think about, the one she didn't trust and held her body rigid.

Petra's heels made their height difference less, and she brought her lips close to Elaine's ear and whispered. "Poor Elaine. Surrounded by women who want you and don't know you. Women who don't understand how utterly alone and out of place you feel in the world." She pressed a soft kiss under her ear. "Do you know there's a word for constantly feeling out of place? Monachopsis. Even here, in a home you have lived in for years, because it's not about where you are, it's about you." Petra's closeness and words wrapped around Elaine and settled over her, soothing, and warm.

She released Elaine's hands and stepped away from her. A rush of coolness where Petra had been startled Elaine. Petra turned and left the room, closing the door with a quick click.

Elaine shivered. She opened and closed her hands, remembering the sweet touch of Petra's lips and the sensation of being known, heady and unsettling. She threw herself into her chair. *What the hell were they thinking? A therapist, they fucking left me with a therapist and didn't tell me.*

Chapter Nine

ELAINE LED MARCO to the ring. Petra was mounted on him, her mouth set in a firm line like she was being led to a punishment and not one she'd enjoy. "Relax. He can feel you if you're tense. He'll think there's something to be worried about."

Petra's face relaxed marginally. "I'm sorry. I am not used to being out of control."

Elaine snorted. "You're still in control. Now, pick up the reins like I showed you."

Petra positioned her hands on the reins. Elaine released Marco's bridle. "He's steady as a rock and gentle. To make him go forward you need to give him a little squeeze with your legs and relax your hands. When you pull back it tightens the bit and signals him to stop. If you squeeze your legs and don't relax your hands, it's like leaving a car in park and stepping on the gas."

Marco started walking forward and Petra laughed. A giddy laugh more like a young girl's than a woman of forty. *Joy. She loves it.* "To go to the right, pull back steadily on the right rein. Soft now, their mouths are tender. And press in with your right knee, relax the left one, bend him around your leg. Once he's going the direction you want, relax your hands again and even out the pressure of your legs, using just enough to keep your seat."

Elaine walked next to Petra as she rode slowly around the ring. She glanced up at her face. Petra's expression was a mix of delight and concentration.

"I can see why you like this." Petra grinned at Elaine.

"I don't think I could survive without Luna and a place to ride." They reached the end of the ring and Petra guided Marco around the turn.

"He's so beautiful. His mane is magnificent."

"Veronica is a miracle worker. She's an excellent teacher too, if you want more lessons. It's like breathing for me, and it's hard for me to teach someone how to ride." Elaine stepped away from Petra's side. "I'll watch from here. Keep your heels down and be sure your hands are still."

Petra rode Marco around the ring, heeding Elaine's instructions as she circled in one direction and then in the other.

"Now, try walking him in a figure eight." Elaine rested her hand on the top of a jump. Petra's happiness was palpable, and Elaine marveled at her own feeling of sharing something she loved so much with someone else. Someone who understood. Roxy tolerated Elaine's obsession with Luna and riding, but her face had never held the joy Petra's did just walking around the indoor ring on a cold rainy day.

"We should probably stop soon. Your thighs will be screaming later, and not in a good way."

Petra laughed again. "No wonder yours are so magnificent."

Elaine arched an eyebrow. "Thank you. And now you know my secret."

"One of them." Petra brought Marco around and stopped in front of Elaine. "I'd like to know the rest of them."

Elaine reached up and clasped Marco's bridle. "What about yours? Quid pro quo?" She led the horse over to the mounting block.

Petra dismounted. She pulled her hardhat from her head. "One of my secrets for one of yours?"

Elaine ran up the stirrups and pulled the reins over Marco's head. She led him out under the covered walkway back to the barn.

"Yes." Elaine kept the horse between them, giving herself some breathing room.

"What do you want to know?"

"You're so brave. Ready to tell me anything." Elaine let the snark show in her voice.

"Yes. But it goes both ways. You ask first."

They walked along in silence. Elaine sorted through the many questions she wanted to ask, surprised by how much she wanted to know Petra.

"Why were you so worried when you arrived there would be issues because you're not white?"

"When you first read my name what did you think I looked like? Were you imagining some tall white blonde goddess?"

"I don't know about tall, but yes, I did imagine you were white and blonde."

"Right. You and everyone else who has seen my name first and me second. I've had people miss picking me up at airports, deny me reservations until I show photo ID, and more than one client reject me after they had contracted for an experience deciding they did not want to interact with me because I was not what they envisioned. I've been accused of pulling a prank, because someone could not possibly have my name and appear as I do, and once, when I was a child, they would not release me to my mother from after-school care because no one believed she was my mother."

Elaine stopped walking and moved Marco to the side. She caught Petra's hand in hers and squeezed it gently. "I'm so sorry you've been through so much. No wonder you asked."

Petra pulled her hand free. "Sorry, I went on about it. I don't need your pity."

Elaine stepped back. She turned Marco toward the barn and resumed.

"Is it my turn now? Or are you tired of playing? Too much information? Sorry you asked?" The edge in Petra's voice cut Elaine to the core.

"Not sorry. I'd like to talk with you some more. We need to get Marco put up first. Veronica will take care of him once we get to the barn. Would you have tea with me?" Elaine chewed her lip, her palms sweaty. *Please say yes.*

"Talk? Are you expecting this to go as our other conversations have?" Petra's crisp footsteps rang on the walk.

"No expectations. Just conversation."

"Understood. I'd prefer to have our conversation someplace private."

"Would my quarters suit?" They had arrived at the barn. "Hold him, please."

Petra took hold of Marco's reins.

Elaine rolled the door back.

Petra handed her the reins and met her gaze. "Yes. In an hour." She turned and left Elaine wondering if she would ever understand the woman who had handed her the reins and walked away.

TESSA ROLLED THE cart into Elaine's room. "Where do you want me to set up, Mistress?"

"In front of the fire is fine." Elaine pulled at the pins holding her hair up and shook it out. "Leave everything covered."

"Yes, Mistress." Tessa rolled the cart to the small rug by the fire and opened the leaves to turn it into a small table and placed it between the two chairs. "Anything else, Mistress?"

"No, thank you."

Elaine sat down and drummed her fingers on the arm of the chair. *Late or not coming? The tea will be cold if she doesn't hurry up. Too much. I pushed too hard. Fuck.*

A rap on the door yanked Elaine out of her thoughts. "It's open," she called from her chair.

Petra walked into the room and closed the door behind her. "Should I lock it?"

"Depends." Elaine shifted in her chair and turned to face Petra.

"On what?" Petra crossed her arms over her chest.

"On you."

"If I'm more comfortable with it locked, or if I need to leave it unlocked to have a ready exit?" Petra laughed. "Is this a test of trust? After what we've done together don't you think this is silly?

Elaine pursed her lips. "Not silly. It's one thing to scene in a public space. To be here alone with me in my room, my private space, where no one ever comes unless they are summoned or invited is very different."

"If I was afraid or didn't trust you, why would I have agreed to meet you here?" Petra crossed the room and sat down opposite Elaine.

"True. I also noticed you didn't lock the door. I had them bring tea, but I could get Tessa to bring us coffee if you prefer."

"Tea is fine. And if no one comes uninvited why would it be necessary to lock the door?"

Elaine poured out the tea. "Milk? Sugar?"

"No. This is fine." Petra picked up her cup. "You didn't answer my question."

"I slept with my door unlocked for years, but after the business with the extortionists I've become more cautious."

Petra's gaze fixed on the scar that bloomed across the back of Elaine's hand and flowed up over her wrist and under her sleeve.

Elaine unbuttoned the cuff of her shirt, folded it back over her forearm, raised her hand, and extended it toward Petra. "I've noticed you staring at it before. Go ahead. I'm not offended."

Petra set aside her teacup and clasped Elaine's hand in both of hers. She rubbed her thumb over the smooth scar. "Does it bother you?"

"It doesn't hurt if that's what you mean. The burn was deep enough it's numb. It doesn't hurt physically."

"But?" Petra held Elaine's gaze.

"But, knowing a woman I had slept with, had taken to my bed and trusted, left a pan of grease in my oven, sabotaged my kitchen, knowing the burn could have been worse, knowing I might have died, or my sister or one of the others could have been killed, knowing my family home could have burned to the ground. Yes. I'm reminded of the horrific reality every time I see it. And every time I burn it again because the skin is numb and I've bumped the back of my hand on the oven rack. That bothers the fuck out of me." Elaine pulled her hand from Petra's grasp.

Petra picked up her tea and took a sip. Elaine avoided Petra's eyes as she unrolled her sleeve and buttoned the cuff in place. She waved her hand over the assortment of biscuits, cheese, and a plate of savory tarts. "What would you like?"

"You choose."

Elaine filled a plate and passed it to Petra before she made her own selection.

Petra placed her cup on the table, picked up a napkin, and spread it over her lap. "Your turn." She took a bite of mini mushroom and spinach tart.

Elaine waited until Petra had finished the tart. "Where did you grow up?"

"I grew up in Vadsø, Norway."

Elaine dabbed at her mouth with her napkin. "I've never been to Norway."

"Have you always lived here?" Petra gestured to the room. "Has this been your room since you were a girl?"

"That's two questions, but I'm feeling generous. Yes, I've lived in this house since I was a girl, except for time spent in cooking schools and interning. I've lived here. Martha and I shared this room until she went to university. We returned here when we had completed our studies. She, Lucia, and Myfanwy occupy the suite of rooms on the opposite side of the main stairs. The illusion of privacy."

Petra bit into a lavender lemon shortbread from her plate. She closed her eyes and chewed, a blissful expression on her face.

Elaine laughed. "Robin has many talents. That is her signature shortbread."

"That is sinful." Petra took a sip of her tea.

"How do you know Lucia?" Elaine bit into her favorite chocolate biscuit.

Petra's eyes shuttered. "Pass."

"Why?"

"Why do you want to know?" Petra's expression was neutral, but her eyes were hard.

"Lucia is part of my family now. You're the first person she has ever mentioned in her life other than Madame. I'm curious. I don't care if you were involved. And neither will Martha if you're concerned."

Petra snorted. "Involved. That's one way to put it." She took another sip of her tea. "I met Lucia in Japan. Madame sent me to her."

"As her what? Sub? Chaperone? Minder?"

"She was studying shibari and was required to bring someone with her to be her canvas."

"You went willingly? Or was it Madame's will?" Elaine twisted her napkin in her hands.

"I wanted to go. There was no place for me at the Onyx." Petra's tone revealed nothing, her face a mask.

Elaine placed her plate on the table. "I don't understand what kind of hold Madame had. How she was able to draw strong women such as yourself, Lucia, and my sister to her side, have them beg to be hers."

"Don't you?" Petra tilted her head to the side. "How many women have asked or begged to be yours?"

Elaine shifted in her seat. "That's different."

"How so? Because they were subs?"

Elaine picked up the teapot. "More tea?"

"No, thank you."

Elaine could sense Petra's eyes on her.

"Not going to answer?"

"I don't know what to say." Elaine sat back in her chair.

"Probably enough sharing for today."

"Goddess, I hate that word. I don't like sharing. I don't want to know. I think we should all keep our secrets and fucked-up feelings inside where they belong."

"So they can fester? Fuel your anger and pain?" Petra snorted. "And here I thought you were a sadist."

"I am." Elaine studied the pattern on the carpet. "And what good does it do to share? It's not like anyone really cares."

"Or stays around? That's the rest of it, isn't it? You don't expect anyone to stay if you're honest." Petra's gaze burned. "If you keep everyone at arm's length, hold back, always stay in control, you don't have to worry, do you? And yet you were surprised when Roxy left."

Elaine stood abruptly. "You don't know me. Three scenes, a few chats, and you think you know me. The audacity."

"I didn't say I did. I said I wanted to." Petra placed her plate on the cart before she pressed her napkin to her mouth. "Thank you for the lovely tea. And the conversation." She stood up and turned to face Elaine.

"What? It's over? You don't want to answer any more questions? Did I offend your sensibilities? I expected more from a Domme." Elaine's anger knotted in her belly, low and tight.

"No point is there?" Petra's voice was soft. "You've made up your mind about me already."

"I didn't say that." Elaine stepped closer to Petra. "I'm sorry."

"So am I." Petra skirted around Elaine and walked out, closing the door behind her with a hard click.

Chapter Ten

ELAINE OPENED THE mail program for the house. Another reason she hated Martha being gone; the tedious task of email left her clenching her jaw on a good day. She scanned the list and a flagged email from Jaya Pomroy caught her attention. Her hand trembled as she tapped the keys to open the email. She opened the middle desk drawer and pulled out the code list Martha had left her. It took her a few minutes to decipher the email, but the message was clear. Robin was free, the extortionists no longer an issue. Elaine closed the program and set her laptop aside.

Tell her. I need to tell her. And then. And then it will be what it will be. Will she leave? What if she does? What if she wants to leave with Petra? What if they both leave? What's wrong with me? Of course, they'll leave together. Why would they stay with me? A pair of hands and a hot time, no heart. I never share my heart, not so they would know, because I never tell them. I thought I loved Roxy, thought she loved me. How wrong I was about all of it.

PETRA FOLDED HER napkin and placed it next to her plate. "I've had another offer. A house on Bygdøy, Oslo. It's for the head mistress position."

Elaine took a sip of water. "And? Do you wish to end your audition early? Withdraw your application?" She rolled the edge of her napkin between her fingers.

Petra pursed her lips. "No. I only wanted you to be aware."

Nothing, she's giving me nothing. She'd make a mint as a card player. "Are you planning on going there to interview before you make your decision about the job here? If we were to offer you one?"

A frowned creased Petra's forehead. "I'd be foolish not to at least visit and see what they are willing to offer. Even if you extend an offer, I wouldn't have any say in how the house is run here."

"It's customary to wait until after the second audition to make any offer. I'll also need to discuss it with Martha and Lucia. As far as having a voice in how the house is run, we have recently moved to a cooperative model of organization."

Petra smiled and took a sip of her coffee before she spoke. "But who makes the ultimate decisions about how the house is run? You? Or all of you?"

Elaine cleared her throat. "Final decisions are made by Martha, Lucia, and me. We are the owners, we view our workers as partners."

"But not full partners." Petra inclined her head toward the kitchen. "They are submissives pledged to the house. How much can they negotiate? How much would I be able to negotiate?"

Elaine rubbed her fingers over her brow. "We've not had the occasion to work with other Mistresses who were members of the staff. Lucia came to us as a legacy from Madame. After she and my sister pledged to each other and decided they were not going to interact with our clients we find ourselves in need of another Mistress. We haven't made firm decisions as to how to proceed. Obviously we wouldn't expect a Mistress to pledge to the house."

"Obviously?" Petra arched an eyebrow. "And why not? Why not expect the type of commitment from a Mistress as from a submissive if they were to become part of the house?"

Elaine frowned. "I don't know. We haven't discussed it. But it seems wrong. I don't know. But until I discuss this with Lucia and Martha I can't make you an offer. As I said."

"So you did." Petra picked up the coffee press and poured herself another cup of coffee.

Elaine opened and closed her hands over the arms of her chair. She pushed it back. "I have some work to do."

"I would like to complete my audition here before I leave."

"Tell Millie what you need for your travel arrangements. As before, tell the others what you need for your scene and they will set it up." Elaine left Petra at the table.

On the walk to her office she chewed her lip as sadness and foreboding settled into her soul. Old friends. *She'll leave. Why stay when she would not be in charge? She loves power. Loves it as much as I do. She gave over to me. Sought me out to submit. Maybe she would pledge to the house. Or me?* Elaine was giddy at the idea of Petra pledging to her, remembering what it felt like to have her under her. *Is this what Lucia feels with Martha, having someone under you who can turn the tables in an instant but who surrenders their power to you?*

ROBIN SAT ON the floor. A pair of light blue nitrile gloves covered her hands. Heavy brown craft paper surrounded her. A pair of black knee-high riding boots and Elaine's favorite black pumps rested on the paper. The fire threw off a warm heat and the reflection of the flames on the glass doors of the gas fireplace lit Robin's face with a soft glow. She picked up a boar's-hair brush from the kit and one of the black pumps. With brisk strokes she brushed the shoe, a first pass to get any dirt off. She repeated it with the second shoe. A satisfied expression settled over her face as she set the brush aside. Meticulously Robin applied black polish to the pumps with an old toothbrush. Elaine sat in her chair and pretended to read as she watched Robin working at her task, admiring the way she focused on what she was doing, as if the only thing in the world, the only thing that mattered, was polishing Elaine's shoes to perfection.

Robin tucked her hand inside a pump and selected a wide brush, the bristles stained black, and brushed the leather, smoothing out the fresh polish until the shoe took on a dull shine.

It was easy, in moments like this, for Elaine to imagine what it would be like if Robin was hers. Cozy evenings spent with each other; together but respecting your lover's need to be near but not engaged. *Is this what love is like? What are we to each other? Partners? Lovers?* Elaine craved Robin. Not only sexually. All of her. She cared for her. Loved her. Loved her enough to not accept her devotion until she was truly free to give it. *If she were free would she still be so anxious to be mine? Or would she move on, happy to be out of the life? Lucia and Martha promised to find her a place to work, a safe place. Jaya would be able to provide her with a new name and new life if she wanted it. What will she want? What do I want?*

Robin set the shoe aside and picked up a pair of old hose, wrapped it around her hand, and dipped it into a small dish of water. She picked up the pump, slipped her hand inside to hold it, and began rubbing the leather in tiny circles. The dullness of the fresh polish gave way to a reflective shine. Robin's tongue peeked from the corner of her mouth. Sweet, innocent, and in total contrast to the woman at Elaine's feet dressed in a short Clan MacLeod tartan kilt and tight white blouse unbuttoned to display her modest cleavage.

Her sleeves were rolled back and the scars of her prior addiction caught the light. *Something else to think about. Would she be able to stay clean and sober without the support and discipline of the house? So many temptations in the outside world.* Rowan House's zero tolerance regarding drugs had drawn more than one former addict seeking a supportive place to work.

Elaine stared at her glass of whiskey. Was she as much an addict? No. If she had to stop tomorrow, she would. She hadn't had any alcohol when she was recovering from her burn, fearful of the effects combined with the pain medications she had been prescribed. And then after, when she had been so sad and angry after Roxy left her, when she had feared crawling into the bottle and never returning, she had been forced to evaluate her use of alcohol.

"I need some water, Mistress. Would you like something?" Robin turned her face to her. She wore a dreamy expression, evidence of the subspace she had drifted into serving at Elaine's feet. She peeled the gloves off her hands, carefully avoiding the polish.

"Yes, please. And dump this. I'm not feeling it." Elaine handed her the glass of whiskey.

"Yes, Mistress. Would you like lemon in the water?"

"That would be lovely." Elaine placed her book on the table.

"Back in a few minutes, Mistress."

Elaine rested her chin in her hand and her elbow on her knee. Her pumps gleamed. Two more pair of shoes and her tall boots remained. *Maybe she should polish the boots while I wear them.* She flushed as she thought about how she would reward Robin for a job well done, and a surge of wetness soaked her briefs. While Robin was absent, she stripped off her clothes. After she donned her emerald-green dressing gown and black thigh-high hose, she took down her hair and brushed it out. With one eye on the clock, she tugged her boots on, picked up her book, crossed her legs, and waited.

Robin returned with a tray holding two glasses and a crystal water pitcher. Slices of lemon floated in the pitcher. She paused and swept her gaze over Elaine, lingering on her boots and thighs where the gown fell open. Robin licked her lower lip, hunger in her eyes. She poured a glass of water. She walked toward Elaine, kneeled by the side of her chair, and offered the glass to her with both hands. Elaine marked her place with a bookmark and set her book aside. She took the glass from Robin's hands, brushing her fingers over hers as she did. She took a long drink before she placed the glass on the side table. "I thought it might make it easier if you polished these while I wore them."

"Oh, yes, Mistress." Robin crawled on her hands and knees to her polishing supplies. She picked up two towels and returned. "Would you spread your legs, Mistress?"

Robin waggled the towel. "I don't want to get any polish on the carpet."

Elaine opened her legs wide, and her feet on either side of the chair. Elaine smiled when she caught her stealing a glance beneath her robe. She shifted and opened her legs a bit wider, letting Robin see the effect she had on her. Robin spread the towel on the carpet.

"May I touch you, Mistress?"

"Yes."

Robin lifted Elaine's boot-shod foot and placed it on the dark brown towel before she repeated the move with the other leg until Elaine's boots were centered on the terry cloth.

Robin donned another pair of nitrile gloves from the kit. She brushed the loose dirt from each of the boots, lifting and moving Elaine's legs as she needed to access each one. Elaine settled back in her chair. Robin applied polish to each boot, her breath coming faster as she worked. Watching Robin as she kneeled at her feet, hands working quickly and her breasts rising and falling as she buffed and polished the boots, made Elaine ache with desire. Her boots gleamed. Robin tugged off her gloves, bent her head, and pressed a light kiss to the toe of each boot before she sat back on her heels, her gaze fixed on the carpet.

"Robin." Elaine touched the top of her head.

Robin met her gaze. "Yes, Mistress."

"You've done a beautiful job. Come here."

Elaine patted her lap.

Robin licked her lower lip and rose up on her knees. She stood and then settled herself on Elaine's lap. Elaine circled her arm around her shoulders. Holding her on her lap, she traced her fingers up and under the hem of the skirt. She stroked her thigh and drew small circles over her smooth skin with her fingertips. "You've earned a reward." She moved her fingers higher and plucked at the edge of Robin's thong.

Robin shivered in her arms, and Elaine moved her hand higher and gripped the back of her neck. "Pull your skirt up for me," she whispered.

Robin grasped the edge of her skirt and pulled it up to her waist.

"Don't let go." Elaine pushed under the thong, moving it to the side. She dipped her fingers between Robin's legs, gathered the wetness there, and brought her fingers to her mouth. She licked her fingers. "So sweet." She shifted in the chair, so Robin was straddling her. She rubbed her thumb over Robin's clit while she mouthed her breast through her shirt. She moved her hands over Robin's ass, grabbed both sides of the thong, and ripped it, tearing it clear of her body. Robin gasped and swayed.

Elaine placed one hand in the middle of Robin's back and moved her other hand between her legs to tease her clit. Robin groaned in her arms and arched into her touch. Elaine fingered her, pressing into her body. Robin panted. Elaine took her time, relentless in her goal to draw out Robin's pleasure.

"Please. Please, Mistress. Let me come for you." Robin's breath was ragged, her hips rolled into Elaine as she held her there and fucked her.

Elaine bit her nipple through her shirt, cursing the clothing that kept her from feeling the rough hardness of Robin's flesh in her mouth.

"Come as you wish."

Robin clenched around her hand and rocked her hips faster. She let go of her skirt and clutched Elaine's shoulders, clinging to her as she ground her hips against her hand, fucking herself into orgasm.

Elaine growled as Robin's nails dug into her shoulders. She stilled, letting Robin ride out her pleasure. Her breathing slowed, and Elaine lowered her hands, scooted forward in the chair, and gripped Robin's ass as she stood up. "Wrap your legs around me."

Robin clasped her legs around her waist, and Elaine walked to her bed and lowered Robin to her back.

The short kilt tore as Elaine yanked at the buttons at the waistband. "Raise your hips." Robin planted her heels and arched up. Elaine drew the remnants of the skirt from her and tossed them to the floor. With both hands, she clasped the front of Robin's blouse and ripped it open. Robin's lacy bra opened in the front. She unhooked it and shoved it aside. She wrapped her hands around Robin's wrists, holding them to each side, and lowered her head to her breasts. She licked and bit her thick nipples. Robin thrashed and moaned under her. Elaine moved lower, biting and nipping Robin's skin, rolling the soft flesh in her teeth, marking her as she went.

Robin moaned. "Oh yes, Mistress. Please."

Elaine covered her with her mouth. She thrust her tongue deep, savoring the salt honey that flowed from her. Robin's hips rocked into her mouth. Elaine tightened her grip on her hands, and Robin whimpered. Moving to her clit, Elaine teased her, circling it with her tongue slowly, sucking it into her mouth. Robin panted. "Oh Mistress, I can't. I'm going to come."

Elaine was relentless, not letting up, never lifting her head. Knowing Robin wouldn't be able to stop, she kept on. Robin shrieked and came. A gush of fluid surged over Elaine's chin. She kept on, and drove her up again, licking her clit directly, softly, until Robin cried out again, her arms rigid in Elaine's grip. "Oh mercy, Mistress. Please. No more. I can't. I can't."

Elaine lifted her head, raised Robin's hands over her head, and captured them with one hand. With her other hand, she pushed deep with four fingers into the raging wet heat between her legs, the heel of her hand grinding against Robin's hard clit, rocking into her.

"Look at me." Elaine fucked her slow and deep. "You will."

Robin trembled under her. She spread her thighs wider and lifted her hips to meet Elaine's strokes. Robin's breathing deepened, and her eyes held Elaine's as she came again in a low slow orgasm. Her body opened to Elaine, and Elaine tucked her thumb and entered her fully and stilled. Robin's mouth was open, and she panted. Her pupils blown wide, her jaw slack.

"Slow down. Slow your breathing." Elaine waited. Robin's eyes never left her face. Her cheeks were flushed, the deep blue of her eyes a fine rim around the black pools of her pupils.

Elaine formed her hand into a fist inside Robin. Robin's eyes closed, and she moaned.

"No. Eyes open."

Robin obeyed.

Elaine rocked her hand and a deep groan rattled Robin's chest. She released Robin's hands and moved her head lower to suck Robin's clit into her mouth. She thrummed her tongue over her clit as she pushed deep, and Robin screamed as she came again. Elaine buried her head into the curve of Robin's neck. Robin brought her hands up and dug them into Elaine's hair as her body shuddered and trembled with aftershocks.

Robin's body pulsed around Elaine's hand, and she waited until her body relaxed before she eased her hand from her. Robin carded her fingers through Elaine's hair. Elaine caressed Robin's stomach and the under curve of her breasts, the pads of fingers scribing small circles of wet across her skin. Elaine pulled away from Robin's arms. Her brow drew down, her eyes fearful, and she made a mournful sound of disappointment. An animal sound, it seared Elaine's heart and branded her soul.

"Shh. I need to get these boots off." Elaine kissed Robin's forehead. She sat on the side of the bed and pulled her boots off and dropped them by the bed. She lay back on the mattress and lifted her arm. Robin slipped under it and lay with her head on Elaine's chest. She pressed her palm over the satin gown, and Elaine's nipple hardened under her touch. Her breath was warm against Elaine's skin. She kissed the side of her neck. "May I, Mistress? Let me pleasure you, please."

Elaine swept her hand down Robin's back. "As you wish."

Robin rolled on top of Elaine and straddled her. She tugged at the robe's ties and the knot came undone in her hands. She leaned down and kissed the space between Elaine's breasts. Her tongue swept over Elaine's skin, and she burned in its wake. Her thighs were slick with want. Robin sipped at her skin, barely there kisses as she moved lower until her warm breath surrounded Elaine's clit. Robin spread her hands out over Elaine's thighs. She circled Elaine's clit with her tongue, a delicate touch, before she closed her mouth over it. She suckled gently, her tongue touching the tight knot of nerves directly, making Elaine ache. Elaine moved her hands to Robin's hair and held her in place, closing her eyes against the sensations. Robin licked with the flat of her tongue, and

Elaine grit her teeth, the pleasure so intense she wanted it to go on forever. *Forever. To have this. To have her.* The thought crashed through her as she came in Robin's mouth with no thought other than how much she didn't want it to end.

ELAINE BRUSHED HER hair and left it loose, red flames around her shoulders. She checked her outfit in the mirror one last time. *I can do this. I need to do this. Need to tell her. Last night was magical. She loves me. Really loves me, not just the idea of me. Time to make my intentions clear. Time to tell her she's free. To see if she wants more.* She swallowed on a dry throat as she pushed away the thoughts of what would happen if she said no. If she laughed in Elaine's face as Roxy had. *She won't. That's not her style. She'd just stare at me with those huge blue eyes and say no. No drama.* She hurried down the stairs and to the dining room.

Elaine looked through the round window of the door leading to the kitchen and immediately wished she had not. Petra was leaning over Robin. One hand under her skirt, the other planted in the middle of Robin's back as Robin lay face down across the table. Robin's cheek rested on her folded arms and her eyes were closed, her face blissful.

Elaine couldn't see what Petra was doing, but she could imagine what was going on. She held her breath, unable to turn away. Petra's lips moved, her words muffled by the heavy door. Robin's moan made Elaine's stomach hurt and her heart ache. Robin's hips lifted and her body undulated as she rocked back, seeking more of Petra's touch.

Elaine rested her head on the window frame and closed her eyes against the pain. Robin's high-pitched wail as she came, a sound so familiar to Elaine she would recognize it anywhere, made her risk a final glance in the window. Robin's eyes opened at just that moment and her gaze locked on Elaine's. Elaine bit her lip to keep from crying out. She backed away from the door and fled the room. *Out. I need to get out. And there's her answer. What she would do if she had the freedom. Why did I give her permission? Stupid. So stupid.* She dashed her hand across her eyes and swept away the liquid evidence of her heartbreak. She ran from the dining room, through the hall and took the stairs to her room two at a time. Once she was in her room, she closed the door and leaned her back against it. Her heart pounded. Her breath was ragged from running the stairs. She reached behind her and turned the knob to seat the deadbolt. Her knees gave out and she slid down the door. She crossed her arms and rested them on the top of her knees, turned her head to the side, and rested her cheek on her arms.

Everything she had wanted to say to Robin turned to ashes in her mouth. *Being alone is better than this heartache. And Petra. She'll leave too, no doubt. The offer is too good to pass up. And Robin will go with her. It's for the best. No one to worry about. Or disappoint. Or want. Don't tell her. Keep her here. Don't say anything. She'll get over Petra. But will I? How can it hurt this much? How can I pretend not to care? How long can I hide the truth? Martha will tell her if I don't, and then she'll hate me. Why? Why did I check the damn email? What am I going to do?*

She chewed her thumbnail. A soft tap at the door drew her attention, and Petra's gardenia perfume tickled

Elaine's nose. She ignored the knock and held her breath, willing Petra to go away and leave her in peace as she gathered up the pieces of her shattered heart.

Another knock, more insistent.

"I'm not receiving," Elaine shouted.

"Open the door, Elaine."

"Go away. Is that clearer?" Elaine covered her face with her hands.

"We need to talk. Hiding is not going to make it better."

"Thank you, doctor. Tell me where to send your final bill." Elaine rested her arms on her knees and leaned her head back against the door.

"I'm not leaving until we talk."

The thump and vibration of what had to be Petra's shoulder against the door shook the door where Elaine leaned against it and rattled the knob.

"Open the door Elaine. Now."

"Or what?"

An explosive kick against the door rattled the hinges.

"This door is older than you are, and if you damage it I will take it out of your skin."

Another kick, louder than the first, made Elaine jump to her feet. She twisted the deadbolt knob and yanked the door open. Not caring if the murderous thoughts in her head were reflected in her expression.

Petra strolled past her and turned to face her.

"I didn't invite you in."

"What are you? A vampire? For fuck's sake, Elaine, stop acting like you're thirteen and just lost your first girlfriend."

Elaine slammed the door shut. "Is that supposed to be therapeutic? Make me angry so I stop feeling sad?"

"If you were honest, none of this would have happened."

"Oh so it's my fault?"

"Yes."

Elaine clenched her hands into fists. "What?"

Petra's gaze was steady. "If you were honest about how you feel about Robin, you never would have given her to me. And she would never have agreed."

Elaine studied the toes of her shoes, her anger morphing into resignation. "You're a better fit for her." She walked to the window. The sky was the dull gray of old silver. How often had she stared out of this window as if it held the answer to her fucked-up little life? As if some great source of knowledge would write the answer out across the gunmetal sky.

Petra's arms clasped her around the waist. The warmth of her body as she pressed against Elaine twisted the double-sided knife of betrayal deep into Elaine's heart. *I care for her, love Robin, and they care for each other. And isn't that just dandy?*

Petra rested her cheek against Elaine's back. "So much sadness in you Elaine. I hate the sad loneliness I see in your eyes, the way sorrow flashes across your face when you think no one is near to see. I know how that feels. Robin does too. Why do you think what we feel for each other means we feel less for you?"

Elaine relaxed into Petra's arms. "I came to tell her she was free. It's safe for her to leave. To ask her to be mine. I couldn't do it. She deserves more than this. Me."

"Why don't you let her decide?"

Elaine snorted. "I have eyes. I saw her face when she was with you. Her guilty expression when she glanced up and realized I was watching you two."

The warmth of Petra's body against her back and her soft voice was a balm to Elaine's heart. *She's not afraid of me, she's not a brat. So calm. Soothing. Would she lie with me? Hold me? And then what? Suffer more when she leaves. And when Robin goes with her? Live with the memories of her body and her mind, and how much she makes me feel cared for? She sees me. Sees all of me. Like Robin and yet not. Robin sees me too. What I've let her see.*

Petra moved back and Elaine missed the heat of her against her body. She grasped Elaine's shoulders and turned her. Elaine let herself be moved. *Trust. I trust her. More than I've trusted anyone. More than I trust myself.*

"I can't speak for Robin. I don't know what she'll do with her freedom. But I can tell you I don't want to leave Rowan House." Petra's voice was husky. She raised up on her tiptoes and brushed a kiss over Elaine's mouth. Elaine held herself rigid, but Petra's gentle kiss surprised her. *She means it. She cares. She cares for me.*

Elaine relaxed, let Petra take the lead, and let herself drown in the sensation of someone else being in charge. Petra broke their kiss. She reached up and placed her hand on Elaine's cheek. "Come, lie down with me." She kissed her again, taking her time, and then took Elaine's hand. Elaine let herself be led. Petra toed off her shoes. She stretched out on the bed and opened her arms in invitation. Elaine kicked off her shoes and lay down with her head on Petra's breast. Petra wrapped her arms around her and held her. The sense of dominos falling in order, bits and pieces of herself falling into place, filled her as she lay in Petra's arms. Petra's steady heartbeat in her ear and the sensation being held tightly but not too, of her letting Elaine be, just be, of not expecting Elaine to do it all, sheltering her. *Is this it? Is this what Martha has with Lucia? Safe. Secure. Happy. Cared for. Love? Does she love me? Is this what love is?*

Petra carded Elaine's hair, her fingernails dragging over Elaine's scalp. Elaine sighed and closed her eyes. The tension in her shoulders relaxed under Petra's touch.

"What about the other job offer?" Elaine chewed her lower lip.

"I leave on Thursday."

So, it was just about leaving Rowan House. She likes it here. But it's not about me, she just said it to make me feel better. Fuck me. Why did I ask? Of course, she needs to go. What can we offer her here? Something to make me feel better. She doesn't mean it. She's leaving. I'm an idiot.

Petra's hands caught Elaine's hand and she intertwined their fingers. "Don't."

"Don't what?"

"Don't go to the place you just went. I agreed to an interview with them because I need to make a good decision. This has nothing to do with how I feel about you."

Elaine raised up on her elbow to see into Petra's face. "And how do you feel about me?" *Might as well get it out there.*

Petra traced Elaine's face with the edge of her nail, and then smoothed the red line with the pad of her finger. "I care for you. How do you not know this?"

"You care for me." Elaine drew in a breath. She quirked her mouth and moved away from Petra, rolled to her back, and tucked her hands behind her head. "What does that even mean? Like you care for a certain wine? Or care for dessert?"

Petra sat up and glared at Elaine. "You're a real stinker, you know?" She rolled over and straddled Elaine, her knees on either side of her waist. "I tell you I have feelings for you and you act like an ass." She pushed her hair back from her face. "And I'm just as bad because when you say shit like that I want to make you understand. It's like fucking catnip to me."

"Make me understand what?'

Petra leaned over Elaine, her face close, her hair surrounding them like a curtain. "Make you understand you deserve to be cared for." She framed Elaine with her arms, her hands over her forearms, pinning her down, and kissed her, softly at first, then deeper. Elaine's body betrayed her and she opened her mouth, opened herself to Petra, opened her heart to the fearless woman above her who took her breath away with her brutal kisses and stark honesty.

Chapter Eleven

THE DUNGEON WAS warm and Elaine opened another button on her shirt. She sat on the dais. Restless, she left her chair and pushed aside the heavy tapestry hiding the surveillance equipment and checked the time. She was early, had been too antsy to stay in her room. *Will she take the other job? Return after her interview? Why would she? She only "cares" for me. Doesn't mean she loves me, or wants to belong to me, or anything more than that. She's fond of me. Likes me. Nothing more. Nothing I can hold onto or hope for. And Robin. I still haven't told her. Tonight. I'll tell her tonight.*

Elaine let the tapestry fall back into place and stuffed her hands in her pockets. She paced around the dungeon, pausing by the rack, remembering Petra's body under her hands. She moved on, cursing herself for indulging her desires. *Will she do the same with the owner of the other house?* Elaine bit back a wave of nausea as she contemplated it. She didn't mind sharing, but on her terms, where she could see it, be part of it. Tonight, Robin was at Petra's mercy. The mindfuck audition was key. So many clients came to the house not knowing exactly what they needed, only aware of their craving for something to make them feel alive. And cherished. And enough.

The door to the dungeon opened. Petra led Robin on a leash. Robin's hands were cuffed and buckled in front of her. A black mask covered her eyes. Elaine crossed the room and took her place on the dais. Petra nodded to her and brought her finger to her lips, signaling for Elaine to remain quiet. Elaine nodded her understanding and took her seat. Petra placed her hand on Robin's shoulder and pushed her to the floor. Robin knelt with her head up, back straight.

Petra moved to block her from Elaine's view. "Safe words?"

Robin's voice was quiet. "Red is stop. Yellow is slow down."

"Very good." Petra yanked Robin to her feet. She stumbled a step before she righted herself. She led Robin to the whipping post, slipped her hands over the top of the post and clipped them in place. Robin's feet were free; only her arms around the post would hold her.

Petra took a wide flogger from its place on the wall. She trailed it over Robin's shoulders and down to her ass. Robin's breath hissed from between her teeth. Petra lifted the flogger and brought it down lightly over Robin's back. The marks from their last session had healed for the most part; only one small red square remained where the whip had broken her skin.

Petra whipped her in smooth rhythm until her back was an even red. She placed the flogger back on its hook and took two short signal whips down from their hooks. She tapped Robin's shoulder with the handles. Robin turned her face and kissed the handles of the whips. Petra stepped back and took a whip in each hand.

She brought the first one down and snapped it across Robin's ass; the second one arced and cracked across the other cheek. Petra continued working in an easy rhythm, maintaining the crossing pattern, Florentine style. The strong curves of Petra's body were displayed by her movement as she rolled her shoulders into her work. Robin's hips rocked back as if seeking contact, her ass an exquisite pattern of red stripes.

The Florentine style of whipping left no break for a submissive to gather themselves, no respite from the sharp sting of the whip. Robin moaned, a deep sound that reverberated off the stones and filled the dungeon. The only other sound in the room, the sharp rhythmic snap of the whips.

The effect was hypnotic. Elaine shifted in her seat. The echoes of whip cracks and searing sounds of Robin's reaction made her clit hard, and a surge of wetness soaked her briefs. Robin's thighs gleamed in the gaslights, and Elaine wanted to run her fingers up the inside of her thigh and sample the sweetness there. Her body burned, and she opened her shirt, exposing her half-hard nipples to the cool air. She cupped her breast and squeezed her nipple. A sharp current of pleasure rippled through her body.

Robin's moans shifted into groans, her mouth open and panting, and tears streamed down her face from under the blindfold. "Mercy, Mistress. Please. Mercy."

Petra snapped the whips two more times. She strode forward and cupped Robin's ass, smoothing her hands over the pattern of stripes and red flesh. "Ssh. You've done well." She returned to the wall and hung up the whips. She walked back to Robin and unbuckled the cuffs from the front of the post. Once Robin was free of the post, Petra guided her hands behind her back and snapped the cuffs together.

With her hand on Robin's shoulder, Petra led her to the blue-and-gold wool carpet in front of the dais. "Kneel."

Robin lowered herself to her knees. Her legs were spread wide, her arms cuffed behind her forced her shoulders back, and her breasts were displayed to perfection. Her blindfold was darker in places, evidence of her tears. Elaine gripped the arms of the chair, fighting her urge to go to Robin, to rip the blindfold from her face. To lick and kiss her tears. Her mouth watered at the thought of the bitter-salt taste of her tears, and how she would taste lower down.

Petra stood over Robin and planted her feet wide. She unsnapped the button on her pants and drew the zipper down slowly before she pushed her pants down her legs. They bunched around her boots. She smoothed her hand over her belly. Elaine's pulse pounded in her ears as Petra thrust her fingers between her legs and fucked herself. She groaned softly when she withdrew them. Her fingertips gleamed in the light. She teased Robin's lower lip, eliciting a whimper before she shoved them into Robin's mouth. Robin sucked greedily, and Petra pulled them back and pushed forward once more before she pulled free of Robin's mouth.

Petra stepped closer. She wrapped her hand in Robin's curls and forced her face between her thighs. "Show me how much you enjoyed your punishment. Please me, and I might have a special treat for you."

Robin whimpered once before the noises of her licking and sucking Petra were the only sounds in the room. Elaine's body clenched as she thought of Robin's mouth, how soft her lips were, how skilled her tongue when she sent Elaine tumbling into deep pools of pleasure. How often she had left Elaine boneless, giddy, and feeling loved. *Love. I love her. It won't matter. She'll leave. She'll fly from Rowan House. She was forced to work here by those disgusting men. I won't take advantage of her. No matter how much I want to keep her here.*

"Enough," Petra panted. Her face glowed with gratification, and she yanked Robin's head away.

Robin whined. Her face was shiny and wet. Elaine wanted to kiss her. To taste Petra on her lips, to have them both. *Oh goddess. I want both of them. So much.*

Petra balanced on one leg and pulled her boot off and slipped her pants down, then she did the same with the opposite leg. She was bare from the waist down and her short-sleeve shirt fluttered about her hips. She held Elaine's gaze as she stripped her shirt off and stood before her naked. Robin's shoulders shook; her breath was ragged.

Petra clasped her by the arm. "Stand."

Robin rose. She swayed, and Petra steadied her. She tilted her head at Elaine and raised her hand and motioned for her to join them. Elaine opened her mouth to give voice to all the reasons why it was a bad idea and closed it with a snap as Petra placed a finger over her lips, her gaze sharp. Elaine swallowed every protest she had planned.

She raised herself from her chair. Petra silently mouthed "strip" and Elaine hesitated. Petra placed a hand on her hip, her expression mocking.

Elaine frowned, yanked her shirt from her body, and tossed it to the floor as she toed off her shoes. She shoved her skirt down and stepped out of it, slipped out of her briefs and added them to the pile. She stepped off the dais, the carpet soft under her feet. Robin turned her head and cocked it to the side.

Petra unclipped her cuffs and rubbed her shoulders. Elaine glared at Petra.

Petra patted Robin's shoulder. "Down. Lay on your back. Hands over your head. Legs spread."

Robin lay back and lifted her arms. Petra crooked her finger at Elaine.

Elaine bent her head to Petra's mouth.

Petra whispered. "Your throne awaits, my queen." She pressed a kiss to the space under Elaine's ear, eliciting a shiver.

Elaine straddled Robin. The sight of her on the floor, her hands clasped over her head, expression serene, made her heart ache. Elaine lowered herself to her knees. Stopping short, she pressed herself to Robin's mouth.

Robin's tongue flicked out and she lifted her head, seeking more. Elaine rested her weight on her hands and pressed the wet ache between her legs to Robin's mouth. She swirled her tongue over Elaine's clit. Petra bent down, her breasts swaying temptingly in front of Elaine's face.

"Keep your eyes closed." Petra removed Robin's blindfold. Robin's tongue slid over Elaine's swollen slick lips before swirling over her thick clit. She held Elaine on the razor's edge of agony and ecstasy. Elaine rocked on her face, seeking what she craved, biting back her need to wrest control from Petra, allowing her the freedom to run the scene. She glanced over her shoulder.

Petra lay between Robin's legs, her breathing harsh. Petra slid her hands under Robin's hips. Lifting her to her mouth, she held Elaine's gaze. "Open your eyes."

Elaine shifted her attention to Robin's face between her thighs. Robin blinked as her eyes adjusted to the light before their gazes locked. She paused, moaned, and shifted her hands to Elaine's thighs. She dug her nails into the tender flesh and clung to her as she licked and sucked her clit, consuming Elaine, eyes wide as she worshiped her with her mouth.

The wet sounds of Petra's attention as she devoured Robin filled Elaine's ears. Robin's chest heaved beneath her, her cries muffled as her body went rigid, and she screamed her pleasure, their gazes locked. Elaine fell forward on her hands, gasping as her orgasm crashed through her like heat lightning. Robin pulled at her, urging her to come back, to lower herself to her mouth again. A hand on her ass, a quick thrust, and Petra's fingers were deep inside her. Elaine lowered her head to the carpet, and spread her knees wide to accommodate Petra's thrusts . She rolled her hips into Robin's mouth.

Satisfied moans and whimpers from Robin rolled over her, and she shuddered when Petra found the spot that made Elaine gyrate and buck her hips, desperate for more. More of what Petra had to give, more of what Robin gave, more of both of them. The twin sensations of being fucked and licked at the same time overwhelmed her even as she fought herself, fought to keep from coming, wanting to make it last, knowing it couldn't. She shouted when she came and jerked her hips away from Robin's mouth. "No more. Please." Petra slowed her strokes and Elaine shook again with a violent aftershock.

Petra withdrew her fingers, and Elaine collapsed to her side. She covered her eyes with her hand. A hand on her cheek, the brush of soft lips against her own, the scent of herself. She uncovered her eyes and Robin leaned over her, a gentle smile on her face. She tucked a lock of Elaine's hair behind her ear. *Love. Love her. So much.* She cupped the back of Robin's head and pulled her in for a kiss. Robin moaned and kissed Elaine, her mouth soft, her tongue darting over Elaine's lower lip, and she sucked it into her mouth gently before releasing.

They stared as if seeing each other for the first time. The world fell away but for the two of them in this moment. Together. One. Hearts and eyes open to the desire and love between them. If their love had been a fire, not one scorched stone of the house around them would still stand.

Chapter Twelve

ELAINE PACED THE office. Morning sun streamed through the windows. *Ride?* She checked the weather app on her phone. *Too cold. Damn it.*

Petra walked through the open door precisely at eight o'clock. "You wished to see me?"

The sight of her brought back memories of her touch, and Elaine shivered. "Why did you leave us last night?" Elaine chewed her lip. Lost in their own desires, she and Robin had been so enthralled with each other, they had failed to notice when Petra had left them.

"It was the right thing to do." Petra clasped her hands in front of her waist. "What was necessary."

"For who?" Elaine shoved her hands in her pants pockets to keep from shaking Petra.

Petra tilted her head to the side. "It was Robin's experience. My role was as facilitator. Have you worked much with couples? It is key to leave when you've gotten them where they wanted to go. If you overstay, you intrude. It spoils the intimacy and the experience. For everyone."

"No." Elaine raised her shoulders and straightened them. "We've not had that kind of clientele. Usually singles. The couples who visit us usually want to have a place to live out their fantasies. And Robin and I are not a couple."

Petra smirked. "Right."

Elaine stepped closer. "We're not."

Petra held her ground. "You close your eyes to things that are real and imagine things that are not."

Elaine stepped back and huffed out a breath. "Did you study philosophy too?"

"No, I just like to quote that movie." Petra's smirk was back.

"And I've had many threesomes. You left before aftercare. I didn't like it." Elaine closed the distance between them to peer into Petra's eyes. "Would you consider another scene?"

"With you?"

"With both of us."

Petra raised an eyebrow. "Because you want to watch me work again? Have some question about my skills?"

"No." Elaine avoided her gaze.

"No?" Petra pursed her lips. "Why then?"

"Because I wish it. Isn't that enough?" Elaine studied the toes of her boots.

"And if I don't wish it?" Petra's voice was soft.

"Then that is that." Elaine waited, unwilling to meet Petra's gaze, fearful of what she would see there.

Petra placed a hand on her shoulder and squeezed. "When?"

Elaine lifted her head and met Petra's gaze. "Tonight?"

"Meet me at eight."

"Where?"

"My favorite room." Petra's sly smile was back.

"Which is?" Elaine rested her hands on her hips.

"Figure it out."

"What if we don't?"

"Then I guess you'll miss me." She turned and walked away from Elaine.

THE WARM SMELL of rosemary and olive bread rose from the breadbasket, and Elaine's mouth watered. She glanced across the table at Robin on her right and to Petra on her left. They dined alone. An intimate feast. More than Tessa would be capable of, and Elaine could taste Robin's hand in every dish. Her uncanny ability to season food to perfection was a gift Elaine coveted and appreciated in equal measure.

Robin was dressed in a light blue, diaphanous dressing gown, the color bringing out the brilliant blue of her eyes. Elaine pulled herself back before she drowned in Robin's eyes, tempted to get so lost she did not know where she ended and Robin began.

She shifted her gaze to Petra. Instead of her usual somber black she wore a traditional áo dái. Bright red, it set off the dark brown of her eyes. Her hair was swept up and held in place with carved wooden combs. The fine dark hairs along her nape begged for Elaine's touch. *A perfect evening, a perfect bubble of contentment, a memory to keep me from going completely mad when they leave me. Later. I'll have plenty of time later to dwell. Tonight, we are together. I'm not going to ruin it worrying about what I can't control.*

She leaned back in her chair. "The food is amazing, Robin. I think Tessa has been hiding her skills."

Robin blushed. "She might have had help."

Elaine touched the back of her hand. "I would know your cooking anywhere. You have outdone yourself this evening."

Robin raised her head. "Thank you. I wanted it to be special."

Petra placed her fork on her plate. "I don't think I've had a better meal, ever. Or better company."

Elaine touched her finger to her plate and mopped up a bit of the delicate loganberry sauce from her dinner with the last bit of her bread and popped it into her mouth. She chewed slowly and swallowed before she spoke. "On that I would agree."

Robin sipped her water and then dabbed at her mouth with her napkin. "Should I ring for pudding?"

Elaine shifted her gaze between Petra and Robin. "Later. Unless you two are too impatient to wait?

Petra leaned back in her chair. "Not hungry for dessert. At least not now." She folded her napkin. "If you would excuse me. I need to prepare for our appointment."

Elaine inclined her head at her. "Of course. I'm sure we can find some way to entertain ourselves."

Petra raised an eyebrow. "Try not to wear yourselves out."

Robin snort laughed before she smothered it with her hand.

"We'll do our best." Elaine traced her fingertips along Robin's arm, enjoying the way the small hairs rose in the wake of her touch. The gown Robin was wearing did nothing to hide the way her nipples peaked with Elaine's attention. Petra pushed her chair in to the table and left them.

A cheeky grin splashed across Robin's face. "Whatever will we do while we wait, Mistress?"

Elaine scooted her seat back from the table and patted her lap. Robin sauntered over to Elaine's chair. Elaine looped an arm around her hips and pulled her into her lap. Robin curled into her body, fitting perfectly against Elaine.

Robin fingered the buttons on Elaine's shirt. "You're tense, Mistress." A statement, not a question. Robin knew her, understood her, never missed the tells of her mood. Elaine's nipple hardened when Robin smoothed her warm palm over her breast. "Maybe I could help you relax?" Robin's lips brushed against the triangle of skin where her shirt was open. "Please." Her breath tickled Elaine, and she wallowed in the wave of need that washed over her. *Need. I need this. Someone who understands me. Reads my moods. My desires.*

"As you wish." Elaine lifted her chin, giving Robin access, and Robin nuzzled her neck, mouthing the skin, scattering soft nibbles as she unbuttoned Elaine's shirt. The cool of her fingers as she brushed against Elaine's skin made her skin pebble and her nipples responded, pressing against the lace of her bra. Robin slipped her hand inside the bra and cupped Elaine's breast. She rubbed her thumb in a tight circle over her nipple. A current of heat traveled in a direct line to Elaine's clit. Elaine hissed a breath when Robin closed her fingers over her nipple and squeezed.

Elaine shifted in her chair. Robin grabbed the hem of the dressing gown, rose up on her knees, and hiked its length up as she changed position and settled her bottom against Elaine's thighs. She ground her hips in a slow lap dance as she opened Elaine's shirt. Elaine leaned forward, and Robin reached behind her and unhooked her bra with one hand while she kept up her attentions on Elaine's nipple. She shoved it out of the way and lowered her head. Her soft curls tickled Elaine's chin as she sucked a nipple into her mouth, her tongue lapping at the tight bud before she tugged it with her teeth and then sucked hard.

Elaine groaned and latched her hands on to Robin's hips and bucked against her, her clit pressing against the heat and pressure of Robin's body. She moved her hand between them, rubbing her thumb over the satin of Robin's panties. The fabric was damp, and she tapped her fingers in a rhythm over Robin's clit. Robin gasped and rolled her hips forward. She bit down lightly on her nipple, forcing a deep groan from Elaine. Robin lifted her head and kissed Elaine, tongue teasing, mouth begging silently. She broke their kiss and held Elaine's face in both her hands, her eyes laser sharp with need. "Fuck me."

Elaine swept the plates and silverware off the table with her arm, ignoring the crashing and shattering of china. She stood and lifted Robin to the table. The white damask cloth bunched and shifted around her hips. In one smooth motion she dragged Robin's panties off and tossed them to the floor. Robin panted as she rested on her elbows.

Elaine inhaled the scent of Robin's arousal, the essence of her. "No." She pinned her in place with her gaze as she kneeled. "I want dessert." Spreading her fingers wide, she cupped Robin's ass and brought it to her mouth like a chalice. The vessel she desired more than any other, her salvation, her life. She licked a long wet line from Robin's core to her clit and thrust her tongue deep, savoring her flavor. Robin groaned, lifted her hips, and opened her legs, her knees drifting wide as she offered herself to Elaine. With the flat of her tongue Elaine teased slow circles over her clit. She shifted her grip and pushed her thumb into Robin.

"Oh. Yes. Please, Mistress." She trembled, her thighs and body tense under Elaine's hands. "Oh, please. More. Let me feel you, please, Mistress."

Elaine hummed with her lips tight around Robin's clit and she withdrew her thumb. Robin whimpered. Elaine lifted her mouth and blew across her clit gently. "Greedy girl."

"I am, Mistress. I am. Please. Fuck me. Please." Her strident plea laced with desperation spurred Elaine's desire to hear more.

Elaine growled and thrust three fingers deep, curling them up and over Robin's sweet spot, knowing her body as well as she knew her own. She leaned down and pressed her brow against Robin's forehead. *Love. She loves me. So much.* Elaine turned her head, unwilling to etch the memory in her brain, turning away from the truth. Knowing it would change when Robin learned she was free, that she didn't have to love Elaine out of obligation.

Robin stilled under her. She released the tablecloth balled in her hands and looped an arm over Elaine's neck before she clasped Elaine's chin with her hand and tugged. Elaine closed her eyes and let Robin move her head. "Don't turn away, Mistress. Please. Let me know it's me you're thinking of when you fuck me. See me. Please."

Elaine opened her eyes. Robin's gaze locked on hers as she moved her hand and touched her fingers to Elaine's lips. "No words, Mistress. Please. Let me see you."

Elaine kissed Robin's palm as she stroked slow and deep. Robin met her stroke for stroke. She locked her ankles over Elaine's hips as she clung to her. Her body clenched around Elaine's fingers.

"See me. Mistress. See me." She came, eyes wide open. Elaine held her gaze, giving over, letting Robin see the love that filled her until it overflowed and ran down her cheeks.

THE WALK TO the dungeon was long after their intimacy. *Call it off. I've got enough information to make a decision. How can I let her go? I crave her. Crave her addicting coolness. I'm addicted to shattering her, addicted to making her lose control, flipping her. How did that happen? Years avoiding tops and those who fancied themselves as such What is it about her?*

Robin tugged at her hand.

Elaine stopped. "What?"

"We're here, Mistress." Robin gestured at the door.

No emotion. What does she want? Does she still want this? Want to go through with the rest of the audition? Ask. I owe her.

Elaine entwined their fingers and pulled Robin close. She rested her chin on the top of Robin's head. "Do you still want to do this?" She rubbed her hands in small circles over Robin's back.

"Do you?" Robin placed her hand on Elaine's chest, her hand over Elaine's heart.

Elaine held her, sorting through her thoughts, unable to answer, not wanting to give either of them up, knowing she would most likely lose both. "Yes. If you do."

"Yes. But"—Robin drew back from Elaine's arms—"it doesn't change how I feel about you."

Elaine lifted her chin with her fingertips and kissed her. "Nor the way I feel about you."

The sound of the door opening behind them made them start. Petra stood in the doorway. She was naked. A pair of leather cuffs dangled from her hand. She cocked her hip and placed her hand on it. "Are we starting out here? Or do you want to bring it inside?" She inhaled sharply through her nose and pursed her lips. "Unless of course you came to tell me you are no longer interested."

The cocky light in her eyes was replaced by a flash of sadness and want.

Robin pushed away from Elaine and kneeled in front of Petra. "It's my fault we're late, Mistress." She bent and kissed the top of Petra's foot.

Elaine's pulse raced as she made eye contact with Petra. *No. Not giving this up. Until they leave. They are what I need. What I want.*

ROBIN SAT BACK on her heels. Petra leaned down and kissed her forehead. "Not to worry. We have all night."

She turned and walked into the dungeon. Robin crawled after her on her hands and knees.

Elaine followed and closed the door. She turned the lock and set the deadbolt, unwilling to risk being disturbed.

Petra kneeled on the carpet in front of the dais, mirroring Robin's pose of the house, knees wide, palms up. Elaine crossed the floor and stepped up on the dais. She sat in her chair and studied the two women. The contrast between them, the set of their shoulders and posture. Robin owned her position, comfortable in her role; Petra's body was rigid, her back arrow straight, her jaw set. Elaine drummed her fingers on the arm of the chair. *What to do? Does Petra think this is what she has to do? That she has to be this for me?*

Petra had placed the cuffs on the floor next to her thighs.

"Petra, eyes to me."

Petra lifted her chin, her eyes full of pain and hurt.

Jealous? Of Robin? Or of me? How much did she hear through the door? She wanted me to be honest.

Robin still doesn't know she's free. Tomorrow. I'll tell her tomorrow. Tonight it will be as if the outside world doesn't exist.

"Come to me. Bring me the cuffs." Elaine reclined in her chair. Petra rose to her feet. "Did I tell you to stand?"

Petra lifted her chin, picked up the cuffs, and stalked to the edge of the dais. She held Elaine's gaze as she walked up the two steps and approached her chair. She tossed the cuffs to the floor in front of Elaine. "No. Ma'am."

Elaine exploded out of the chair, picked Petra up, and turned her over her shoulder. She slapped her ass once when she wiggled. "I warned you before. Disrespect. Will. Not. Be. Tolerated." She punctuated each word with a hard slap of her ass. The scent of Petra's arousal tickled Elaine's nostrils and she licked her lips. Petra relaxed against her shoulder. *This. She needs it this way. So do I.* Elaine placed her on her feet, wrapped her hand in her hair, and kissed her hard and bruising. Petra latched her hands on to Elaine's forearms, digging her nails in as she responded to Elaine's kiss.

Elaine pulled back. She manacled Petra's wrists with her hands and held them in front of her body. Petra's breathing was ragged, eyes heavy-lidded. "Robin, walk to me. Bring the cuffs." Robin obeyed and arrived at Elaine's side, the cuffs in her hand. "Put them on Petra." Robin placed the cuffs around Petra's wrists, avoiding Elaine's eyes.

Elaine looped her finger through the D-rings of the cuffs and, with one hand, held them together in front of Petra's body. She led her over to a low bench. She shifted her hand to her shoulder. "Face down over it." She pushed her into place. Elaine clipped one cuff to each side of the bench. The length of the bench supported her body. Elaine swept her hand over her ass and then her shoulder. The faint red marks from Elaine's earlier lesson were warm under her touch. She patted Petra's cheek. With a deep moan Petra turned her face to kiss and nuzzle Elaine's palm.

"Robin." Robin stepped to Elaine's side. With two fingers she tipped Robin's chin up, forcing her to meet her gaze. "Would you like to serve Petra?"

Robin trembled under her touch. "Whatever my Mistress commands."

Elaine rubbed her thumb over Robin's lower lip. "I would like you to assist me in showing her what respect means."

Robin's hungry expression was back. "Yes, Mistress."

Elaine turned Robin so she faced Petra. "Observe."

She wrapped her arms around Robin and reached between her legs. She pulled the gown up slowly, exposing her legs inch by inch until the harness she had asked her to wear was displayed. The O-ring was empty. Petra's gaze fixed on the space between Robin's legs.

With her other hand Elaine cupped her breast. Robin's nipple pressed into her palm through the thin gown. "I'm going to let Robin fuck you."

Petra licked her lower lip, her breathing harsh in Elaine's ears.

"After I apply my lesson to the seat of your disobedience." Elaine firmed her gaze. "Robin, bring me my favorite paddle."

Bound over the bench, Petra's back dipped into a hollow and the smooth cheeks of her ass rounded perfectly. Elaine studied her face, the way her mouth was open just a bit. The scent of her desire rose from her and her rasping breaths were loud in the stony silence of the dungeon. This was her world, her domain, a wild kingdom of savagery and desire, and Elaine was the queen. Robin approached and kneeled at her feet. She lifted the paddle with both hands.

Elaine took it from her. "Well done." She hefted the thick leather paddle in her hand, the weight comforting and familiar. She held it in front of Petra's face. Petra raised her gaze and locked on to Elaine's eyes. She kissed the black smooth surface presented to her, and Elaine's body responded as if Petra had pressed her lips to Elaine's mouth instead of the paddle.

Elaine's belly tightened, and desire twined around her body, a dull ache between her legs. She pulled the paddle away, leaned down, and cupped Petra's chin. "Same words?"

"Yes." Petra's voice was firm, and her eyes never wavered.

"Robin." Robin kneeled at Elaine's side. "Why don't you keep her mouth occupied?"

Robin crawled to Petra and sat back on her heels. She stroked Petra's hair before she kissed her. Elaine watched them for a moment, the way Robin's nipples hardened and her back arched as she leaned in to kiss Petra. Small whimpers of need sounded from Robin, sending another wave of heat through Elaine.

She pinched the skin over Petra's hip and she yipped, the sound muffled by Robin's mouth. Elaine brought the paddle down hard. The impact of her blow shook Petra's body. She screamed into Robin's mouth. She broke their kiss and scattered kisses over Petra's forehead, her cheeks, and her eyelids before she returned to her mouth. Elaine waited until Petra's breathing returned to normal, and then she raised the paddle again and brought it down on her other cheek. The snap of leather against Petra's skin sent a rip current of desire through her as she screamed into Robin's mouth.

Elaine smoothed her hand over her ass before she bent and kissed the red marks, the heat of her skin lush against her lips. Petra moaned when Elaine straightened. She struck two more lighter blows in quick succession, and this time Petra groaned, a deep, sensuous sound that made Elaine want to toss the paddle aside and have her. *Not yet.* Robin's sounds of want mingled with Petra's. Elaine closed her eyes and reveled in the sounds of them together. She opened her eyes, kissed Robin on the crown of her head, and then kissed Petra's shoulder.

Straightening, she set her feet and paddled Petra in earnest, alternating her blows, light and heavy, spreading them out over her ass until it was bright red. Elaine stopped. A trickle of sweat stung her eyes, and she wiped it away. Petra wailed and lifted her hips.

Elaine trailed a finger down the seam of Petra's ass. Her thighs were wet and slick, her clit swollen and thick. Elaine pushed two fingers in slowly and groaned at the searing heat that encased her. "Petra, do you want to show Robin how much you appreciate the way she drank in your pain and soothed you?"

"Please, Ma'am. Let me." Petra's voice was hoarse.

"Robin, go to the cabinet. Select whatever size toy you want to fuck her with. I'm sure Petra will be accommodating." At the word fuck, Petra moaned, and rolled her hips, pushing back on to Elaine's fingers.

Elaine raised the paddle and slapped it against Petra's ass and then thrust her fingers in and out. Petra rocked back violently. "Oh please. Ma'am. I want you to fuck me, please."

"Later." Elaine withdrew her fingers. She moved to Petra's field of vision and licked her fingers. "You taste divine. So sweet. I like you like this. So eager. So willing."

Robin returned with a thick purple dildo fastened in the harness and a bottle of lube clutched in her hand. A clitoral stimulator ringed its wide base.

Elaine nodded at her choice. "Excellent."

She unclipped Petra's cuffs from the bench. "Support yourself on your hands and knees. I want to move the bench." She waved a hand toward Petra. "Robin, get in position. Enter her." Elaine dragged the bench clear of Petra's body.

Petra's eyes widened; her breath came hard and fast. Elaine cupped her chin, forcing her head back. "Breathe. Slow down, slow your breathing."

Robin kneeled between Petra's legs. She dribbled lube over Petra's core and then slicked the dildo. She set the head, gripped Petra's hips, and inched forward. Petra's body stilled, her face a grimace. Robin patted Petra's hip. "She's tense, Mistress."

Elaine leaned down to stare into Petra's eyes. "Relax and breathe."

"Oooh." Petra's breathing slowed. Elaine nodded and Robin pressed forward again.

"Yellow." Petra panted. Robin stopped.

"Do you need her to rub your clit? Would it help you?" Elaine rubbed the back of Petra's neck.

"Yes. Please, Ma'am. I want to please you." A tinge of tears filled Petra's voice.

"Shh. No matter how this goes now, you've pleased me." Elaine kissed Petra, a gentle brush of her lips over her mouth. She lingered on her damp lower lip. "Robin, can you reach her clit?"

Robin smiled at Elaine and reached under Petra. A deep groan and twitch of Petra's hips let Elaine know Robin had achieved her goal. Petra's body relaxed under Robin's skillful attention and she pushed back, seeking more of the fat toy between Robin's legs. "Oh god. Ma'am, I'm going to...I can't stop." Her body shook violently, and Elaine nodded at Robin to continue. Petra came with a keening sound and Robin pushed forward until her hips were fitted against Petra's ass, the toy buried to the hilt. Petra trembled as the rich sounds of her satisfaction filled the room. Robin moved her hands back to Petra's hips and gripped her tightly.

"Oh no. Please don't stop. More. Please let me come again. Please. I need..." Her voice was bereft, and tears streamed down her face. Elaine touched the tip of her fingers to Petra's tears. She licked the tip of her finger, the bitter salt taste on her tongue, a sweet gift.

Elaine rubbed Petra's shoulders. "I'll let you come again. As soon as you complete your task." She grabbed her jaw, forcing Petra's head back. She summoned her most menacing tone. "Squeeze down on her. Hold the toy inside you. If it slips out, game over, you don't get to come. Deny your pleasure for mine. If you come before I tell you, game over, I'll beat you with my flogger, you won't get to pleasure me. Or Robin. Do you understand?"

"Yes. Ma'am." Petra's voice wobbled.

"Good. Robin, move with her." She hardened her gaze. "If you come without permission, or cause her to lose the toy, you don't get to pleasure me, or Petra. Do you understand?"

"Yes, Mistress." Robin's voice was breathy but sure, the expression on her face one of determination. Her knuckles were white where she gripped Petra's hips.

Elaine reached between them and touched the button to turn on the vibrating ring before she walked to the far side of the dungeon. The low hum of the vibrator and the sighing moan from Robin made her hard. "Eyes to me."

Two gazes fixed on her and she stripped off her clothes. She sat in her queening chair, spread her legs wide, and rested her feet on the floor. "Come and get what you want. Show me how much you want to please me." Elaine dropped her hand between her legs and cupped herself. "Hurry. Or I may get impatient and decide to take care of myself."

A sharp sound of longing slipped from Petra's lips. She moved forward on her hands and knees. Robin moved with her, holding on to her hips to keep herself buried deep in Petra. "Oh." A deep groan broke the quiet and Petra shuddered. "Oh. Ma'am."

Elaine inclined her head. "Yes?" She couldn't suppress her smile, knowing each time Petra moved and Robin moved with her the toy would hit her g-spot. The vibrating ring alone was enough to make any woman come. Combined with the deep penetration and g-spot stimulation, this was a true test of discipline.

Robin moaned softly. Petra shifted forward, and Robin lagged behind a moment, the bright purple dildo visible. Robin moved forward quickly to close the gap and buried the toy again. Petra whimpered.

Robin lay over her and grabbed a nipple in each hand and squeezed. "Focus." Her voice was harsh and Petra's breath hitched.

Elaine rubbed her clit, enjoying the tableau, torn between her desire to have Petra's tongue on her clit and the chance to flog her and listen to her screams again.

They moved again in sync with Robin over Petra, one hand on her tit, the other on her hip. Petra crawled forward with her gaze fixed between Elaine's legs. "Oh god. I can't. Oh please, Ma'am. Oh, no. I'm—oh oh oh… Robin, don't move. Wait, please. Oh, god." Petra's body shook as she fought to regain control.

Robin chewed her lip as she waited. Petra shuddered. "Slap me. For both our sakes. Slap my ass. Now."

Robin pulled her hand back and slapped Petra's ass.

"Harder." Petra's voice was harsh.

Robin's eyes glittered. She raised her hand high and cracked it against Petra's ass.

Petra's breathing slowed. "Okay. I'm okay now."

They began again. Inch by inch they made their way across the floor until they were in front of the chair.

Petra focused on Elaine's face. "Please, Ma'am. Please let me pleasure you. Please."

Elaine grabbed her hair with both hands. "Yes. Now. Worship me."

Robin's face was a mask of strain. Her chin trembled. "Please, Mistress. Please let me."

"Fuck her. Until you both come." Elaine locked gazes with Robin. "For me."

Robin locked both hands around Petra's hips, pulled out to the tip, and slammed it home. Petra's face was pushed into Elaine and she moaned as she sucked on Elaine's clit. Hands on her tits, pinching her nipples, Elaine basked in pleasure as Robin fucked Petra, never taking her gaze from Elaine's face. A gift for Elaine, her offering, her reward.

Petra groaned as she licked and suckled Elaine's clit and begged with her mouth for Elaine's favor. A torrent of pleasure swept over Elaine. Petra's mouth was perfection.

Elaine panted in an effort to extend her pleasure, but the vision of Petra's head between her legs combined with the hypnotizing sway of Robin's breasts as she fucked Petra from behind detonated her orgasm. Elaine came with a shout, grinding herself onto Petra's face. Petra came then, the sound muffled as she screamed her pleasure, her body going rigid as Robin continued to fuck her. Robin's cries as she finished against her ass echoed in the playroom. Bound together, they floated on an ocean of bliss, as the waves of pleasure ebbed and flowed between them.

Chapter Thirteen

ELAINE BENT OVER and picked up Luna's hoof. She held it between her knees and worked the hoof pick to clear the mud from around the frog to inspect it. Satisfied the horse's hoof was sound, she replaced it on the floor of the barn. She worked her way around the horse methodically examining each hoof. "You're right. I don't think it has to do with her hooves either."

"I watched her when I turned her out in the ring. Her gait seems fine. No lameness." Veronica passed Elaine a towel.

Elaine wiped her hands before she patted Luna's shoulder. She ran her fingers along her back, pressing against her spine gently. She reached a point over her mid-back and Luna shied away from her.

"Ho. Easy." Elaine stepped back and away from Luna's restless stomping. Luna's eyes were large, the white showing, and her breath huffed out. "Easy girl." Luna settled, her eyes wary.

Veronica came and stood next to Elaine. "That's the spot. When I was grooming her yesterday she tried to bite me when I touched it."

"Have you called Doctor Franz?"

"She'll be here this afternoon."

Elaine chewed her lip. She grimaced as she sorted through the reasons Luna's back could be touchy, some fixable, some not. Elaine rubbed Luna's cheek and scratched under her neck. Luna rubbed against her. "Call me when she gets here." She gave Luna a final pat and left the barn.

ELAINE POURED HERSELF another cup of tea. She drummed her fingers on the table. *What if it's cancer like Billie? Please let it be something easy.* She yanked the lid off the tin and rummaged around for her favorite chocolate biscuit. She bit into it, the crumbs falling on to her plate. *Where's Robin? She should be here to help Tessa. And where the hell is Tessa?* She squinted at her watch, unwilling to fish her reading glasses out to see the face. *Market. That explains Tessa.*

A chill stole down her spine when she realized she had not seen Petra this morning either. *Together. They're probably together. Well, they're both free to.* Elaine stuffed down her rankled feelings over being left out of whatever they were doing. Her biscuit gone, she sipped her tea.

The kitchen door swung open and Petra entered followed by Robin. "There you are." The happy tone of her voice made Elaine grit her teeth. *What is she so fucking happy about?* Elaine shifted her gaze to Robin, who blushed and bowed her head under her scrutiny. She hunched her shoulders and pushed past Petra to the cabinets behind Elaine. *Just like I thought. What's up with Robin? So what. It's a phase. As soon as the others are back I'll want to be with one of them. Benita, or maybe Fallon.*

Elaine lifted her cup of tea and took a sip before she placed it precisely on her saucer. "Been right here, so I'm not sure how hard you looked."

She could hear Robin working behind her as she filled the electric kettle and turned it on. More sounds, the clink of glass and metal as she busied herself with setting up the French Press, and then the sharp scent of fresh coffee wafted to Elaine as she scooped the grounds into the press. *Why won't she look at me? Embarrassed? Ashamed?*

"And so you are." Petra shifted in her chair and straightened her shoulders. "I want your permission to take Robin with me for my audition in Oslo."

White-hot anger ripped through Elaine. She gripped the edge of the table to keep from flipping it. "What?"

"It's safe for her to travel, so why not?" Petra crossed her arms over her chest and leaned back in her chair.

Robin had stilled behind her. Elaine sensed her gaze on her. She fought a wave of nausea. *No. No. She knows. And knows I didn't tell her as soon as I knew. Why didn't I tell her? Why did I tell Petra? Why did I trust her?*

Elaine smacked both hands flat on the table. "You couldn't wait, could you? Couldn't let me tell her in my own time? Couldn't wait to spirit her away."

Elaine stood and her chair clattered to the floor. Robin let out a squeak of fear behind her. A common sound when she had first come to them anytime someone made a sudden move or dropped a dish. It crushed Elaine's heart. What was left of it.

She turned to Robin. She had her back to the counter, her face a mask of fear. *Afraid. Of me. I have well and truly fucked this up.* Elaine scrubbed her hand over her face. "Robin, I'm—" The sheen of unshed tears in Robin's eyes dried up everything Elaine wanted to explain. "I'm sorry. I should have told you right away." Elaine took a deep breath, raised her shoulders and lowered them, squaring her body like a soldier before a firing squad. "Of course, you can go." *Please don't go. Please don't want to go.* She spoke the biggest lie of her life. "I don't care. Go with Petra. I'm not your..." *Mistress? Lover? Are we even friends now?* She faded out, unable to say it. "It's not for me to say anyway."

Robin's shoulders relaxed. Her face morphed from fear to sadness. "Why didn't you tell me?" She turned away from Elaine. "I wouldn't have left you."

Her use of the past tense hit Elaine like a rock to the face. "Wouldn't have?"

Petra cleared her throat behind her.

Elaine spun on her heel and leveled a glare at Petra.

"I'm sorry, Elaine. I overheard you talking in the hall outside the dungeon the other night. I thought you'd told her."

Elaine lifted her chin. "Fuck you. Fuck you and fuck me." She picked up her teacup and saucer and placed them in the sink, walked out of the kitchen, and away from what she thought would have been the rest of her life. *Don't run. Don't run. Don't run.*

She waited until she was away from the kitchen before she broke her promise to herself and bolted to her room. Once there, she closed the door. *A ride. That's what I need.* And then she remembered Luna, the vet, and all the what-ifs that had occupied her morning. Elaine kicked off her shoes, locked her door, and pushed the bar lock in place. *No Petra coming to counsel me this time. Maybe that's why she's here. Maybe Lucia and Martha thought I needed someone to help me let go of Robin. Meddlers. No. I need to get over myself. Robin deserves this. A new start. With someone she chooses. Not me, another in a long line of jailors.*

In the bathroom, she turned on the water and set the taps. Steam rose from the water. She stripped off her clothes and flipped the switch on the heated towel rack. Her heart stuttered when she thought about the last time she had done this, when she had taken care of Robin after her first scene with Petra. Elaine poured lavender-scented bath salts into the tub. *Wonder if they have one just for heartache? Fuck me. I'm an idiot. Should've told her. Should've trusted her. Should've done so many things.* She turned the water off and lowered herself slowly into the bath. The water soothed her, and she closed her eyes and let her thoughts drift. *Stop fighting myself. Ignore the drama. So what if I lose Robin. I never had Petra to lose. Luna. Dear goddess, what if I lose Luna?* A sob twisted inside her. *No. I can't lose her. I refuse. She's the only love I can count on.* A bitter taste rose in her mouth. *The only unconditional love I've ever known has four legs and can't talk.*

DR. FRANZ RAN her hands along Luna's back. Luna shuffled and tried to move away from her.

Veronica held Luna's halter. "Easy. Ho now. Easy."

"I'll draw some blood work. We need to get a sonogram and an X-ray." A deep frown furrowed her brow. "It may be kissing spines from your descriptions of the changes. Can you trailer her to my office tomorrow?"

Elaine stood with her hands on her hips. "Tomorrow? Why not today?"

"Because it's not going to make a difference if we get a diagnosis tonight or tomorrow." Her face softened. "I know you're worried. It's not like Billie. I'll have the physiotherapist examine her too."

Elaine sighed. She took hold of Luna's halter. "I've got her, Veronica. Make the necessary arrangements." She led her to her stall and settled her with soft words and tender touches. "We'll get you fixed up, girl." She swallowed against her fear. *Goddess please let her be okay, let it be a simple fix. I can't lose her. Not right now. I can't deal with more.*

Elaine closed the door to her stall and latched it. She walked back to the office. Veronica was working on the computer. Elaine sat on the couch. Veronica leaned to the side of the computer screen to meet her gaze. "You okay?"

"Do I look like I'm okay?"

"Nope. That's why I asked." Veronica pointed to the file cabinet. "Do you need anything? I moved the emergency supplies."

Elaine chewed her lip. "No. It's too early and too easy."

Veronica got up and came and sat on the couch. "Wanna talk?"

"Not really. Won't help. Not with this."

"'It's more than Luna."

Elaine glared at Veronica.

"You can look evil at me all you want, but I know you and you're a wreck because Robin is leaving."

Elaine inhaled sharply through her nose. "We're not talking about it."

"We? You mean you and me? Or you and her? Weren't you the person who told me not to take anything for granted?"

Elaine pursed her lips. "And your point?"

"My point is, you don't have to talk to me about it, but if you care for her, you sure as hell owe it to both of you to talk to her."

Elaine leaned over and rested her elbows on her knees. "It's too late. It won't matter what I say now. She thinks I'm like everyone else in her life who has forced her into doing things. Why did I ever open that email? And why didn't I just tell her right then?"

Veronica tapped her shoulder. "Because you were afraid. And because you don't fucking trust anyone might be telling you the truth."

Elaine stood up. "I trusted Roxy. Where did that get me?"

Veronica crossed her legs. "You going to bolt now? Run away when the conversation gets real?"

Elaine grabbed her hair with both hands and shoved it back. "What the hell? Is everyone a fucking therapist now?"

Veronica snorted. "No. But you might think about seeing one. For fuck's sake, Elaine. One person turns you down and you'll never take another chance?"

"So what if I don't?"

Veronica stood. "You'll spend the rest of your life asking yourself why you didn't." She crossed the room and plucked their coats from the coat rack. "Come on."

Elaine took her coat. "Where're we going?"

"I'm not going to sit around and watch this train wreck play out. Not on my watch." She crossed her arms. "And you can quit trying to melt glass with that look because I'm impervious to it."

Elaine shoved her arm in her coat. "It won't do any good."

Veronica held open the office door. "Well, you can tell me 'I told you so' later if it doesn't."

VERONICA WALKED ELAINE back to the main house. They entered the mudroom, toed off their boots, and hung their jackets up. Elaine jammed her hands in her pants pockets. "What are we doing?" she whispered.

"I'm going in there and getting Tessa out, and you're going to talk to Robin."

Veronica grabbed her arm and pulled her toward the door.

Elaine planted her feet. "No. This is stupid. She's not going to believe me. Not now."

Veronica yanked her along. "You are going in there and say your thing. If she doesn't believe you, that's on her, but if you don't say anything and she leaves here not knowing how you feel, that's on you."

She shoved the kitchen door open and dragged Elaine inside. Elaine stumbled before she caught her balance. Tessa raised her head, her eyes streaming from the onions she was chopping. "Mistress?"

Robin turned from the pastry bench, her hands covered in flour from where she was kneading bread. "Elaine?"

Veronica blocked Elaine's exit. "Hey, Tessa, leave off with the onions. I need to talk with you about, um, something."

Elaine glared over her shoulder. "Smooth."

Tessa scraped the onion she had chopped into a bowl and placed a lid over it. "Give me a minute." She washed her hands, picked up the knife, washed it, and dried it carefully before she replaced it on the metal magnetic strip. She placed the cutting board in the sink. Veronica rolled her eyes. "Come on, Tessa." She held the door open, and Tessa walked out ahead of her.

Robin continued to knead the bread dough, not breaking her rhythm.

Elaine turned a chair around and sat down to face Robin. "Is that the orange rye raisin?"

Robin glanced up before she returned her attention to the dough. "A riff on the recipe."

Her voice was stiff, and Elaine's heart ached. Ruined. They had been so easy together. Easier even than Roxy.

Elaine cleared her throat. She hadn't rehearsed this part. "I truly am sorry."

Robin turned the sticky dough over and tossed another handful of flour over the bench. "So you said."

Elaine knotted her hands in her lap. "I don't know why I didn't tell you right away."

Robin skewered her with a hard expression. "Don't even try that. You know why. You didn't trust I'd stay. Didn't believe I would stay unless I had to."

Elaine knotted her hands together. "Yes." Her throat burned. "I love you."

Robin stilled. "I know."

Elaine frowned. "You're going with her, aren't you?"

Robin patted the dough into a rectangle. "I haven't decided."

Elaine's heartbeat was loud in her ears. "You haven't?"

Robin sighed. "No." She inclined her head toward a small bowl filled with raisins. "Move the bowl closer, please." Elaine stood and moved the ramekin, the scent of the raisins saturated with orange liqueur rose from the dish.

Robin reached into the bowl and dropped the raisins over the dough, spreading them evenly over the rectangle. She rolled and patted the bread into a tidy log. Once it was formed, she took a large knife and cut it into rounds before placing them onto a parchment-lined baking sheet.

"A new presentation?" Elaine dipped her finger into the ramekin and the dregs of the soaking liquid. She sucked the sweet orange liqueur off her fingertip.

"I like cinnamon rolls, and I had the idea the rye raisin would be good this way if I tweaked the dough and finished them with an orange glaze." Robin covered the rolls with a cloth and moved them to the proofing cabinet.

"You are so very talented. A natural cook. You're creative and your instincts about food are bang on." Elaine cleaned the top of the bench, scraping up bits of dough and flour. "I went to school for three years, interned in the finest kitchens in the world, and you have more natural talent in your pinkie than I have in both hands. It will be difficult to replace you in the kitchen."

Robin moved to the sink and washed her hands. She contemplated Elaine as she dried them. "And in your bed?"

Elaine met her gaze. "I don't expect to find another, anyone like you."

"I don't know what I'm going to do. I have to think. I've not had a time in my life when I've been free. My parents were tyrants. Abused the hell out of me when I came out. I left home at fifteen. And then was a slave to my habit and various pimps."

Elaine winced at the word pimp. "I understand."

"Do you?" Robin tilted her head. "Really?"

Elaine shoved her hands in her pockets. "No. I don't. I can't imagine. I want you to have what you want. I want to give you what no one else has ever given you."

"And what is that?" Robin came and stood a breath away. She tugged at Elaine's hands, pulling them from her pockets. She laced their fingers together.

"Your freedom." Elaine gazed into Robin's eyes, memorizing them, so that after she left, she would be able to close her eyes and remember how she had once cared for her.

Robin lifted up on her toes and kissed Elaine. A gentle kiss, soft, unhurried. She stepped back and let go of Elaine's hands. "Thank you."

She left Elaine standing in the kitchen. *What will she do? What will I do? Does it matter?* She rubbed her chest, a fruitless attempt to soothe the ache in her heart, the pain more acute than Roxy's departure, more devastating because she finally realized what Roxy had said was true. Elaine hadn't loved Roxy the way she loved her own freedom. Elaine loved Robin more than her own happiness. She would give Robin whatever she wanted, do whatever she could to make her happy even if it meant ripping her own heart out.

"THE PHYSIOTHERAPIST LEFT some instructions. At least it wasn't kissing spines." Veronica passed the sheet of paper to Elaine.

Elaine pressed her lips together. She had been so caught up with the drama with Robin and Petra she had been distracted from Luna's health.

"She's confident this is something we can fix?"

"Yes. She's going to come the next time the blacksmith comes. She wants to try different shoes."

Elaine sat on the leather couch and rested her head in her hands. "I had convinced myself it was kissing spines, and I'd have to make a horrible decision. Sorry, if I was difficult."

Veronica sat down on the couch. "You've been kinda wacky lately. Even for you."

Elaine turned to Veronica. "Have you ever"—*what to call this? A triple? A couple plus one? A ménage?*—"had feelings for more than one woman, at the same time?"

Veronica stared at her. "Like become involved with someone while I was with someone else? Like an affair?"

"No." Elaine huffed out a breath. "I'm in love with Robin."

"Yeah. Tell me something I don't know."

"I have feelings for Petra."

Veronica's face pulled into a frown.

"I think Robin does too." Elaine shrugged.

Veronica raised an eyebrow. "You know I'm not your magical negro, right?"

"What the hell are you talking about?"

"I'm not the one you need to talk to. I have no idea what you should do, and you've got to figure your own stuff out. I have no frame of reference for this. I'm a one woman at a time woman."

"I know. I was at your wedding, remember?" Elaine stood up and paced the office. "I know I need to sort this."

"You're worried Robin will choose Petra over you."

Elaine stopped pacing and drummed her fingers on the desk. "Yes. And I can't do a damn thing about it."

"You said you had feelings for Petra too."

"I do." Elaine sat down hard on the couch.

"Talk to Martha. She knows how to do the poly thing. They're happy."

"I promised not to bother her unless it was an emergency. This hardly qualifies." Elaine drummed her fingers on her knee. "I hate this. Things are so much easier when you don't feel anything. I thought I loved Roxy. I had no idea how miserable a feeling it is. I hate how out of control I feel when I think about Robin not being here, of not seeing her every day."

Veronica smirked at her. "You are some piece of work. You sulk around here for months, miserable because Roxy left. And now, you finally notice the woman who would have laid over burning hot coals for you so you wouldn't burn your feet, and you can't figure out what to do because you have 'feelings' for someone you just met?"

"It's not that simple."

Veronica stood up. "Yes it is. You tell her how you feel, and you let her decide. I have to turn them out. Want to help?"

"Yes." Elaine took her coat off the coat rack and shoved her arm in the sleeve. "And thank you. You may not be magical, but you're the only one here besides my sister who is honest with me. Everyone else scuttles away from me."

"Maybe if you didn't spend all your time perfecting your Ice Queen persona and being an ass, maybe they wouldn't be so afraid of you."

Elaine snort laughed. "Maybe, but I wouldn't have near as much fun."

ELAINE SPENT THE day pacing her room, resisting her urge to break Petra's door down. Her gut roiled when she imagined Robin was behind the door. She knew, knew in her gut Robin would leave. She would want to see the world as a free agent. The money Robin had made at the house, invested by Martha, would keep her for quite a while. She would have security, could have her own life, do whatever she wanted.

Elaine had never had to worry about money. She had no memory of her parents, but after listening to so many people's horror stories about coming out to their families she thought maybe it wasn't so bad, but she had ached for parents as a child.

As adults, she and Martha had made their own family. But now Martha was bound to two women, happy, busy with them. She was not as available as she once was, and Elaine felt the loss keenly. She had thought that was what she craved, the idea of one person who was hers alone. To have someone who cared for and loved her above all others. So, she had asked Roxy, and she had laughed in her face, convinced it was a joke. And now, because she had dawdled in telling Robin she was free, she was going to lose a woman she loved.

Elaine had not spoken to Petra since their argument in the kitchen over her revelation to Robin. And she suffered that loss too. She shook her head. *No. Not for me. It's not to be. At least not now. There will be others. Maybe I'm supposed to be alone. Some people are.* She stared at the dismal rain painting rivers across the windowpanes. Veronica had left with Luna early this morning, another trip to the physiotherapist. Elaine tugged on her jeans and her favorite old sweater. *The barn. There'll be something to do.*

ELAINE ROLLED THE door back on the barn and slipped in, closing it behind her to shut out the bitter wind. *Why didn't I go with them to Lake Como? Because Petra. And now I'm stuck here, having fucked up an audition with someone who could have fit in the house, and fucked up with Robin, so I don't even get to see her every day.* And that was the worst of it. She wouldn't have Robin's company. The cheerful smile she gifted Elaine like she was truly glad to see her. Hardly anyone ever smiled at Elaine.

Imperious, cruel, and haughty, she had worked hard to let everyone know she expected perfection and was more than capable of taking anyone to task who did not do as expected. Even those who erred on purpose, hoping to draw her attention. *And what do I have to show for it? Empty bed. Empty arms. Broken heart. Goddess, listen to me. So emo. Fuck this. Fuck me.*

She walked the length of the barn and opened the door leading to the paddock. Marco and Bruno were on the far side of the field. She whistled and they both raised their heads. "Bruno!" She yelled over the wind. Marco snorted, his ears forward. Bruno lowered his head and ignored her. Elaine whistled again.

"Impressive."

Elaine turned on her heel, her body in a defensive posture, one hand cocked back in a fist.

Petra stepped back from her.

"Stop sneaking up on people." Elaine did nothing to hide the anger in her voice. "I warned you before." She lowered her fist.

Petra tilted her head. "Do you have time to talk?"

"No. I have an urgent appointment with Bruno's mane." Elaine turned her back on Petra and opened the paddock gate, walked through it, and closed it behind her. *Fuck her. Wanting to talk. About when she and Robin leave. Who fucking cares. I don't need to know. I don't want to know.* She stormed across the muddy field. Bruno ambled over to her. She caught his halter and attached the lead shank to it before she gathered the excess in her hand. Marco fell in behind them. He would follow. As devoted to Bruno as Martha was to Lucia. *What if Lucia talked Martha and Myfanwy into relocating to Italy? A* cold sweat broke out along Elaine's back. *What if this was their plan? They would move into Madame's old house. And then I'd be alone. Truly alone. Fuck, oh fuck they can't. They can't do that.*

At the gate, Petra waited. *Still here. I don't need this today. Not when I'm worried about Luna and paranoid as hell.*

Elaine unlatched the gate and swung it open. Petra stepped out of the way as Elaine led Bruno into the barn with Marco following behind him. Marco walked into his stall and buried his head in his hay box. "If you insist on hanging around and badgering me, make yourself useful, and lock Marco's stall door." She led Bruno to the cross-ties and clipped one to each side of his halter. She unclipped the lead shank and hung it up. She picked up the hoof pick. She cupped Bruno's hoof and lifted it, settling it between her knees.

Petra came and sat on the bench next to the grooming box. She leaned back against the wall and crossed her ankles. Elaine finished with his other hooves, working her way methodically around the horse. She picked up the curry comb and raked it over his coat. The red mud caked on his hide fell away. Elaine sensed Petra's gaze on her. *What does she want me to say? I don't forgive her. I won't ever. I would have told Robin. Eventually.*

Petra broke the silence. "I didn't intend to intrude on your relationship with Robin."

Elaine kept her back turned. "Right. And you didn't mean to tell her the one thing that would turn her from me, so you could take her with you."

"I made her an offer. It remains to be seen if she will come with me."

"And why wouldn't she? You're her shero now. Delivering her from the evil employer bent on keeping her here against her will."

Petra sighed. "You're being overly dramatic and ridiculous."

Elaine turned. She placed the curry comb into the grooming box, keeping her gaze averted from Petra's face, picked up a stiff brush, and turned back to Bruno. She started at his neck, brushing with short flicks to get rid of the dirt and loose hair on his coat. "If you are done insulting me, why don't you leave me in peace? I'm not going to make you feel better by saying I forgive you or understand. You can assuage your guilt with someone else. Robin is particularly good at that. I'm sure you'll be very happy together."

Petra's hand closed over her elbow. She yanked hard, and Elaine stumbled back. The brush fell to the floor.

"What the hell is wrong with you? If this had been any horse other than Bruno we could have both been hurt." Elaine placed a steadying hand on Bruno's shoulder.

Petra stepped back. "We are going to talk. This is not about Robin. Or you and Robin." Her lips pulled back in a snarl. "This is about us. Or what I thought we might be working toward."

Elaine affected a bored expression. "Sorry. That ship sailed when you decided to ask the woman I love to leave with you. So, if you'll excuse me, I need to get back to work."

Petra stepped into Elaine's space, dug her hands in Elaine's sweater, and tugged her into a kiss, raw, ravenous, and everything she craved. Elaine clasped Petra's elbows and crushed her to her body, letting herself get lost in her hot, hungry, punishing kiss. *This. Pushback. Fury. Insistence. Brutal passion. I need this as much as I need Robin's sublime submission.*

Petra broke the kiss. "Stop being an ass." She met Elaine's gaze. "Don't shut me out. Don't shut either of us out."

"What? You speak for Robin now?" Elaine's barely contained rage boiled up.

"No. And neither do you. Not talking to either of us is as good as shoving us out the door. We don't have agency because you refuse to talk to us, to even explore what could be because it's not how you want it, or think you want it."

She pressed herself into Elaine's arms. "This. You. This feels right. Righter than anything I've ever known." She lowered herself to her knees. "You want me to beg? Like this? Plead with you?" Petra kept her gaze focused on Elaine's eyes. "I'll do whatever it takes for you to see what you mean to me, and how serious I am about more with you."

Elaine stared down at Petra's face. Bruno, ever curious, nuzzled the top of Petra's hair. Elaine couldn't stop herself from laughing as a horrified expression spread over Petra's face. She scrambled away from him. Elaine reached out and pushed Bruno's muzzle away. "Maybe not declaring your intentions in the middle of the barn might be better."

Petra glared at her as she swept her hand over her hair in a vain attempt to wipe away Bruno's saliva.

Elaine chuckled and helped Petra to her feet. "Let me put him up. And then we'll talk."

Chapter Fourteen

Elaine passed Petra a towel and turned away to hide her grin as Petra scrubbed at her head. Still chuckling, she led Bruno back to his stall. She tossed a hay flake into his hay box and closed him in. Petra waited for her in the aisle. Elaine linked their arms. "Come on. You'll need a shower to get that out of your hair."

Petra fell into step beside her. "So, you believe me now?"

"After your display in the barn?" Elaine smirked at her. "I believe you want something with me. I'm not sure what it is. I'm not sure what I want. I thought I knew." She glanced up at the gray sky. "I planned on figuring it out during a long talk with Bruno."

Petra leaned into her. "Will you talk with me now? Will you at least tell me what's going on with you?"

"If I knew myself, it would be easier. I've been in a funk since Roxy left. I'm not myself. Or maybe this is me. I haven't felt this unsure since I was a baby butch, trying to figure out which end of the whip I belonged on." Elaine held the door open for Petra. "I need some tea for this discussion."

They left their boots in the mudroom and washed up.

Tessa was in the kitchen, a frown on her face. "Mistress, I'm going to need help to serve lunch on time."

Elaine turned to Petra. "Maybe you should go to your room and rouse Robin." Her gut churned as she thought of Robin in Petra's bed. *My Robin. No. Not mine. Her own person. She belongs to no one.* It stung Robin had chosen to sleep with Petra, and Elaine's annoyance with Petra returned twofold.

"She's not in my room. And hasn't been." Petra tilted her head at Elaine. "Did you think she'd been with me this whole time?"

"Well, yes. Hasn't she?"

"No. She's never spent the night in my room." A rueful smile crossed Petra's face. "Said she couldn't sleep unless she felt safe."

"Tessa, when was the last time you saw Robin?" Elaine pushed aside her rising panic. *She wouldn't leave without saying goodbye. Would she? Millie would have to drive her. She wouldn't take her anywhere without telling me. Would she?*

"Yesterday morning, Mistress." Tessa pressed her lips together in a thin line. "She was distracted after you talked. She burned the orange rye raisin rolls she was working on. I haven't seen her since."

Elaine turned from Petra and rushed through the door leading out of the kitchen. Robin hadn't burned anything since she first started in the kitchen. In the beginning she had burned so much food they had taken to preparing twice as much, figuring Robin would ruin at least half of it. But she had settled, stopped jumping at shadows, and grown confident. Once she got her feet, her talent had shown. And now... And now she was distracted enough to burn a special project she was working on.

Elaine stopped at the door leading to the room under the stairs—the small windowless room close to the kitchen with the thick door and solid locks Robin preferred to the dorm. *Please let her be here. Please.*

PETRA FROWNED AT Elaine. "This is her room?"

The judgment in her voice rankled Elaine. "Don't. Don't even try to judge things you know nothing about. You're a latecomer to this party. You don't know her."

A dull red blush stole over Petra's face, and she stepped away from the door, giving Elaine space.

Elaine tapped gently on the door. "Robin? Please open the door. Let me see you. If you don't want to talk, that's fine. I want to make sure you're okay."

The tick of the hall clock was the only sound. Elaine kneeled and pressed her ear to the door. She pulled back and spoke close to the keyhole. "Robin. Please. Even if you don't want to open the door, just tap on it. Let me know you're okay." Elaine kept her voice gentle and her tone even. *Please be here. Please be safe.*

A soft tap sounded on the other side of the door. Elaine's heart clenched hard. *She's still here.* "Thank you."

Elaine sat down with her back against the door. "Will you come to lunch? Please. I miss you. You don't have to decide now."

Petra sat down next to Elaine. She reached over and clasped her hand and whispered, "What do we do now?" She shifted her gaze to the door and back to Elaine's face. "You've been through this before with her, haven't you?"

"Yes." Elaine pitched her voice low. "We wait. We don't push." She let her head rest against the door to Robin's room. So many times. So many nights she had sat with the door between them, worried to leave her alone, fearful of her needing something and not having it, fearful of losing her to the demons of depression and its dark lies.

Petra leaned her head on Elaine's shoulder. Elaine squeezed her hand.

They sat on the floor. Not speaking. Waiting. Elaine stretched her legs out and lifted her arm. Petra leaned against her, her head on Elaine's chest. As willing to wait for Robin as Elaine was.

Unbidden images of Roxy's impatient expression and harsh tones as she spoke to Robin during her time at Rowan House filled Elaine's thoughts. Angry over Elaine's willingness to wait for Robin, Roxy had railed at her. She had hated it, found it annoying, hard to handle. She would roll her eyes and leave Elaine sitting on the floor as she stomped away in a huff, insisting that Robin was playing a game to garner Elaine's attention.

Elaine knew it was no game, knew Robin needed to know she mattered, not just as a piece of ass, but as a person. Elaine had known the first time she had met Robin, known under the hard woman brassing out her existence was one who needed to know she was more.

Elaine started when the latch to the door turned, the deadbolt loud as it clicked open. Elaine and Petra shifted away from the door. Elaine kneeled in the hallway and sat back on her heels. She kept her eyes on the door. It opened and Robin stepped out into the hallway. "I'm hungry." Her voice was as flat as her expression, eyes dull, her hair knotted and tangled. Elaine rested her hands on the top of her thighs, fighting her urge to wrap her arms around Robin and never let go.

"Do you want to eat in the kitchen? Or would you like to eat in my room? Just us?" Elaine remained kneeling.

Robin met Petra's gaze. She inclined her head toward Elaine. "I need to talk to her, Petra. Would you excuse us?"

Petra gracefully rose from the floor. "I'll go see if I can make myself useful in the kitchen."

Elaine rose to her feet and offered her arm to Robin, and she clasped it, leaning her body into Elaine as they walked to her room in silence. At the door, Elaine opened it and stepped back to allow Robin to precede her before she closed the door and locked it. Robin crossed the room, entered the bathroom, and closed the door after her. Elaine pressed her ear to the en suite door. *Shower. Good. Food, she'll want food.*

Elaine called the kitchen. Tessa picked up on the third ring.

"Tessa, bring lunch for two to my room. Yes, Robin's fine." *Is she? Please let her be.* Satisfied Tessa would know Robin's food preferences, she disconnected the call and rang Millie.

Millie's deep voice rumbled through the speaker. "Yes, Ma'am?"

"Make sure Petra and Tessa don't destroy my kitchen and take care of the house for the rest of the day."

"Aye, Ma'am. Robin?"

"With me."

"I'll take care of things, Ma'am."

"Thank you."

Robin stepped out of the bathroom wrapped in Elaine's robe. She sat in the wingback chair next to the fireplace, tucked her feet up under her, and pulled the dressing gown over her feet. Her hair was wet and hung in dark strands about her face as she leaned forward and dried her hair with a towel. Elaine flipped the switch and ignited the gas fire before she sat in the chair opposite Robin.

"I love you." Robin's voice was clear and strong as she separated her curls with her fingers. "I want you to understand, even if I leave, I'll always love you."

Elaine bit her lip. "How can you be so sure?"

"That I love you?" Robin twisted a lock of her wet hair around her finger. "How does anyone know if they love someone?"

Elaine crossed her legs. "I don't doubt your love. But there's a wide world out there. A world where you have a chance to start over. To be with someone who knows nothing of your past."

Robin lifted her chin. "I'm not ashamed of who I've been. I survived."

"You did. And thrived. You should take the opportunity Petra is offering you. I can't ask you to stay."

Robin's eyes locked on Elaine's face. "Can't or won't?"

Elaine held her gaze. "It wouldn't be right for me to ask you to stay, no matter how I feel about you."

"I don't care if it's right." Robin turned away from Elaine. "You're so damn noble."

Elaine shifted in her chair and crossed her legs. "If I were noble, I'd have told you immediately you were safe to leave."

"Why?" Robin's voice was harsh. "Why didn't you tell me?"

"Because I wanted a little more time with you before you left me. Because I didn't want to remember what my life was like before you came. Because I love you and I wanted to pretend you loved me for me, and not because you didn't have a choice. Stockholm syndrome is real. Once you're away from here, away from Rowan House, you'll hate me." Elaine knotted her hands in her lap. "They say if you love someone you should let them go and if they come back it's real."

Robin snorted. "That is complete and utter rot."

She left her chair. She yanked Elaine's hands apart before she shoved Elaine's leg off her knee and climbed into her lap, straddling her. "If you love someone you should let them know. Tell them you don't want them to go." She grabbed Elaine's face with both hands. "Right or wrong, I don't want to leave you." She kissed Elaine. "I sat in my room, trying to imagine what it would be like without you. I can't. You're the first person to see me. To see someone beyond the addict, the whore, the submissive." She leaned her forehead against Elaine's brow. "I need to know you trust me, trust me enough to know, even if I leave with Petra, I'll come back to you."

Elaine wrapped her arms around Robin. "I'll be here. Your room will be here."

Robin kissed her eyelids, her cheek, and then her mouth, her kisses tender. "I'm yours, collar or no, I'm yours."

Elaine held her gaze. "Mine. Always. No matter where you go, or with who, you are mine. And always will be. I don't want anyone else, Robin."

"Not even Petra?"

Elaine shifted her grip on Robin's hips. "I could ask the same of you. What about Petra?"

"She's not you."

"Exactly. She's not you. I like her. I care for her. But she's not you." Elaine smoothed her hand over Robin's back. "Do you want more with her?"

Robin tilted her head. "Do you?"

"Yes. Do you?"

Robin's eyes were wary. "Yes. And no."

Elaine frowned. "Explain."

"I don't want more with her if you think it means I want less with you."

Elaine rubbed Robin's back, massaging the tight knots of her muscles under her fingers. "I don't want more with her if it makes you unhappy." She pushed a damp lock of Robin's hair behind her ear. "I hate it when you're unhappy."

Robin leaned in and pressed a kiss to Elaine's mouth. "We are in agreement then; we both want more, but only if the other is okay with it."

Elaine snorted. "Yes, so it seems."

Robin pressed her lips together. "What if I wanted you to stop seeing clients?"

Elaine shifted in the chair and studied Robin's expression. "What if you did?"

"Would you?"

"Is this a test?"

"No. I hate the idea of anyone but me with you." Robin lowered her chin to her chest and half-turned away from Elaine. "I've managed to survive the last three years, but I don't know if I can now."

The sadness in her voice cracked Elaine's heart. Elaine raised Robin's chin with two fingers. "Is it a condition of remaining here? Of being with me?"

Robin swallowed visibly. "Yes." Her voice wobbled. "I couldn't tolerate it. Not now."

Elaine quirked her mouth. "You want me to give up everyone else in the world for you? To be exclusive?"

Robin's gaze was steady. "Yes."

"And you, you would give up everyone else as well?" Elaine studied Robin's expression.

"Yes."

"Including Petra?"

Robin quirked her mouth. "Depends."

Elaine scowled. "On what?"

"On Petra."

Elaine huffed out a breath. "Robin Broadacre, I would give up whatever you asked of me. I can't imagine my life without you. As far as Petra goes, we can decide together."

"We?" Robin smirked.

"Yes." Elaine shifted her grip, one hand behind Robin's head and the other on her ass. Crushing her to her chest, she kissed the gorgeous smirk off her face, claiming her mouth even as she surrendered her own soul. She pulled back, breathless. "Yes, we."

THEY HAD STAYED in bed late. Snuggled under the heavy blankets, Elaine lay on her back with Robin's leg over her thighs, her body plastered to Elaine's side. In the night, Elaine had woken to Robin's strangled cries and thrashing. She had woken her from her nightmare and rocked her until Robin had curled into her, clung to her, and settled. *Petra. Will she go with her? Maybe. Maybe not. Doesn't matter. She's mine. No matter what she's mine. Mine.*

Robin stirred and lifted her leg clear. "Morning." She slid out from under Elaine's arm and went into the bathroom. Elaine stayed under the covers waiting her turn in the bathroom. Robin came back, her nipples hard in the cool air. She nipped back to the bed and slipped under the covers.

Elaine went to the bathroom. The minty smell of mouthwash made her smile as she brushed her teeth. *Need to get her a toothbrush. Would she move in with me? Or would she still want her space?* She spit the toothpaste into the sink and rinsed her mouth.

Robin was propped up in the bed with pillows behind her back. The duvet was tucked around her. She crooked a finger at Elaine. "I'm cold. Come warm me up?"

Elaine stopped long enough to pick up her hairbrush from her dressing table. She flipped the covers back, slid into bed, and leaned back against the headboard.

She patted her lap and Robin lay across her legs. Elaine tucked the covers around her body, leaving her ass exposed. Her skin pebbled in the cool of the room. She drew the bristles of the brush over Robin's ass, lightly scratching her skin. She moaned quietly and wiggled her hips. "Please. Mistress. Mark me."

Elaine lifted the brush and brought it down. A light blow and Robin sighed her contentment. Elaine rubbed her fingers over the red oval-shaped spot left from the brush. She rotated the handle and dragged the stiff bristles over the mark. *My mark. Mine.* Elaine raised the brush and brought it down again, harder this time.

Robin pressed her hips into Elaine's thigh. "More, Mistress. Harder please, Mistress."

Elaine hummed with pleasure and brought the brush down hard twice.

Robin trembled and ground against Elaine.

"Lift your hips for me."

Robin rocked back on her knees, raising her hips.

Elaine reached under her and touched her fingertips to Robin's clit, thick and slick with her desire. Elaine shoved the covers down and spread her legs. "Turn around, I want your face between my legs."

Robin complied, the position offering Elaine unfettered access to what she desired most, and the delectable scent of Robin's excitement had her desperate to possess every bit of sweetness she could wring from her willing body.

The puff of Robin's warm breath on her thighs was intoxicating. She gripped her hips and brought her to her mouth.

Elaine licked a firm stroke over her slickness before she thrust her tongue deep, making Robin gasp. She pulled back and nibbled her ass cheek, drawing a squeal from Robin. "Lick me."

Robin settled her mouth over her and swirled her tongue before she sucked hard. Elaine gasped and buried her face in Robin's lush folds and lost herself in the sensation. Soft wet sounds of their attentions broke the quiet; loud moans and deep growls of pleasure echoing in Elaine's room. Unable to focus with Robin's skillful mouth on her, Elaine surrendered, rested her cheek against Robin's thigh, bucked her hips into her mouth, and came with a shout.

She moved her mouth back to Robin and sucked hard before she whispered. "Give it to me, love. Give me what's mine. Now." Robin rocked her hips back, pressing herself into Elaine's mouth, and came with a gush and a whimper. "Again. Please, give it to me. Now." Elaine kept licking and Robin groaned and thrust her hips wildly as she gave to Elaine what was hers to have, and only hers to have ever after this, unless Elaine gave her permission.

Elaine cherished her gift. Her love. *All of her, forever mine.* Elaine released her. Turning Robin around, she cupped the back of her neck and brought her up to her mouth. She kissed her, sealing their agreement, savoring their combined essence.

Chapter Fifteen

PETRA SAT BETWEEN them at the small round table. She wore Channel and a closed expression. Her forearms were on the tabletop as if braced for impact.

Elaine reached out and rubbed her fingertips in small circles over the tense muscles of Petra's forearm. "We need to talk about this."

Robin touched Petra's hand. Petra turned her hand over, palm up, and Robin clasped it. "Are you okay?"

Petra quirked her mouth. "I don't know."

Robin lifted her hand and kissed the back of it. "I needed to talk with Elaine first. And now we need to talk to you."

"We?" Petra pulled free from Robin's grip and away from Elaine's touch.

"Yes." Elaine leveled her gaze at Petra. "We need to discuss you and us."

Petra pressed her lips in a thin line. "It's fine. I was planning on leaving soon." She pushed back from the table, stood, and shoved her chair into place under the table.

Elaine cuffed her wrist with her fingers. "You're going to talk to us. We can't leave it like this."

Petra lifted her chin, her gaze hard. "Let go of me. I'm not your property. You're not my Mistress." Petra's voice wobbled.

Elaine released her and rose from her own chair. "Maybe you're right. Maybe we don't have anything to discuss."

Robin tapped the table. "Petra." Elaine and Petra turned toward Robin. "Please talk with us." She tilted her head and met Petra's hard gaze. "Is your version of love so narrow you think it has to be either-or? Is there no room for both?"

Petra lifted her chin. "I don't know, is there?"

Robin stood up and glared at Petra and Elaine. She pointed to their chairs.

"Sit down. Now. We are not leaving this room until we get this sorted."

Elaine blinked. *Who is this fierce woman? I've never heard that tone before. Impressive.* She lifted her hand to her mouth to cover her smile before she inclined her head toward Robin. "As you wish."

Petra frowned at Robin as she pulled her chair out and sat on the edge of the seat, her back stiff and straight.

Robin rested her hands on the table, palms up. "Elaine and I have discussed where we are with each other."

Petra glanced between the two of them. "And where is that?"

Robin held her gaze. "We are for each other, will pledge to each other." Sadness roiled over Petra's face before she smoothed her expression.

"And"—Robin reached over and clasped Elaine and Petra's hands—"we want to explore more with you. If you're interested."

Petra traced her fingers over the pattern on the tablecloth. "When you say you're going to pledge to each other, what does it mean?"

Elaine covered Petra's fingers with her hand and laced their fingers together. "It means we will be for each other. We will be exclusive."

Petra's head snapped up. "But you just said you wanted to explore more with me? How is that? You want a third when you want to spice things up? A toy to pick up and put down whenever you feel like it?" She tugged at their hands to pull away. Elaine and Robin held fast.

Elaine met her gaze. "We would never treat you as a plaything. And it would be however the fuck we three wanted it to be. Robin and I are clear. We don't expect you to be exclusive. I will no longer see clients. As for us and you—" Elaine brought Petra's hand to her mouth, turned it over, and placed a kiss in the center of her palm. "That depends on you. Do you want to explore more with us? To see where this might lead?"

Petra's eyes shone. "Yes. But I can't commit to being exclusive. I can't, not now. I'm about to be offered what I've spent years working for—my own house, my own space in this world."

Robin laced her fingers with Petra's. "We're not asking you to give anything up."

"Then what are we talking about?" Petra frowned.

"We wanted you to know going forward, in intimate matters, we scene with you together or not at all."

Petra quirked her mouth. "And what if I don't want that? What if I only want one of you?"

Robin jerked her hand away from Petra's. "Then you need to go, and don't let the door hit you on the way out. I'm not going to tolerate it. I've spent the last three years dying a little inside each time Elaine was with anyone else. I won't live like that anymore."

Elaine swallowed hard, hearing the pain in Robin's voice, kicking herself for not seeing it before. She released Petra's hand slowly. "I was sick at heart when I thought Robin had chosen you over me. If you don't want us on our terms, we understand. But we're not going to change our minds." She reached over and clasped Robin's hands. "We're not going to pretend, not anymore, not with each other, and not with you."

Petra pursed her lips. "I'm the odd woman out here."

"No. You're not. We want you, to know you, to have you join us. But we just met you. We need time to get to know you. And you need to get to know us, to know who we are outside the playroom, not only our sexual side." Elaine raked her gaze over Petra. "We already know we're compatible sexually."

"Are you asking to date me?" The incredulous tone of Petra's voice made Elaine grit her teeth.

Robin tapped the top of the table, drawing Petra's gaze. "Yes. We are. And don't act like we're crazy—well, we probably are, but yes. Date us."

Elaine released Petra's hand.

Petra crossed her arms. "What does that even mean?"

Elaine smiled at her. "It means dinners, and teas, and walks, and quiet evenings talking, or lying about reading together. It means learning your favorite foods and colors, what agitates you, and what makes it better, what keeps you up at night, what makes you sad and happy, and how you like your coffee. It's hundreds of mornings after where we don't get out of bed until noon, and a thousand other small things you do together, to discover and remember when you are trying to see if someone is for you, if you need them in your life like air."

Petra's breath came quickly. "You're serious?"

"Of course we are. For fuck's sake, we wouldn't say it if we weren't."

Petra pressed her lips together. "I need to think. I've never…I've never considered anything like this."

Robin stood up and placed her hand on Elaine's shoulder. Elaine reached up and rested her hand on top of Robin's. "We understand."

Petra stood. "I have to go. I've got to start packing."

"You're still going to Oslo?" Robin's fingers dug into Elaine's shoulder.

"I have to. If I don't, I'll regret it." Petra glanced at Robin, a rueful expression on her face. "And now I need to go early since I will have to learn someone new for my audition."

PETRA FOLDED HER shirt and placed it in the packing cube on the table.

"I could have Tessa or June do this for you." Elaine lay on the bed with her hands clasped behind her head.

"I know. I'm more comfortable doing it myself." Petra slipped another shirt off the hanger and folded it.

"Will you let us know you've arrived safely?" Elaine rolled to her side and rested her head on her hand. "Please?"

"Yes. If you want me to."

"You don't have to. You don't owe us anything."

Petra sat on the edge of the bed, her back to Elaine. "Why? Why do you care? You have one woman who would walk on hot coals for you. Why do you care what happens with me? Or for me?"

Elaine sat up and touched Petra's shoulder. "Loving Robin does not mean I can't care for you. Robin cares for you too. What is hard to understand about that?"

Petra turned to her. "All I can see when I look at you is all the years I wanted Madame to notice me, to want only me."

Elaine sat up and pushed her hands through her hair. "I am not her. I have no intention of starting a harem, or whatever she had with her collection of women. But I do want more with you, so does Robin. We'd be lying if we said we didn't. Are you willing to give us up in search of someone you may or may not find?" She reached out and touched Petra's cheek. "Someone who may not want all sides of you? Robin craves your dominance as much as I crave your submission."

"But you'd want me to stop being who I am." Petra's mouth was firm.

"No. We didn't say that. We know you want to continue your work. We would come to an arrangement or agreement. We understand the difference between clients and lovers."

"So, what is it you want from me? How is it different from just engaging my services when you want them?"

"As your clients? In practice it might not be any different. But would it be the same for you? Knowing we care not just about your body and how you make us feel? Knowing we care about you?"

Petra stood and walked to the closet. "I'm sure I have other clients who care about me."

Elaine snorted. "Right. You're worse than I am."

Petra rested her hands on her hips. "What?"

"You keep telling yourself that. I lied to myself for years. We can't and don't want to stop you. We'll be here. When... If you return, there will be a place for you. I know my sister and Lucia will agree. We will need someone to take over my clients."

Petra quirked her mouth. "And what? Come back here and suffer Robin mooning over me? Watch you pretend it doesn't matter to you when I'm with clients? No thanks."

Elaine stuffed her hands in her pockets to keep from shaking Petra. "Fine. Call Millie when your bags are packed, and she'll take care of them."

ROBIN POURED ELAINE'S tea. She sat opposite her. The empty tin of biscuits between them was open. Scattered papers and chocolate biscuit crumbs littered Elaine's plate.

Robin sipped from her cup. "She's leaving, isn't she?"

Elaine met Robin's gaze. "Yes." She reached out and touched Robin's hand. "I'm sorry."

"You're sorry?" Robin snorted. "The only one who should be sorry is Petra."

Elaine focused on Robin's face. "I hate when I can't give you what you want."

Robin set her teacup aside, left her chair. Elaine scooted her chair back and Robin settled herself in Elaine's lap. "You've given me you. I've more than I ever dreamed I'd have."

Elaine touched her chin and kissed the corner of her mouth. She spoke against her lips. "You won't regret it? That you didn't go with her?"

Robin brushed her hand over Elaine's hair. "No. The first trip I take from here will be with you. Some people come into your life, a fortunate moment, and then leave. Trying to force people to love you never works."

Elaine hugged Robin close. "Do you love her?"

"Do you?"

Elaine chewed her lip. "Not yet. But..."

"But sometimes you imagine it could become more?" Robin sat up and smoothed a hand over Elaine's hip. "I feel the same way, and then think I should be grateful for what I have, not sad I didn't get a chance to explore a relationship with her."

"How could she turn us down? I mean really."

Robin laughed. "Exactly." She palmed Elaine's breast. "Thank you for trying, Mistress, even if she said no. I'm happy with you. And will be. Always."

Elaine cupped the back of Robin's neck and smiled as a shiver ran through her frame. "I couldn't ask for more than you and your sublime submission. But you'll miss her, miss the way she punished you."

Robin quirked her mouth. "As you'll miss having her submit to you, a powerful bratty Domme at your feet."

Elaine kissed her. "Yes. And watching her punish you. She's the best I've ever seen with a single tail."

Robin settled into her lap. "What will Mistress Martha and Lucia say? Will they be angry?"

"No. For once it wasn't about me being difficult."

Robin snorted. "Yes. Asking someone to stay and explore a relationship shouldn't make them run away."

Elaine moved her hand from the back of Robin's neck and rubbed her back. "She's searching for something, or someone else. She doesn't trust we'd be equal. She believes I would dismiss her when we tired of her."

"She said that to you?" Robin's face was a mask of indignation.

"And some other things. She's worried you would be unhappy if she kept seeing clients."

Robin pursed her lips. "I wouldn't love it, but it's not like with you."

Elaine smiled a smug smile. "Because you love me and don't want to share? For the very first time in my life I find myself feeling the same way."

Robin rolled the button on Elaine's shirt between her fingers. "I am deeply honored. I know so many women who will grieve it was not them."

Elaine laughed. "My sister will be intolerable. She's been after me to settle down since she pledged to Lucia and Myfanwy."

Robin pressed a kiss to Elaine's neck. "Mistress, are you tired?"

Elaine lifted her neck to give Robin access. "Not too. What did you have in mind?"

"Could we try once more? To convince her to stay?"

Elaine's nipples hardened. "Mmm. Actions do speak louder than words. Do you still have the white peignoir I bought you?"

"You gave me several white peignoirs. Which one?" Robin nibbled her way along Elaine's jaw.

"The copy of the one Grace Kelly wore in *Rear Window*?"

"That one is in the front of my closet."

Elaine tipped her chin up. "Excellent. Meet me in the large playroom in an hour. I'll extend our invitation to Petra."

Robin kissed her. "Yes, Mistress."

ELAINE TAPPED ON Petra's door.

"Just a minute," Petra called.

Elaine wiped her sweaty palms on her pants.

Petra yanked the door open. "Yes?"

Elaine stared at the dark smudges under Petra's eyes. "Are you okay?"

Petra swiped at her face. "I was testing some new mascara. Not so waterproof."

Elaine raised an eyebrow. "Do you have plans for this evening?"

Petra gestured to her room. "Other than finishing my packing and washing my face? No."

"Would you be interested in participating in a going away scene?"

Petra pursed her lips and rested a hand on her hip. "Where?"

Elaine tilted her head. "The large playroom."

Petra's mouth curved into a blade-sharp smile. "Is there a theme?"

Elaine rested her hands on the doorway to stop herself from grabbing Petra and kissing the cheeky expression off her face.

"Innocence lost."

Petra's smirk was replaced by a feral smile. "Time?"

"Eight."

"I'll be there."

ELAINE ROSE FROM her bath and dried herself. In the mirror she studied her face. *Make-up? Or bare face? Innocence. Only lip color.* She chose a pale pink lip color, so light it was if she was wearing no color at all. *And what does innocence smell like?* Forgoing her signature Chanel Coco Mademoiselle perfume, she chose a light citrus scent, barely there. *What to wear? Innocence, innocence. Not white. What will go with Robin's elegant peignoir?*

She stood naked in front of her wardrobe, and her nipples pebbled in the cool of air of her room after her bath. Heat built in her body in anticipation of the evening. She had never performed innocence lost. *Can I do it? Will my pride get in the way? What will Petra do? What does she want? Besides a dead woman. Shouldn't speak ill of the dead. She loved her, like Martha, like Lucia. Like so many over the years. She said I was like her. I'm not. Time to change her mind.*

She slid the hangers along the closet rod, perusing her clothes. *Innocence lost. But whose? Petra's or mine? So hung up on what she couldn't have with Madame. Or Lucia. No, she didn't want Lucia. She did it trying to win Madame's favor. What a bitch. And then she says I remind her of Madame. I hate that. She thinks she can't compete with Robin. How to make her see this is not just a game for us? That we are sincere? Show her. Innocence. What is innocence? Maybe let Robin have her way with her? Maybe have my way with both, have them confess what they want, truly want, make them put on a show? Maybe make them show each other their deepest desires? She won't go down easy tonight, not as sad as she is. Maybe she'll be up for a little competition? But what stakes?*

She cupped her breast and rolled her nipple as she thought, relishing the delicate threads of desire swirling low in her belly and stiffening her clit.

Her fingertips lingered on her favorite hunter-green silk wrap dress, before she bypassed it in favor of a dark-gray tailored suit. She selected a white shirt and maroon silk tie to complete her outfit. After laying her clothes out on her bed, she drew a binder over her breasts, not wanting to spoil the line of her suit. She chose her favorite black belt, soft enough to be comfortable to wear, stiff enough to swing for more intimate impact play. Onyx cuff links, one pair of black oxfords, and a full Windsor knot later she was ready to go. *What stakes indeed? What do I have she wants?*

Chapter Sixteen

ELAINE ARRIVED AT the playroom at half seven and set about checking her equipment. She adjusted the thermostat and the heat panels came on. The mini-refrigerator was stocked with water, fruit, and juice. She moved the queening chair, her favorite item of furniture, to the middle of the room. After she placed two kneeling benches close to each other, she surveyed the room. From the equipment cabinet Elaine chose three white low-melt candles, arranged them on a sideboard, and placed a lighter near them. *I'll go with what Petra gives me. How she presents herself. And then we'll see.*

She placed several small bottles of lube in strategic places, and an ache settled between her legs. *Should've taken care of myself before I got dressed. Too late now. Easier to master the desires of others when my own is in check.* She selected two spreader bars and cuffs and two small bullet vibrators whose remotes she set on the table next to her chair. She closed her eyes as she imagined the scene. Robin and Petra cuffed to each other, their legs spread for Elaine's pleasure. *Will Petra submit tonight? Or will she and I share Robin, competing to outdo each other, to be the one who makes her come first? Too fraught. What did she want from Madame? To be hers? Or to serve her as she wanted, not as Madame commanded. To be given freedom to explore and touch and do as she pleased with Madame's body. Submit. Give*

Petra permission to do as she wishes. What does she want from Robin? Elaine chewed her lip. *Perfect. This has to be perfect. She has to see. See how much we want her.*

"You're here early. Are you anxious, Elaine?" Petra's tone of mock concern made Elaine smile. *Pure bitch. Goddess, I love that.*

Elaine turned and perused Petra's costume of long black skirt, a matching long-waisted under bust Victorian corset, and a peasant blouse. She raised an eyebrow. "*Phantom of the Opera*? Didn't Emmy Rosen wear that in the 'point of no return' scene?"

"As close as I could do on short notice. It seemed appropriate." Petra sauntered into the room. "On several levels."

"Am I to play the Phantom?" Elaine held up her scarred hand. "If my arm had been shorter, my face would have been burned." She closed the distance between them and leaned to inhale Petra's signature scent, the warm smell of gardenia, a sharp contrast to the cold expression on Petra's face. "Are we there?"

"Are we where?"

"The point of no return. Are we there?" Elaine ran her fingertip along the low neckline of Petra's blouse, deliberately avoiding her skin. She smirked as Petra's dark nipples tented the sheer white cloth.

Petra opened her mouth as if to respond and shut it when Robin tapped on the door frame.

She was a vision in an exact copy of Grace Kelly's spectacular nightgown from *Rear Window*. Chaste and wanton in one smooth white satin package with a diaphanous overlay. "May I enter, Mistress?"

The rich tone of her voice and undercurrent of her excitement sent a torrent of want through Elaine. "Yes. Walk to me. I want to watch the way the gown moves about you."

Petra turned as well, her expression keen. "That is lovely. Where did you have it made?"

Robin arrived at Elaine's side. "There's a woman in Milan, Aurora Rossi. She can replicate anything." Robin blushed. "It was a gift from Mistress Elaine."

Petra arched a brow. "It's almost virginal. Almost." A tight smile crossed her face. She turned her gaze to Elaine. "So, what's the plan? Or do you have one?" Her insolent tone matched the feigned innocence of her outfit.

Elaine turned on her. "We need to establish safe words and boundaries."

Petra sighed. "You feel compelled to ask every time?"

Elaine frowned at her. "Is it wrong?"

"You don't ask Robin, do you? When you play you don't worry about crossing lines with her, do you?"

"We've known each other for years. We've played many times."

Petra pinned Elaine in place with her eyes. "You trust your assessment of her, your knowledge of her body. You know just when to push and when to hold back. And you know whatever happens she won't leave. You'd work it out."

Elaine tilted her head to the side. "And your point?"

"I want." Petra lifted her chin. "I want you to stop treating me like I'm made of glass." She tugged the shoulders of her blouse down. "I want to go beyond the invisible barrier you've placed around your heart. Past the point of no return." She lowered her chin to her chest. "With you too, Robin. You gave me what you thought I could handle, what I needed for my audition. But you've never given me all of you."

Robin leaned into Elaine's body, a subtle press against Elaine's side, and she reached for Elaine's hand, laced their fingers together.

Petra spoke through her teeth, her eyes bright. "You say you want more with me, and yet you hold back. Prove to me you do want me, all of me, not just the parts that get you off." Her bare shoulders glowed in the gaslight.

Elaine squeezed Robin's hand once, and Robin gave a quick squeeze back, signaling her agreement. She released her. Robin approached Petra, stopped a step away, and lowered her gaze. "May I touch you?"

"Please." Her voice a harsh plea.

Robin raised her hands to Petra's hips before she tugged her closer. She lowered her mouth to her chest and traced the swell of her breasts with her tongue.

Elaine lifted Petra's hair and kissed the smooth skin of her neck. She bit down, hard enough to mark her. "Do you want us?" She bit again, harder, forcing a sharp intake of breath from Petra. Robin tugged Petra's blouse down and exposed her breasts, settling the stretchy neckline under them. She took a step back and admired the display before she wrapped her lips around her nipple. Her cheeks hollowed as she sucked hard. Elaine looped her arm around Petra's waist. "Ready to give us what's ours?"

Petra moaned. "Yes."

Robin ground her hips against her as she sucked Petra's nipples, lapped at them. She brought her hands up and pressed them together, licking the channel between Petra's breasts before she lowered herself to her knees.

She pressed her face to the apex of Petra's thighs. "I love your scent, Mistress. Let me. Let me taste you. Please."

Elaine captured Petra's wrists and pulled them behind her back to hold them in one hand. Robin used her palms to slide Petra's skirt up, licked and nipped her way along her thigh. Petra turned her head to her, and Elaine captured her mouth in a deep kiss. "You want this? To have this with us?"

"Yes." Petra leaned back against her. "Yes. Ma'am."

Elaine shifted her hands to cup her breasts. "Or is there something else you want more? Something I've never given anyone else."

Petra's breath hitched as she peered into Elaine's eyes.

Delicious sounds filled the air between them as Robin, given permission to do as she wished, worshipped Petra with her mouth. Elaine banded Petra's waist with her arm and Petra leaned back into her embrace. She swept her hand up to her neck and traced Petra's delicate throat with her fingertips, relishing the rapid beat of her pulse and the way her breath quickened under their attentions. *Longing. Desire. So much desire. She wants us. Wants me. All of me.*

Petra closed her eyes and groaned. "Yes. So much." A whisper, a petition.

Elaine released Petra.

"Robin. Stop."

Robin whimpered her disappointment. Elaine turned Petra to her, cupped her chin, and ran her thumb over her lower lip. "Sit on the queening chair." Petra raised an eyebrow and held Elaine's gaze for a moment. Her breathing evened out, and she raised and then lowered her shoulders before she strode to the queening chair. She lifted her skirts as she mounted the chair. Her mistress mask firmly in place, she tucked up her skirt, placed her elegantly shod feet on the footrests and spread her legs wide. Elaine trembled with need as she savored the view of the sweet delight between Petra's thighs.

Elaine snapped her fingers. "Robin, undress me."

Robin quirked her mouth. "Yes. Mistress." She crawled over on her hands and knees. She untied both shoes, and Elaine lifted her foot. With firm hands, Robin took her shoe and sock off before repeating it with the other foot. She rose and unknotted Elaine's tie. Looking into Elaine's eyes, she pulled it free before she rolled it around her fingers and then tucked it into the pocket of Elaine's suit jacket. After moving behind her, she slid her suit coat from her shoulders. Elaine focused on Petra's face, enjoying her reactions to the show she and Robin were providing their Mistress. *Mistress. For tonight. And then what?* Elaine shoved aside all thoughts of the future and relaxed under Robin's touch and their Mistress's gaze.

"Slow down, Robin. It's too good to rush." A slow smile spread across Petra's face. Elaine surrendered to Petra's power as she assumed control of the scene.

Robin's fingers feathered over Elaine's skin as she unbuttoned her shirt. She took the cufflinks off and settled her arms around Elaine's waist and pushed them into Elaine's front pocket. Taking advantage of her proximity, she rubbed against Elaine's ass drawing a soft groan from Elaine.

Robin reached up and drew the shirt from Elaine's back, folded it, and placed it on top of the suit coat before she kneeled in front of Elaine. Her gaze fixed on Elaine's face, she rested her hands on the waistband of her trousers, the backs of her knuckles warm against Elaine's skin. A sharp wave of want washed over Elaine as Robin unbuckled her belt. The sight of her kneeling and the brush of her fingers against the taut skin of Elaine's belly made her tremble, and she curled her fingers into her palms to keep from wrapping her hands in Robin's hair. Robin opened the buckle, and in one smooth movement pulled it free of the belt loops.

Elaine held out her hand. "Give me the belt."

Robin turned to Petra. "Mistress?"

Elaine flushed. *Damn. I should have asked permission. So hard to remember. To give over.*

"That's one, Elaine. Don't test my patience. Lucky for you I'm feeling generous tonight. Robin, you may give her the belt."

Robin placed her belt in Elaine's hand. Petra raised her eyebrow and said nothing more, regal as an empress on her throne.

Chastised, Elaine lowered her chin to her chest and let Robin remove her pants.

Robin turned to Petra. "I can't reach to remove her binder, Mistress."

"Leave it. I like this binder and boy short look." Petra rested her chin in her hand. She lowered her hand between her legs and arched in her palm. She drew her fingers up and over her clit, before she held out her hand, fingers glistening with her desire.

Robin whimpered and lowered herself to her knees. She crawled to Petra and lowered her head to the floor. Her gown bunched and flowed around her, an oasis of white against the dark-gray stone floor.

Elaine walked forward. She stopped next to Robin and lowered herself to one knee, bowed her head, and held out her belt with both hands. An offering. A gift. A plea. A drop of sweat tickled the back of Elaine's neck. *Will she take it? Accept my surrender? Trust me? Please take it. Take me.*

Petra's hands brushed hers as she took the belt. She folded it and popped it, the sound of slapping leather sending a rill of desire through Elaine. *I can do this. Give to her what no other Domme has ever given her. The surrender of a powerful woman.* Elaine had never kneeled to anyone, but she was ready to kneel to Petra. Ready to give to her all she had, all she had held tight to, ready to trust Petra, to let go, to experience what her submissives experienced. She watched Robin's face from under her lashes, the incredulous expression on her face half hidden by her gown.

"Robin." Petra's voice was sharp. "Place those cuffs on Elaine's wrists and ankles. Be quick." Petra snapped the belt again. "Mmm. Nice and stiff. I might use this later. Beat you with your own belt, mark you so you remember to ask permission before ordering subs around when you are not in charge."

Elaine kept her gaze fixed on the floor. *Her marks. To carry her marks. To be hers.* She gasped as fear and desire ratcheted up her need. Robin's gown rustled as she kneeled next to her. With trembling fingers, she applied the cuff to Elaine's wrist and buckled it into place. Elaine glanced at Robin. Her nipples were peaked under her gown, but her teeth were clamped to her lower lip. *Worried. She's afraid. For me? Or us?*

Elaine held out her other wrist, a signal of her desire to Robin. Robin applied the second cuff with more confidence. She moved behind Elaine and applied the cuffs to her ankles.

"Elaine, stand." Petra swept two fingers over her clit and held them out, gleaming with her desire. "You'd like a taste, wouldn't you?"

"Yes." *What to call her? She hadn't said. Mistress? Ask.* "What would you like me to call you?" Elaine kept her tone respectful.

"Look at me."

Elaine raised her head and met Petra's gaze.

"Ma'am. Wasn't that what you said to me?"

Elaine bowed her head. "Yes, Ma'am."

"If you want to call me Mistress, you'll have to earn it."

Petra's steely voice sent a shiver down Elaine's spine. *No going back now.*

"There is one thing we have not discussed." Petra stood and walked to Elaine.

Elaine focused on her shoes, the hem of her skirt. The delicious scent of her, wafting from under her skirt, made Elaine's mouth water. Petra lifted her chin with two hard fingers under her jaw. Elaine closed her eyes, swallowing her desire to turn the tables, to fling Petra down, flip her skirt up, and lick her until she didn't know her own name.

"Open your eyes, Elaine. No hiding." Petra's voice was husky, her command harsh.

Elaine opened her eyes slowly. Petra's face was inches away. Her gaze burned, a dark fire in her eyes.

"Your safe word?" Petra dug her fingers in, forcing Elaine's head back sharply, the angle straining her throat. Petra closed her fingers over Elaine's exposed throat and scraped the skin with her nails. The threat behind her grip sent a sharp current of adrenalin-laced desire through her, and she groaned before she answered. "Fire."

Petra leaned down and kissed Elaine, fingers wrapped around her throat. She held her still, her grip like iron on her chin as she took what she wanted. Elaine shuddered with the sensation of being taken, out of control, knowing she trusted Petra with her life, her soul, and she wanted to give her everything. *Is this what it's like for Robin? To trust like this? To feel precious? Cherished. Safe. Robin. Where is Robin? Is this hard for her?*

Petra broke their kiss. She slapped Elaine's face lightly. "Pay attention."

Elaine flushed. "I was."

"No. You don't argue." Petra's hand snaked out and slapped her again, harder this time. "Obey."

Anger bubbled up in Elaine's soul, followed by something unexpected. She craved Petra's correction. Her attention. Her cheek stung. The ache between her legs grew. Her clit hard, she pinched her thigh to keep from touching her face, to feel the heat of her skin where Petra had slapped her, wanting to savor her attention.

"Robin, bring me the short spreader bar." She shoved Elaine hard, knocking her off balance so she sprawled on the floor. "On your back. Arms over your head."

Elaine rolled to her back and lifted her arms over her head.

"Spread your legs." Petra nudged Elaine's thigh with her foot.

Elaine complied, conscious of the need between her legs, tickling as it slipped between her ass cheeks.

Robin presented the spreader bar to Petra. "Mistress?"

Petra took the spreader bar from Robin. "Get the longer one. Strip her and then fasten her legs to the bar." Petra straddled Elaine's body. She lifted her skirt and placed one foot on either side of Elaine's head, shifting her feet until the smooth leather of her strapped pumps rested against Elaine's ears and her head was locked in place. She lowered her skirt. In the dim light filtered through the fabric Elaine could see the shadowy outline of Petra's sex. The warm scent of her excitement had saliva pooling in Elaine's mouth, and she bit her lip to keep herself from begging for a taste. Petra bent from the waist and fastened Elaine's arms to the spreader bar. As she did, the skirt lifted enough Elaine could see her glistening flesh. She turned her head and pressed a kiss to Petra's ankle, desperate for contact with her skin.

"That's enough." Petra's voice was soft.

Robin's warm breath on her thigh raised gooseflesh. Elaine trembled, wound tight as a clock spring. Elaine lifted her hips, seeking contact, and groaned when Robin's hands grazed the curve of her stomach. She lifted the waistband of her boy shorts and drew them down her legs. She stopped when they were around Elaine's ankles and blew a warm breath over Elaine's clit before stripping her bare. Robin locked one ankle cuff to the spreader bar, the click of the clip loud in Elaine's ears. Panic welled in her chest. She was almost naked, on her back, spread-eagle, held in place by cuffs and spreader bars. Vulnerable. Exposed. Out of control. Petra moved from her place over her and stared down at her. A sensation of peace washed over Elaine as she gazed up into Petra's obsidian eyes. *Safe. I'm safe. To feel. To just be.*

Petra leaned down and slipped a finger under the binder. "This—" Petra yanked up on the elastic edge of the binder and released it. Elaine yipped at the sharp sting when she popped it against her skin. "Is in my way." She pulled a folding knife from the pocket of her skirt and opened it.

Elaine followed her movements with her gaze. Petra slipped the edge of the blade under the elastic fabric. The metal was cold against her skin. *Trust. I need to trust*

Petra. I'm safe. With a quick motion, Petra sliced through the binder and it fell away. Elaine's nipples were taut under Petra's delighted gaze.

"Robin?"

"Yes, Mistress."

"Bring me some nipple clips. Your choice."

Robin retreated, her footsteps a whisper as she hurried away to serve Petra. Petra laid the flat of the blade against Elaine's skin, the cool metal tracing a thin line. Elaine's nipples ached as they hardened, and she flushed, heat rising in her face as Petra's eyes followed the path of the blade and Elaine's reaction.

"Do you like edge play?" She turned the blade a fraction, the edge pressing into the skin over Elaine's ribs. Elaine shuddered and panted.

"I don't know, Ma'am." Elaine slowed her breathing. "Do you wish it?" *I'll give her anything. Let her mark me. Hell, she can carve her initials into me.*

A smile ghosted over Petra's face. "Another time then." She folded the knife and placed it back in her skirt pocket. Robin kneeled next to Elaine.

Petra held out her hand and Robin deposited the clips. A heavy silver chain connected them. "Suck her nipples."

Robin bent her head and took Elaine into her mouth. Elaine arched into her, wanting to press all of her breast into her mouth. Robin hummed her enjoyment as she drew Elaine's nipple deep. Petra smoothed her warm hands over Elaine's body, featherlight touches everywhere but where Elaine was desperate for her touch. Legs spread wide, she pulled against her bonds, trying to relieve the raging ache in her clit. Robin switched to the other breast and sucked hard before she scraped her teeth over the tip, drawing a cry from Elaine.

She opened and closed her hands in frustration. She longed to touch Robin, Petra, both of them.

"Poor Elaine." Petra leaned over her, brushed her lips over her mouth, a fleeting touch. Elaine lifted her head, straining for more. "You want and can't have. A new sensation for you, isn't it?" She unzipped her skirt and let it fall. She was a vision in ankle strap pumps, corset, and white blouse, her dark brown nipples a sharp contrast to the white of her blouse.

Elaine groaned as Robin switched back to the other breast. She panted. "Yes. Ma'am."

"Robin, suck her clit. She doesn't come until I say so. No fingers."

"Yes, Mistress." Robin crawled over Elaine's body, settling herself between Elaine's legs. The satin of her gown and the press of her body against Elaine's thighs set her on fire. Robin's lips covered her clit, and she arched into her mouth. Robin spread her hands over her thighs and pressed her down as she suckled Elaine's clit, holding her in place. Elaine's world became Robin between her legs; she closed her eyes and lost herself in the pleasure. *No worries. Feel, just feel. Petra will keep me safe. I'm safe. This. This is why Martha's with Lucia. This is why Petra craved Madame. I can let go. She'll keep me safe, guide my pleasure. All I have to do is take it. And not come. How can I not come? Ask. Beg. I need. Want.* Elaine's body trembled under Robin's attentions. Robin eased off and blew cool air over her clit. Elaine cursed in frustration and struggled against her bonds.

Petra straddled her and then lowered herself. Elaine gasped when she pressed herself into the skin of her belly and ground her clit against her. Petra's hands settled on her breasts and she plucked her nipples rhythmically.

"Oh, Ma'am. Please. Stop, I'm going to come. Please. I can't."

Petra stilled her hands. Elaine hissed when the chill length of chain between the nipple clamps draped over her skin. Petra applied a clamp to Elaine's nipple and tightened it. The white-hot pain focused Elaine. *Breathe. Slow down.* Robin's lips closed over her clit, her tongue teasing the tight bundle of nerves under the hood. Petra squeezed her other nipple hard and applied the second clamp.

The twin sensations of Robin sucking her clit and Petra working her nipples drove Elaine's excitement. She tried to arch up into Robin's mouth, unable to move under the weight of the two women. Pain. Pleasure. Freedom. Free to feel, to let go. To explore what it was like to let someone else guide her pleasure. Her body clenched. She wanted. Wanted to feel more. Wanted it all.

"Oh please. Stop. I'm going to come. I can't... Please." Robin lifted her mouth.

Petra was relentless. "You will. You'll take all of it. Or you'll take your punishment." She leaned down and kissed Elaine, her lips bruising. She scraped a fingernail over the tip of Elaine's nipple. And Elaine arched off the floor and came hard, unable to stop.

Robin's squeak of dismay devastated Elaine.

"Shh. Robin, come here. It's not your fault." Petra twisted against her, grinding into Elaine, making her crave the slick slide of her hard clit against her own. Elaine shuddered and groaned as Petra kissed Robin and smoothed a hand over her head. "You did nothing wrong."

Petra's hum of satisfaction twisted Elaine's insides. "Poor girl. Couldn't wait. Couldn't stop. And now you'll have to take so much more." She dragged her body over

Elaine's, her hard nipples teasing her. "Robin has more control in her little pinkie than you do in your whole body. Why do you think that is?" Petra nibbled and kissed her way along Elaine's neck. Her hands moved lower, and the tension on the clamps increased. Lights flashed behind Elaine's eyes as another orgasm built. Petra took her mouth away and pulled the chain hard. The clamps pulled free, and Elaine came again, her cry swallowed by Petra's hungry mouth.

Petra released her mouth. "Look at me."

Elaine opened her eyes.

"Do you like to be fucked?"

Elaine shivered at the promise in Petra's eyes.

"To be taken?" Petra pushed Elaine's hair back from her damp brow.

Elaine lifted her chin. "I've not—that is, I usually do the fucking." Heat rose in her face. She was the one who fucked. She enjoyed a finger or two, but she was sure that was not Petra's intention. She'd never allowed anyone to take her, to fuck her as they pleased. Petra reached over and clasped the back of Robin's neck. She kissed her, and Elaine groaned as she watched them. She hungered for them, both of them, and seeing them together made her happy, made her heart swell with desire. *Love. Love? Goddess help me, I love her too.*

Petra moved her mouth close to Robin's ears. Elaine saw her lips move but could not hear her words. Robin pulled back, her eyes wide. Petra kissed her again and tilted her head in the direction of the cabinet on the other side of the room. Robin rose and walked out of Elaine's field of vision.

Petra cupped Elaine's face and kissed her, a soothing, seductive kiss. Elaine let herself get lost in it, let her anxiety drift away on Petra's kisses.

"Do you want to find out?" Petra kissed her again. "Would you like that? To be fucked?" She slid her hand up and circled Elaine's throat with her fingers, her touch light.

"Desperately." Elaine lifted her chin, exposing her throat, signaling her willingness to give Petra even this, all of it, to surrender to her. "Please, Ma'am."

Petra closed her fingers over Elaine's throat, a stronger grip now, her fingers pressing into Elaine's flesh. Elaine's pulse sped up under Petra's touch, safe under her control.

"Close your eyes, sweet one."

Elaine closed her eyes and willed her body to relax as a steady hum of excitement burned through her. Petra moved off her, and she was bereft at the loss of her reassuring weight on her body. With her eyes closed, the rustle of clothing and the sharp snap of the cap, the unmistakable sound of a bottle of lube being opened, made her tense. *What will they use? Who will fuck me? Will I be able to handle it?* Restless, she stretched and pulled at the cuffs, before surrendering to the sensation of being at Petra's mercy.

Petra squeezed her shoulder. "I want you to turn over, on your knees, forearms flat on the floor. I'll help you." Elaine responded to Petra's directions. Firm hands guided her and then she was on her knees. She hollowed her stomach, and Petra slid a bench beneath her midsection to support her with her ass in the air, her legs spread obscenely wide, forearms on the floor. She winced inwardly as she thought of the display she must present. Ass up. On display, exposed. She shivered. She had never been fucked in the ass and wasn't ready to today. *I have a safe word. I can use it if I need to. She wouldn't hurt me.*

I'm safe. I can say my word. If I want to. Petra's hand on the crown of her head steadied her.

"I wish you could see how gorgeous you are like this." Her fingers dipped and flowed along Elaine's spine. "If you were mine, I'd want to keep you like this."

Elaine did not miss the wistfulness in Petra's voice. She kept her eyes closed, obeying her Mistress's command. *Hers. I want to be hers. I want this. To feel secure. To know I'm safe. I want to call her Mistress. To give her the power I can never surrender to Robin because she doesn't want it.*

A wash of cool lube stroked over her clit and made her hump her hips in search of relief. Petra placed a hand in the middle of her back. Her touch steadied Elaine. She relaxed and blew out a breath. The tip of a sex toy pressed against her and she tensed in spite of herself. *Relax. Petra knows what she's about. I'm safe.* Robin's hands settled on her hips.

The slick toy rubbed against her clit and Elaine shuddered with the sensation. "Oh. Ma'am. More please."

Petra gripped the back of Elaine's neck. "Shh. Feel."

The tip eased between her thick lips a fraction before Robin pulled back. She teased the toy in again and Elaine rocked back, desperate for more of what Robin was offering. Petra petted her head. "Let her do this. Slow down, or you'll hurt yourself.

Elaine was ready, ready for Robin to fill her, take her, take everything. She burned with need as the thick toy slipped deeper. Petra reached under her to massage her breast with slim fingers, and then moved over her clit. She jacked it, making Elaine gasp. Robin pulled back and eased forward again, and Elaine shuddered and squeezed down, desperate to keep Robin inside. "Oh, don't stop.

Please don't stop. I want it, Ma'am. Please let her fuck me. Please."

Robin's fingers dug into her, and Elaine heard her gasp, the one she loved to hear, the sound letting Elaine know she took pleasure in fucking her. Robin pulled out almost to the tip, and then in one long motion pushed forward. Elaine's body burned and trembled. Petra continued to jack her clit. Waves of sensation and ravenous hunger for more filled her.

Elaine whimpered. "Please. More. Please. Let her fuck me. Mistress, please."

Petra's hand stilled and she pressed a kiss between Elaine's shoulder blades. "Robin, let's give our girl what she wants." She pinched Elaine's clit, and she cried out. "What she needs." Given permission, Robin fucked her, her hips slamming into her, angling the toy so it hit her g-spot with every stroke. Elaine howled, begged, and rocked into Robin's strokes as she came undone under her, letting go, giving over to them both. Petra squeezed her clit in a rhythm with Robin's motions. "Come as you wish."

Elaine couldn't do anything else. She had to, had to come, had to give it to them. All of it. She screamed her release, a tribute, a gift to the two people she trusted above all others to treasure it, treasure her.

ELAINE'S BODY CLENCHED around the toy inside her. Robin rocked against her, sending her spinning into another orgasm, and Robin's strangled cry of her own release sweetened the moment. Petra's hands stilled. Elaine panted.

Petra pulled her hand away from her clit and a sob escaped Elaine. "No. Please, Ma'am. Please touch me."

Petra's hands were in her hair, nails sharp against her scalp. Pulling Elaine's head back, Petra kissed her; savage, raw, unfettered desire. She pulled away and then shoved Elaine's face between her thighs. "Lick me." Petra rocked on her face; her juices coated Elaine's chin as she marked her with her essence. Elaine swallowed and sucked, driven by Petra's deep growls of pleasure.

Robin drew back, almost emptying her before she surged forward, falling into a slow rhythm. The sensation of having Petra's clit in her mouth and being filled by Robin sent her spinning into another space as she served them both, a vessel, an instrument of pleasure with no thought but pleasing them. Her. Her Ma'am, her Mistress. Petra gripped her head with both hands and came, and a surge of sweetness burst over Elaine's tongue and ran down her chin.

Petra rolled her hips, taking everything she wanted, everything Elaine was willing to give. She slowed her movements and drew away. Robin slipped the toy from her body. Elaine felt hollow without Robin's solid presence grounding her and she cried out.

Robin returned and her satin-draped frame covered Elaine as she lay on her back. She mouthed Elaine's skin, pressing tender kisses between her shoulder blades, and stroked her hands over Elaine's ribs. "Shh, I've got you."

Petra released her grip on Elaine's hair. "Open your eyes, love."

Elaine gazed into Petra's eyes and she sank into her words, stunned by the word "love" and the expression on Petra's face. She shivered, and Robin lay her cheek on Elaine's shoulder. Petra stepped away. She unfastened the cuffs around Elaine's ankles, releasing her from the bar.

Robin's hands were on Elaine's shoulders, rubbing and soothing, the familiar weight of her body calming the storm of emotions raging in her mind. Her body's visceral reaction to Robin's presence subsumed her thoughts, and she relaxed into her care.

Petra unfastened Elaine's wrist, and Elaine grasped at her waist, settling a hand on her hip. Petra unfastened the other wrist, and Elaine wrapped both arms around her, hiding her face in Petra's corset. A sob wrenched from her body. *Loved. Cherished. Safe.*

Petra stroked her head. "Shh, love. Let's get you more comfortable." She eased away from Elaine's grip. Robin moved from her back and they assisted Elaine to the floor. Robin wrapped a blanket around her shoulders and Petra hugged her close. Elaine laid her head on Petra's shoulder. Robin's arm circled her waist. Petra kissed her forehead and then her mouth. Elaine closed her eyes against the troubling emotions filling her.

"Water, Mistress?" Robin cupped Elaine's cheek.

Elaine turned her face and kissed Robin's palm. "Yes. Please."

Her throat was sore and she wondered how loud she had screamed when she came.

Petra hugged her tight and kissed the top of Elaine's head. "You were magnificent. Thank you."

Elaine relaxed into Petra's praise. Robin returned with water. Elaine sat cross-legged on the floor and took the glass. The water was cool on her raw throat.

Robin handed Petra a glass of water.

"Get some for yourself as well, Robin." Petra kneeled beside Elaine.

"Are you tired? Do you want to go on?" Petra's hands rested on top of her thighs, palm up. "Ma'am?"

Elaine tilted her head to look at Petra. "Not too, and yes." The part of her that craved submission rose up, demanded to be acknowledged, to be given its due. Elaine let the blanket fall from her shoulders. She reached out and cupped the back of Petra's neck. "Yes. I want to go on. Get my belt."

Petra crawled over to the chair, giving Elaine a view of her sumptuous body. She returned with Elaine's belt. She kissed it before presenting it to Elaine with both hands.

A jagged edge of need rose up in Elaine. "Robin."

"Yes, Mistress?" Robin crawled over and kneeled next to Petra, assuming the position of the house.

"My room."

A gasp from Robin and a similar sound from Petra let Elaine know she had been misunderstood.

"All of us are going to my room. Right now." Elaine snapped the belt to punctuate her direction. "Stand, both of you. Disrobe." Elaine stood, letting the blanket pool around her feet.

Robin and Petra divested themselves of their clothes.

Elaine stepped behind them. "I will motivate you as I see fit. Clear?"

"Yes." Petra squared her shoulders.

Elaine snapped the belt across her ass, a taste of what was to come. "Yes, what?"

"Yes, Ma'am."

"Yes, Mistress." A tremor in Robin's voice signaled her excitement.

Elaine opened the door and indicted with her arm for them to proceed her. They made their way down the hall, the two of them walking in front of Elaine. Elaine admired the way they walked side by side, pacing each other, their bodies a contrast. Robin's petite frame next to Petra's tightly muscled body. They kept their heads high, their pride in being taken back to Elaine's room, to her private sanctuary and what it meant evident.

She chewed the inside of her lip when she thought of how quickly Robin thought she was being dismissed. *Have to fix that. She should know what she means to me.* At the stairs, they paused and Elaine delivered an affectionate pop of the belt to each of them. Their sharp yips and hisses stirred Elaine. Her clit swelled and she was impatient to get to her room. "Faster. I'd like to get there before my next birthday." She snapped the belt against their asses again and the women quick marched up the stairs.

ROBIN AND PETRA kneeled on the small rug near the fireplace.

Elaine locked the door and flipped the bar lock in place. She crossed her arms and let the belt dangle from her fingertips. Wanting to banish the chill from the room, she crossed to the fireplace and lit the gas log. She tapped her lips with her finger. "Robin, lie on the floor face up." Robin complied and stretched out on the rug. The flames cast a yellow glow over her skin.

Elaine walked to her and trailed the belt over her before she leaned down and pinched the inside of her thigh. "Legs spread."

Robin opened her legs. Elaine brushed her clit with the back of her knuckles and then pressed into her with one finger before withdrawing. *So wet. For me. For this. For us.* Robin's hips arched, seeking more. Elaine indulged her and rubbed harder, circling her thumb around her clit. Robin shuddered, and her breathing stuttered. "Oh please, Mistress. Please. Let me come for you. Come under your touch." Elaine shifted her hand and palmed her, rubbing her fingertips over the wet. "You'd like to come for me, legs wide, letting Petra watch you, let her see what a delightful good girl you are, wouldn't you?"

Robin groaned. "Oh please. Please, Mistress."

Petra's low moan sounded behind Elaine.

Elaine leaned over Robin. "Look at me when you come. Let me see you."

"Yes, Mistress. Oh, oh, oh. Please now. Please!"

Elaine pressed down hard on Robin's clit. "Now."

Robin arched up, trembling, legs stiff, eyes never leaving Elaine's face, as she came with a bone-deep groan.

Elaine brushed Robin's hair back with her hand. "Good girl." Robin's smile made Elaine's heart swell.

"Petra, lie next to Robin." Petra shifted on her knees and lay on the floor, mirroring Robin's position.

Elaine teased a finger up Petra's leg, smiling at the gooseflesh that followed her touch. When she arrived at the wet heat between her legs, she touched her clit with the tip of her finger. Petra gasped, and her hips twitched.

"Robin, lie on top of Petra. Align your clits. I'm in the mood to be entertained."

Robin straddled Petra. Elaine reached between them and used her fingers to spread Petra's labia. Robin clasped Petra's hands and interlaced their fingers as she lay over her. She wiggled her hips until her clit was in direct contact with Petra's. Elaine traced a finger over their slick clits, painted them with each other's liquid desire. Petra gasped.

"Robin. Make yourself come, take your time. I want to hear you. Petra, you wait. Feel Robin's pleasure and deny your own. It belongs to me."

Elaine kneeled between their legs. She pushed two fingers into Petra, curling them up to stroke her sweet spot. Robin rotated her hips, and Elaine followed her motions, fucking Petra as Robin started a slow grind, rocking her hips into Petra. Petra tightened around Elaine's fingers. She pushed down and spread them wide, opening her before she added a third, pushing deeper. Her mouth watered as she watched the dance of pleasure play out before her. The salacious sounds of fucking Petra combined with the clutch of her body around Elaine's fingers made her ache for release. She licked a line up Robin's thigh as she cupped herself and squeezed. Petra's breathing shifted and her body opened to Elaine. Elaine curled her fingers and fucked her hard. Robin accelerated the rocking of her hips as she ground her clit against Petra.

Elaine stopped touching herself to concentrate. "Now. Robin, come now." Elaine pushed hard, Robin rolled her hips, and Petra groaned. Robin screamed her delight, and Elaine feathered her fingers. Petra swore, hips bucking, unable to stop herself, and Elaine's palm was filled with liquid as she squirted. Robin hummed her satisfaction and shuddered through another orgasm. Elaine's breath caught. *So exquisite. For me. Mine. Both of them. I want this. Please let Petra want this.* "Naughty girl. Looks like Robin is the only one who can follow directions."

"Sorry, Ma'am."

The contrition in Petra's voice cracked Elaine's heart wide open and she eased her fingers from Petra. She smoothed her hand over her hip and pressed a soft kiss to her thigh. Petra's ragged breathing eased, and she stilled under Elaine's touch. She tapped Robin on the ass, and Robin shifted to the side of Petra.

"Let's try it again. No coming until I say." Elaine lay between Petra's legs and swept her tongue along the salt honey trail on her thigh before she traced a line up her perineum and then stuck her tongue deep. Petra's hips arched. Robin rolled to her side and pinned her in place with her thigh over her hips. Elaine hummed her approval, and Robin lowered her head to Petra's breasts and teased her nipples with short sucks and bites. Elaine covered Petra's clit with her mouth, circling it with her tongue before sucking it deep between her lips to roll her tongue over the stiff tip. The combined taste of Robin and Petra was a sweet ambrosia in her mouth. *More. More of this. More of them.* She licked and sucked, watching as Robin worked on Petra's breasts. Petra's hand was on the back of Robin's neck, holding her in place. Elaine reached up and captured her other hand. She joined her fingers together with Petra's on one side and Robin's on the other. Connected, a circuit of pleasure.

Petra writhed beneath her. "May I come? Please. May I, Ma'am?"

Elaine lifted her head. "Call me Mistress." She bit the inside of her thigh. Robin squeezed Elaine's hand in silent approval. "Come as you wish."

"Thank you, Mistress." Petra's voice quavered.

Elaine suckled her clit, rolling her tongue over it, relentless until Petra screamed and arched into her mouth.

Chapter Seventeen

ELAINE PEERED OUT of the window at the car. The limousine idled in the driveway as Millie loaded Petra's bag into the trunk. The grim expression on her face matched the dread pooling in Elaine's gut.

Robin's warm hand clasped her fingers. "She'll come back."

The hope in her voice made Elaine's heart ache, as much for Robin as for herself. She lifted her hand to her face, cupped her chin, and kissed her forehead. "Of course she will. How could she not?" Elaine swallowed her own fear and anger. They had spent hours talking, twined together naked, exploring each other. And yet it was not enough to convince Petra to stay with them. *Not enough. Again. Fuck, how can she leave us? We'll be okay, we have each other, but what could have been? It would be so sweet. She's perfect. A perfect fit for us. And yet she doesn't believe us, or doesn't want to believe us. How could she not feel the same way?*

The sound of Petra's heels tapping as she entered the foyer made her look away from Robin's face. Her eyes locked on Petra's gaze. Petra's shuttered expression tightened her throat. *Gone. She's already gone.*

Petra's forced smile twisted Elaine's stomach. She glided to them, Mistress mask firmly in place. Elaine missed her genuine smile, the one she had shared at their private goodbye. The one that had given Elaine the courage to give to Petra what she had never given to another. Robin's grip on her hand tightened.

Elaine straightened and lifted her chin. "Millie's got the last of it loaded."

Petra inclined her head at Elaine. She held out her hand to Robin. Robin released Elaine's hand and walked to Petra as if drawn by a string. Petra took her hand, kissed her knuckles, and then drew her into a deep kiss. She released her, and Robin stepped back, her hand to her mouth, fingers touching her lips.

Elaine offered her hand to Petra. In two long strides Petra was in her arms. Elaine crushed her to her chest and kissed her, emptying herself into Petra, saying everything with her kiss she could not put into words. Petra's head rested on Elaine's chest. Elaine held tight to her, unable to speak her desires aloud, fearful of rejection and more heartache. *How can she not know? How much she means to me? To us? How much we want her to stay?*

Petra stepped back. Chest heaving, she lifted her hand to her forehead and covered her eyes for a moment, her lower lip quivering. After a minute, her breathing slowed, and she lowered her hand. Her face was expressionless, her veneer of control and distance firmly in place.

Elaine offered her arm to Petra and she rested her hand lightly on her forearm. Elaine clenched her teeth around her pleas and escorted Petra to the car. Millie opened the door and Petra entered. Millie closed the door. She took her suit coat off before she opened her door and slid behind the wheel. Elaine snatched the rear door open.

Petra lifted her chin, her knuckles white where she gripped the edge of the seat. Elaine swept her gaze over Petra. Her throat closed. *What can I say I haven't already said?*

Petra's eyes glazed with unshed tears, her voice rough. "Close the door. Now. Don't make it harder than it is. Please." And then, in a desperate whisper, she said the one word that reminded Elaine of her duty. "Mistress."

Elaine closed the door gently. She tapped the roof of the car twice, signaling Millie to go.

She stood in the drive, shivering in the cold, and watched as the car exited the long drive, unable to turn away.

"Elaine."

Elaine turned toward Robin's voice.

Robin hugged herself. "Come inside, it's too cold to be out here without a coat." She left the door open and walked into the dark hallway.

Elaine gathered up the bits of her shattered heart, shoved her hands in her pockets, and strode back to the house.

ROBIN LAY WITH her head on her folded hands as her body stretched the length of Elaine, her weight comforting. Elaine wrapped a loose silky curl around her finger. "What should we do today?" She tugged the curl. "It's foul outside."

"I've some ideas for new menus." Robin raised her head to look into Elaine's eyes. "If you want to look at them." She smoothed a hand down and cupped Elaine's breast. "Or you could come tour the greenhouse with me. I need to check on the veg starts. Myfanwy won't be happy if I don't tend to them properly."

Elaine huffed out a sigh. "I suppose it's better than wallowing here."

Robin kissed her softly. "You miss her as much as I do."

"I do. Damn it."

Robin laid her head on Elaine's chest. The wind rattled the panes and she snuggled closer. "I don't want to get out of the bed but I really do need to go out to the greenhouse." She slid out from under Elaine's arms. "Should I bring you tea back?"

Elaine shoved up to sitting. "No. I'll come with you." *Better than lying here alone.* Robin bent to pick up her clothes from the night before. "You should move your things here."

Robin straightened. She blinked at Elaine. "Here?"

Elaine crossed the room and embraced her. "If you want." She rubbed the slim column of Robin's bare throat with the back of her knuckles. "Would you like to stay here? To sleep here with me? Every night."

Robin trembled. "If you wish it."

Elaine cupped her face. "Only if you do." She kissed her softly. "I want you here but only if you want to be. Do you?" She leaned back to look into Robin's eyes.

Robin lifted on her toes and captured Elaine's mouth and kissed her hard. She sucked Elaine's lower lip between her teeth and nipped. Salt copper flavored their kiss and Elaine groaned into Robin's kiss. She reached down and grabbed Robin's slim ass and lifted her up, crushing her tight against her, brand took over the kiss. Robin sighed and relaxed into Elaine's embrace as she wrapped her legs around Elaine's hips.

Elaine broke their kiss, chest heaving. She studied Robin's face.

Robin's eyes were bright. She brought her hands up, dared to cup her Mistress's face. "Yes, Elaine. Yes,

Mistress. I wish it. With everything I am, with all my heart I wish it."

ROBIN SAT AT the dressing table, wrapped in Elaine's robe. She rubbed her damp hair with a towel. Elaine stepped behind her and rested her hands on her shoulders. Robin pressed her cheek to the back of Elaine's hand and she regarded their reflection in the mirror.

Elaine tugged open the robe, exposing Robin's breasts. She smoothed her hands over her chest and cupped them, brushing her thumbs over her tight pink nipples. "You're exquisite." Robin trembled under her fingertips. "I don't know if you need to move your clothes here. Maybe I should just keep you naked and in my bed at all times." She bent and kissed Robin's throat.

"Tempting, Mistress. But I think you'd miss my shortbread." Robin dropped the towel to the floor.

"Stand for me." Elaine released her and stepped back.

Robin stood and Elaine moved the vanity chair from between them and stepped close. She plucked at the shoulders of the robe before she slid it down Robin's body and pulled it free. She closed the distance between them and pressed her body into Robin's.

Robin met her gaze in the mirror, a half smile on her lips. "Wouldn't you, Mistress?"

Elaine reached around her and closed her fingers over her throat. Robin moaned and closed her eyes. Elaine held her still, her pulse hammering under her palm. She rubbed her thumb over the soft skin of her neck. With her other hand she cupped her breast and squeezed hard. Robin's eyes widened and she panted. Elaine hummed her appreciation of Robin's surrender, the give of her body in her arms and the sensation of Robin's nipple hardening under her palm. She tangled her fingers in the tight curls above Robin's sex. "Lift your leg. Plant your foot on the vanity. I want to see how wet you are for me."

Robin leaned back, cradled in Elaine's arms, and planted one foot on the vanity. Her dark-pink glistening labia and swollen clit were reflected in the glass, a wanton display for her Mistress. Elaine touched her fingers to the pool of liquid desire and drew it up over Robin's clit. Robin groaned when she rubbed a slow circle around the base of her clit.

"So immodest." Elaine drew her hand to her mouth and tasted her. "So sweet."

Robin's eyes were a stormy blue in the glass as she gazed at their reflection in the mirror and squirmed in Elaine's arms. "Please, Mistress."

"You want something?" Elaine teased Robin's nipple with her damp finger, tracing light circles over the tip.

Robin shifted her hips, pressing back against Elaine's body. "Touch me, please Mistress."

"Touch you?" Elaine slid her hand down and rubbed her forefinger along one side of Robin's swollen clit. She continued her slow path and then slid her finger deep. "Don't you mean fuck me? Isn't that what you want?"

Robin bucked her hips forward, seeking Elaine's touch. "Yes. Please." Her lower lip trembled. "Fuck me. Please, Mistress. Fuck me."

Elaine pulled back slowly, her eyes fixed on Robin's as she plunged three fingers deep. Robin spread her leg wider, opening herself. The sight of her fingers buried deep in Robin's body sent a wave of desire dripping down Elaine's thighs. She rubbed her fat clit against Robin's ass, the slick slide threatening her control.

Robin bucked her hips, drawing Elaine deeper. "More, Mistress. Please, more."

"Be still." Elaine curled her fingers and rocked into Robin, rubbing her sweet spot. Robin shuddered in her arms as Elaine held her tightly and massaged her g-spot.

"Oh, Mistress, I can't… Please may I come for you? Please." Robin's breath was ragged.

Elaine licked a line along her neck and then bit down hard. Robin shrieked and came, filling Elaine's hand with her liquid satisfaction.

"I'm sorry, Mistress. I couldn't stop." A coy smile played about her mouth.

Elaine smiled at Robin in the mirror. "Naughty girl."

"Am I your naughty girl, Mistress?" Robin arched her back and thrust her breasts forward. Elaine curled her fingers over her g-spot and rubbed hard. Robin groaned and trembled.

"Yes. Very naughty." Elaine eased her fingers from Robin. "And look at the mess you made." She brought her glistening fingers up to Robin's mouth. Robin flicked out her tongue and licked Elaine's fingertips. "Please let me clean up, Mistress. Please."

"You may." Elaine relaxed her grip on Robin's throat and allowed her to lick her hand clean. In the mirror, Elaine's gaze was fixed on Robin's thick clit and glistening labia, the aftermath of her orgasm on display. Robin sucked hard and her tongue slid over Elaine's fingers.

"Enough." Elaine pulled her hand free of Robin's mouth and relaxed her grip on her throat. "Lower your leg. Hands on the top of the vanity. Legs wide." Robin obeyed and Elaine stepped back to admire Robin's ass. From her nightstand she drew her new favorite toy and bottle of lube. She walked back to Robin. She spread her legs wide. "Come here." Robin left her position and sank to her knees in front of Elaine.

Elaine stepped close and gripped Robin's hair. She tugged Robin's head up to look in her face. "Pleasure me."

Robin moaned and leaned in to lick Elaine's clit. She swirled her tongue over her and drew her deep. Elaine glanced in the mirror. The reflection of them with Robin's face buried between her legs pushed her over the edge, and she came. Robin lapped hungrily at her, humming her delight. Elaine tugged her away. "Do you want me to fuck you?"

Robin's eyes were dark, her pupils blown wide. "Oh yes, please, Mistress. Please."

Elaine gestured at the vanity chair. "Bring the chair." Robin rose to her feet and then brought the chair over for Elaine. She tugged the chair into position, making sure the mirror would capture their reflections.

Elaine in the chair, spread her legs wide, and held up the toy. "Put this in me." Robin took the no-harness dildo and small bottle of lube from Elaine's hands with reverence.

"Yes, Mistress." She flipped open the cap and drizzled the lube over the thick end designed to anchor the dildo in Elaine, covering it until it shone. Setting the bottle aside, she set the tip at Elaine's entrance and lifted her face to look into Elaine's eyes. "Now?"

Elaine placed her palm on top of Robin's head. "Now."

Robin pushed steadily and Elaine moaned when the toy slid home, resting against her g-spot, the angle of the twin pressed against her clit.

"Would you like to touch it?" Elaine arched a brow at Robin and palmed the dildo, stroking it.

Robin eyed the toy, a greedy expression on her face. "It's so big. Please may I? Please, Mistress, may I give you an orgasm this way? Please."

Elaine gripped the arms of the chair. "Yes. Be quick."

Robin poured a puddle of lube into her hand, warmed it before she let it drip over the toy. The warm liquid ran down the shaft and over Elaine's clit. She wrapped her delicate hand around the base and stroked upward, the vibration against her clit and pressure on Elaine's g-spot made her shake and groan.

"Mmm. So good. More. Now." Elaine leaned back.

Robin's strokes spread up as she jacked the thick shaft. The vibrations spread, the ridged base pressing against her clit, and Elaine broke, her hips thrusting into Robin's palm.

"Straddle me. Now. Let me see you take this."

Robin straddled the low chair, steadied the toy with one hand, and slowly lowered herself over it. Elaine watched as the wide tip disappeared into Robin's body. Her clit throbbed as Robin shifted and leaned forward. Elaine thrust her hips upward. Robin rocked on her, the sensation, vibration, and closeness of their bodies an exquisite decadence. Elaine grabbed Robin's ass to hold her in place as she hammered into her. Robin's curls brushed her chin as she canted her body forward and rocked her body to meet her thrusts, with her arms looped around Elaine's neck. Her coarse breathing tickled her ear as she groaned. "Oh Mistress. Please. Let me. I won't be able to stop. Please!"

"Come now. With me." Elaine stroked on and Robin clawed at Elaine's back. Her hips a blur, she came, her liquid surrender spilling over Elaine.

They clung to each other, giving over to bliss.

Robin shifted and each tiny movement of her hips sent little aftershocks through Elaine. "Watch me, Mistress, please. Watch me."

She raised herself until the tip was almost clear and slowly lowered herself down. Elaine gasped and juddered. She watched their reflections in the mirror. Robin's slow descent sent deep vibrations against Elaine's sweet spot. She raised her hips in search of more. Robin placed a hand between her breasts. "Please, Mistress. Let me." She kissed the corner of Elaine's mouth. "Please."

Elaine groaned and surrendered to Robin's slow fuck. Robin moved her hands lower, feathered her fingers over Elaine's breasts and rolled her nipples, tugging them gently as she rode her. Sharp shocks of pleasure shot through her when Robin descended, the grind against her clit sweet torture. Elaine gripped the edge of the chair and allowed Robin to control their pleasure. Robin let her head fall back, exposing her throat, and Elaine licked and kissed her neck, relishing the hard beat of her pulse under her lips.

Robin panted. "Are you close, Mistress? Would you like to come?"

The devil in her voice tripped all of Elaine's triggers, and she growled low in her throat. "Finish me."

Robin rose up and dropped down to the hilt and ground against Elaine.

Elaine shouted as she came, soaking the chair beneath them. She grabbed Robin's hips, held her in place as she rolled into her. Robin shuddered through her own orgasm before she collapsed against Elaine.

Elaine kissed the crown of her head and hugged her close. Robin rested her head on her shoulder.

"I love being so close to you when you come, Mistress. I could stay like this all day." She wiggled in Elaine's arms and shifted her hips.

Elaine tightened her grip. "I can't again right now, my insatiable vixen."

Robin rolled her hips again and Elaine shuddered with the sensation. "Are you sure, Mistress?"

"Yes. No. I don't know." Elaine panted.

Robin licked a line up Elaine's throat and nipped at her jaw. "Please. I live to give you pleasure."

Another slow roll of her hips and Elaine hissed as she clenched around the toy, her body responding to Robin's movements. "Don't stop."

"Never, Mistress." Robin kissed her and rolled her hips again as Elaine groaned her satisfaction into her mouth, undone by her words.

ROBIN SETTLED HERSELF in Elaine's lap and twined her fingers in Elaine's hair. "Has she contacted you?"

"No."

"I miss her. More than I should." Robin's teeth rested on her lower lip.

Elaine rubbed small circles over Robin's back.

"What do you miss the most?" Robin kissed Elaine's jaw and snuggled closer.

"Her voice. Her saltiness before she's had her coffee. The way she pushed me." *The way I was safe with her, the way I could let go.*

"Her voice is so sexy. Her hint of an accent. I miss the way she devoured my food. As if it was the most delicious thing she'd ever had."

Elaine tipped Robin's chin up. "You are the most delicious woman I've ever had and she was a fool to leave us." Elaine tamped down her anger, not willing to spoil a tender moment.

Robin met Elaine's gaze. "She was frightened. Of her feelings. Of being out of control."

Elaine inhaled sharply through her nose. "I've half a mind to go to Oslo, throw her over my shoulder, and bring her back here. Then we could keep her chained to our bed until she understands how much we love her."

Robin quirked her mouth at Elaine. "Kidnapping is a hard limit for me, Mistress. Besides, we want her to be here because she wants to be." She cupped Elaine's face. "Love can't be forced. It's only yours if it's given freely."

Chastised, Elaine turned her head and pressed a kiss into Robin's palm.

Chapter Eighteen

"HOLD STILL. IF you move while I'm writing this you'll have ink all over your ass." Elaine swatted Robin's thigh before she settled the notepaper over her bottom.

Robin wiggled again. "I can't help it. It tickles."

Elaine snorted. "You can stay still while I decorate your lovely ass with my single tail and you can't stay still while I write this note to Petra?"

Robin plumped the pillow under her head. "Go ahead. I'll behave."

"Right. Now. What do we want to say?" Elaine set her pen to the paper.

"Come back, please?"

The wistfulness in Robin's plea made Elaine's heart ache. *What kind of Mistress am I? I can't give my girl what she wants? Who she wants.*

Elaine tapped the pen against her lips. "How about come back immediately?"

"Too much. Maybe your idea of kidnapping her is better."

Elaine set aside the paper and pen. "Have you ever been to Oslo?"

Robin rolled to her side. "No." A flicker of fear swept over her face before she smoothed her features.

"Would you go with me?" She picked up Robin's hand and held it in both of hers. "I trust Jaya has neutralized the threat. Do you trust me?"

Robin cupped Elaine's face with her hand. "With my life."

Elaine traced a finger over Robin's shoulder. "Good. She'll have to tell us to our faces she doesn't want to be with us."

"ROBIN AND I are traveling to Oslo. I want to leave as soon as possible."

"It might be hard to find first class seats at the last minute." Millie rolled her cap in her hand. "Anywhere in particular you want to stay within the city? Hotel or Airbnb?"

"Hotel."

"I'll get started." Millie turned to leave and turned back. "May I speak freely?"

Elaine rolled her eyes. "When have you ever been concerned about speaking your mind? Out with it."

Millie frowned. "Are you sure it's safe for Robin? We've only just had the clearance from Miss Pomroy."

Elaine drummed her fingers on the desk. "Are you suggesting Jaya Pomroy doesn't know what she's about?"

Millie flushed. "I'm asking if I could accompany you. Robin is my friend, and my wife's best friend."

Elaine stood up and crossed to Millie. She rested her hand on Millie's shoulder and squeezed lightly. "I appreciate the offer. I'll be careful. I trust Jaya."

"I'll get started on the arrangements."

"NO. NO. IT'S not negotiable. I'm going. Millie and Veronica can manage here." Elaine rubbed her forehead with her fingers, the hint of a headache beginning to bloom behind her eyes.

"Can't you wait? I don't like the idea of you traveling with Robin alone. I'll be home in a week. Wait and I'll go with you." Martha's cajoling tone made Elaine clench her jaw.

"Why is everyone suddenly convinced I can't take care of myself and my submissive?"

"Your submissive? Since when is Robin your property? She's an employee. One we owe an obligation to."

"Since she is. And I know full well what our obligation to her is. So kindly fuck off. I'm going."

"Wait. Please. I'm sorry. Is this woman worth exposing Robin to harm? I'm not questioning Jaya, but why not give it some time?"

"Because we don't have time. If she says yes to the job before I tell her—" Elaine bit off her words, not wanting to discuss her plan to install Petra as head mistress of Rowan House and to no longer serve clients over the phone. *She'd say it's just my pussy talking. I'll change my mind, break Robin's heart.*

"Tell her what?"

"Sorry? What?" Elaine brushed her fingers over the phone's surface. "You're breaking up. Talk to you when you get back. Love to Lucia and Myfanwy." She pushed the disconnect button and ended the call.

Chapter Nineteen

A SHARP WIND buffeted them as they waited for the number 30 bus to Bygdøy. Elaine hunched her shoulders against the cold. Robin moved closer and placed a red-gloved hand on Elaine's arm. The man Elaine suspected was following them stood to the side of the crowd, pretending to read the same paper she had observed him with the day before. His hooded eyes were set in a thick-jowled face. His ungloved hands were bright red from the cold. His gaze skittered to the side when Elaine made eye contact with him. *Still with us. So sloppy. Didn't even bother to buy today's paper. Amateur.*

Most of the people waiting for the bus had their heads bowed, absorbed in their phones. A white-haired couple held hands and talked quietly. *Too many witnesses to take care of him here.* The bus arrived, and they waited in the orderly queue to board. They found seats near the rear of the bus. Robin clutched Elaine's hand. Her mouth was set in a grim line.

"Having second thoughts?" Elaine rubbed her thumb over the back of Robin's hand.

Robin leaned close and brought her lips to Elaine's ear. "Don't look. That man, the one in the navy-blue coat with the newspaper. I saw him yesterday. On the tram, on our way back from dinner. And this morning at the hotel."

Elaine turned her head and kissed Robin's cheek. "I made him yesterday. He's following us. Don't worry. I've plans for our friend." She leaned back and lifted Robin's hand to her mouth and kissed her warm leather-covered knuckles. "Trust me."

THEY EXITED THE bus and started up the steep hill leading away from the stop. The man alighted from the rear door and then turned to follow them.

Elaine clasped Robin's hand and spoke quietly. "I'm going to take care of our friend. You and I are going to have a loud argument, my love. And then you are going to storm off in the direction of the Viking Museum. Just follow the signs. Our friend will follow one of us. I'm guessing it will be you. Stay with people. Don't leave the museum. I'll find you."

Robin squeezed her hand once and then yanked it away.

Elaine raised her hands, palm out. "What?"

"You know what. Flirting with that slut." Robin's voice was loud and shrill enough several people on the sidewalk ahead of them turned to stare at them. Robin strode away from Elaine and hurried to catch up with the group of people ahead of them.

"Fine." Elaine shouted before she turned and walked away. She brushed past the man who had followed them. She listened for footsteps behind her. Hearing none, she pulled out her phone, held it up like she was taking a photo, and switched the direction of the camera to watch behind her. The man stuffed his newspaper in his coat pocket and hurried up the hill in the direction Robin had gone. Elaine turned and quickened her steps. *Gotcha. And I'm going to enjoy this.* She switched her fine leather gloves for the weighted tactical gloves she carried when traveling. As she walked, she flexed her hands. The steel shot over the knuckles added a pleasant weight when she curled her hands into fists. *Who is he? What if this was Petra's plan? What if she's working with them? Maybe she was playing us all along to lure Robin from Rowan House.*

Elaine clenched her jaw as she stalked the man. She had attempted to call Petra since they had arrived in Oslo. Her calls had gone to voicemail, and texts and email were unreturned. Elaine mulled the possible reasons why Petra had ghosted. Unable to reach Petra, Elaine had called the main house number Petra had left them and those messages went unreturned as well. *Maybe Petra was forced into it like Robin. It would be like them. Maybe she's being held. She didn't deliver Robin, now they're using her for bait. Or she was willing. Maybe it was all lies.*

A wave of guilt washed over her. She had not shared her fears with Robin. *What if I'm exposing her? Doing exactly what they wanted by bringing her here.* Cold rage replaced guilt and she clenched her fists in her coat pockets. *I'm ready to be done with this horseshit. We should have gone to war, not let Jaya handle it alone. Fuck that. We need to end this. End him. Then we go get our girl.*

Chapter Twenty

HER QUARRY HAD stopped at an intersection. He glanced up at the street signs with his hand on his hip while talking on his phone. So focused on catching up with Robin, he had not noticed Elaine following him. Large gated homes lined the streets. On her left a large hedge hid the white brick walls of the house. She couldn't hear the man's conversation, but he had become animated, gesturing with the hand not holding the phone as he spoke.

Elaine studied her opponent. She was taller by six inches, but he had at least twenty-five kilos on her. He finished his call and shoved his phone in his coat pocket. Elaine scanned the street. A car passed by them, and the man huffed out a breath as he waited to cross the intersection. Before he could step off the curb, Elaine closed the distance between them and delivered a sharp jab directly over his kidney. He cried out and fell to the ground. She latched her fingers around the collar of his coat and dragged him behind the hedge. He flailed his arms. "Fucking dyke."

She released him, and he rose to his knees. The quiet snick of a blade opening and the flash of metal in his hand made Elaine step back. She spun and delivered a kick to his face. She smiled at the satisfying crunch of bone and spurt of blood from his nose. His eyes blazed with hate, and she kicked him in the stomach. He fell to his side. She stomped on the white-knuckled hand holding the knife. He screamed and she kicked him in the stomach again. He curled into a ball. *Finish him. No. I need information.* She rolled him over and sat on his back. She straddled him, pinning his arms in place. She gripped his greasy hair and yanked his head back. A gush of blood flowed from his nose. His eyes were closed and he groaned.

Elaine yanked his hair, twisting his face to the side. "Who sent you?"

He glared at her and drew his lips back. "Fuck you." He spat blood and bucked under her, trying to unseat her.

Elaine tightened her grip on his hair and slapped his ear. The impact from the extra weight of the glove caused it to instantly swell as the cartilage broke under the blow, and he cried out.

"I'm only going to ask you once more."

He shifted under her, and she held tight.

She flicked the tip of his swollen ear, and he shuddered. "Who sent you? Why are you following her?"

The man remained silent except for his labored breathing.

Elaine sighed. "I hope it was worth it."

"What?"

"This hill you've chosen to die on." Elaine released him, and his head fell forward. One sharp punch to the back of his head and the tension went out of his body. She crouched down and rested her fingers on his neck. His pulse slowed and then stopped under her touch. Satisfied he would not follow anyone anywhere ever again, she rolled his body under the hedge, positioned him as if he was sleeping, laid the newspaper over his face, and left him.

Elaine stood. She grimaced at the maroon splotches of blood on her boots and the mud on her pants and coat. With a handful of wet leaves she cleaned her boots as well she could. Her coat and pants would have to wait. *Robin. Then Petra.* She tugged off her tactical gloves and placed them back in her pocket.

ROBIN'S EYES WIDENED. "Did you fall?"

Elaine smirked. "No. Our friend had a terrible accident."

Robin opened her mouth as if to ask and then closed it.

Elaine glanced around at the crowd in front of the Viking Museum. "I've read about this for so long, I don't know why I've never taken the time to visit."

"There is a burial here of two women. I want to see it."

Elaine smiled at Robin. "I'll buy the tickets. It would be best if we stayed here a bit."

They spent two hours viewing the Viking ships and artifacts. Robin read every display case note and information plaque. They spent most of their time gazing at the burial goods of the two women.

Elaine chewed the inside of her lip. *We can't walk back the way we came. We need to get to Petra, and she needs to come with us. Even if she doesn't want to be with us, it's not safe here.*

*****

They lingered at the museum. Using their code, Elaine texted Millie and asked for the last coordinates of Petra's phone. After Millie texted them to her, she mapped it on her phone.

Elaine touched Robin's shoulder. "I've her last location." She leaned down to whisper. "If you'd feel safer, I can take you back to the hotel."

Robin shivered. "No. I don't want to be away from you."

Elaine held her gaze. "I'll do whatever it takes to keep you safe."

Robin's voice was steady, and she gripped Elaine's hand fiercely. "I know."

They left the museum. At the corner they turned right. The harbor was at their backs and they stopped in the gathering dusk to look at the lights reflected by the dark gray water.

Elaine pulled a small heavy flashlight-shaped object from her coat pocket. "If anyone gets too close or tries to grab you, use this. Point it at them and pull the trigger." She donned her tactical gloves as she spoke.

Robin pressed her lips in a thin line. "Shine it in their eyes?"

"No. It delivers an electric shock. Trust me, they won't be a problem after."

"Will it kill them?" Robin's voice wobbled.

"No. Well, only if they have a heart condition. It's a Taser, and it won't kill them."

Robin nodded and tucked the device in her pocket.

Elaine consulted her phone map. "This way." She led the way as they entered a neighborhood filled with mansions behind locked gates. The tile roofs gleamed as the last of the light faded.

"This is it." Ornate metal gates blocked the drive and a high wall surrounded the three-story house and land around it. A security camera was visible. Elaine reached for the intercom button. A light came on over the door and the gates swung open.

Robin stepped back. "Elaine. Don't." She grabbed her hand. "I don't like this. What if she's one of them? What if this was their plan?"

Elaine hugged Robin to her. "What if she's like you? What if they forced her into this?" She tipped Robin's chin up with her finger and kissed her. "If she's here, we owe her the chance to tell us." She stepped back and laced her fingers together to seat her tactical gloves. "Stay behind me. If I tell you to run, run, don't look back. Get to the hotel and call Millie." Elaine scanned the area as they walked to the door. A short round man opened the door before they arrived. Robin stopped and grabbed Elaine's arm.

The man leered at Robin. "I see you've finally come home."

"Gordon." Robin's fingers dug into Elaine's arm.

He turned his gaze on Elaine. "You've come to make an exchange perhaps?" His simpering face and oily tone made Elaine clench her jaw.

"No. I've come to take back what belongs to me."

Gordon laughed. "You do have a sense of humor. No one here will make the same mistake Hubert did."

"The idiot you sent to follow us?"

Gordon stepped back from the door. "I hate to conduct business outside. Come in."

Robin hung back. "No." She turned to Elaine. "I can't go in there. Not with him." Shrill panic filled her voice, and her eyes were wild. "We need to go."

"Shh." Elaine slung her arm around Robin. "I'm with you. You're not alone." She patted Robin's pocket. "You have a friend." Elaine walked into the house with her arm tight around Robin's shoulders.

THEY FOLLOWED GORDON as he walked up three flights of stairs to a large room at the top of the house. Floor to ceiling windows provided a view of the harbor. In the distance the lights of Oslo glowed. A leather couch filled one side of the room. A low wide coffee table rested in front of the couch. A full bar ran the length of the wall opposite the stairs. Gordon sat down in a dark leather chair, his back to the view.

On one side a stout red-haired man with a large scar on his face flanked him. He sneered at them. "Is that the bitch?" He moved from behind the chair and took a step toward them. A shorter man with jet-black hair studied Elaine from behind wire-rimmed glasses.

Elaine held out a hand. "If you touch me you won't see your next birthday."

The man stopped and turned to Gordon. "Let it go, Roger. I don't have time for you to assert your manliness now. You can have some fun later. With both of them."

Elaine inclined her head. "Oh, I think we'll all have some fun later." She unbuttoned her coat and tossed it over the back of the couch. "Now that we've exchanged unpleasantries, where is Petra?"

Gordon pursed his lips. "You wish to trade this one?"

"No. I don't. But I'm willing to negotiate a truce."

He steepled his fingers. "Are we at war?"

"Not yet." Elaine stepped forward. "May we sit?"

Gordon nodded at the sofa. "Forgive my manners. Yes."

Elaine sat on the couch and crossed her legs. Robin perched on the edge of the cushion next to her.

"Drink?" The man indicated the bar. "Please help yourself."

"No. Thank you." Elaine flicked a bit of dried mud off her trousers.

"What's your proposition?"

Elaine lifted a gloved hand and counted on her fingers as she spoke. "One, you'll surrender Petra to me. Two, you will cease and desist from all attempts to assassinate Robin. Three, you will end your extortion operations and leave Rowan House and its subsidiary houses alone."

The man scowled at Elaine. "And you? What will you give me?"

"You and your men will walk out of here alive." She unbuttoned the sleeves of her shirt and rolled back the cuffs.

"You're ridiculous. These are my terms. One, you will return my property, Robin, as you call her. Two, you will call off that dog of yours, Jaya Pomroy. And three, I let you walk away from here and forget about avenging Hubert."

"And what about Petra?"

"What about her? She's inconsequential. I'll get a fair price for her." His gaze slid over Robin. "Not as much as I would for this one. Blondes are popular in Dubai. Especially one with such a talented mouth. The other one put up too much of a fight. At first. But Roger handled her." Gordon's leer and the innuendo in his voice wormed its way into Elaine's brain. Rage. Hot burning rage blotted out every rational thought in her mind.

Elaine inhaled sharply and then exhaled slowly, controlling her fury. "I want to see her. Now. Or all negotiations are off. We go to war, and I'm sure your boss won't like that at all."

"I'm the boss."

"No. You're a wannabe. Your boss is too smart to get caught up in petty shit like this. The Widow was not into trafficking, nor blackmail last time I chatted with her. But then again, maybe she doesn't know what you're up to."

The leather of the chair squeaked as Gordon shifted in his seat.

"Why don't we call her, let her decide?" Elaine lifted an eyebrow.

"Brian, get the woman." Gordon waved his bodyguard away, and the man with wire-rimmed glasses disappeared through a side door. He shifted his gaze to Roger. Roger moved a half step to the right, and he balled his hands into fists, and a nasty smile spread across his face.

Showtime. I'm going to exterminate every last one of these fuckers. Elaine touched Robin's shoulder. "Why don't you fix us a drink?"

Robin stared at her. "What?"

"Get me a drink. See what kind of whiskey they have. Go on. Check the bottom shelf, see if they have what I like." Elaine tilted her head in the direction of the bar.

Robin rolled her eyes at Elaine. "Now?"

"Yes. Now."

Robin moved to the bar. She bent down. Once she was safely behind the counter. Elaine stood up, stretched her arms over her head, and glanced at her watch. "Time's up."

She hooked her foot under the coffee table and flipped it toward Gordon. He shouted as he fell out of his chair, and scrambled out of the way. Roger charged Elaine. She stepped to the side and cupped his chin, forcing his head back. He sprawled on the floor. She kicked him in the head and then again. She dropped to her knees, straddled him, and ended him with a sharp punch to his throat. Gordon stood behind his chair, his hands white knuckled on the back of it.

Elaine stood up and turned to Gordon. "You murdered Rachel, and you are behind the imprisonment and almost death of my sister-in-law. You are a filthy rapist and a waste of space on this planet." Elaine pulled the glove off her left hand and turned the back of it toward him. "I was permanently scarred when you tried to burn down my house." She advanced on him. He backed up until he was pressed against the large window. She clenched the glove in her hand. "You've kidnapped Petra, and I want her back."

She slapped his mouth with the weighted glove. His face snapped to the side, and his lip split. Globs of blood and spittle flew and splattered the window. Robin shrieked. Elaine turned. Brian stood in the doorway with Petra naked and limp in his arms. Her wrists and ankles were bound. Dried blood stained her mouth.

A flash of movement caught her attention, and she turned back to Gordon. He grunted as he swung at her and landed a punch to Elaine's jaw. She rocked back on her heels. She tasted blood in her mouth. Sharp pain bloomed along her jaw. She set her feet and landed an uppercut on his chin. It snapped his head back. She advanced and punched him again, flattening his nose, and he crashed into the glass wall. The glass spiderwebbed with the impact of his body. He slid down the window, eyes closed.

Elaine turned to the scuffle behind her. Petra lay on the floor, still as death. Robin was on Brian's back pummeling him with her fists. He scrabbled at her and knocked her to the floor. He slapped her face and split her lip. He advanced on her as Robin scuttled away from him, eyes wide.

"Hey, asshole!" Elaine threw the chair cushion at Brian. He batted it aside. She lifted her hand and motioned him forward. "Come get some of this."

Brian advanced toward Elaine slowly, his fists raised. Three steps away he lowered his head, arms wide, and rushed her. Elaine waited until he was close and then spun to the side. She kicked him in the middle of his back. He crashed into the weakened glass. It fragmented around him, and he plunged through it to the ground below.

Elaine wrapped both hands in Gordon's collar and hauled him to his feet. She shook him until his eyes opened. "Say hello to Hubert." She held him up with one hand and punched his face. The crackle and thud of bone splintering as his face collapsed from the blow made her smile as she shoved him out the broken window.

Robin gasped behind her. When Elaine turned to her, Robin's eyes were wide. "You killed them."

Elaine frowned at her. "Yes."

"Thank you."

Petra moaned, and they turned as one.

"Tend to her. Find some clothes for her and her passport. I've got to contact Jaya. I hope she knows some reliable cleaners."

ELAINE SAT IN the chair next to the bed. She checked Petra's pulse for what must be the hundredth time since they had brought her back to the room. She had been unresponsive as they dressed her, and Robin had cried as she wiped away the blood on Petra's face. On the trip through the hotel lobby, they had made it appear as if she had overindulged. Elaine's rage swelled as she inventoried the deep bruises scattered over Petra's body. She wished she could resurrect Gordon and his crew and kill them again.

Petra had roused while they bathed her, mumbling incoherent words and flailing at them while they washed away the last remnants of her nightmare. Afterward they rubbed witch-hazel lotion into her skin and now she slept as loose as a rag doll. The bright-red ligature marks on her wrists and ankles turned Elaine's stomach.

Jaya had connected her with a cleaner. They had arrived, escorted them back to the hotel, and promised to return to deliver them to the airport. Elaine touched Petra's wrist. *Drugged. Bound and beaten. She wasn't part of it. Just bait. Maybe. Have to ask. Have to know.* She brushed a lock of her hair back and tucked it behind her ear.

Robin opened the door to the bathroom. She was wrapped in a white robe too large on her petite frame. "She's still out?" The worried expression on her face matched the fear in Elaine's heart.

"Yes. Whatever they gave her, it's powerful."

Robin sat on Elaine's lap. "There's a mix of drugs Gordon called the silver bullet." She shivered and snuggled closer. "He gave it to the uncooperative ones." She snorted. "He didn't have to give it to me. He threatened to give me heroin, to get me hooked again, and then take it away. Withdrawal is hell. I'd worked so hard to be clean. I could never go through it again."

Petra started awake and screamed. Robin rushed to the side of the bed. "You're safe. You're with us now. You're safe."

Petra's chest heaved, and she clutched the sheet around her. "How?" She stared at Elaine. "Where are we?"

Robin petted her arm. "Hotel in Oslo."

Elaine held out a glass of water. "Drink."

Petra's hand shook and water sloshed over the side of the glass as she sipped. She placed it on the table. "What happened? My last clear memory was arriving at the airport."

Elaine thrust her hands in her pockets. "Some old business we thought was taken care of, was not."

"The job offer was to lure you here with Robin." Elaine pulled her chair closer to the bed. "Petra, I am going to ask you this once and only once and then we will never speak of this again. Were you in any way bribed or manipulated to cooperate with those men? Was this a setup to lure Robin from Rowan House?"

Petra's lower lip trembled. "You think I could ever be involved in something so heinous?"

Robin clasped Petra's hand. "It happened to me. They kept me captive, threatened me. I was too afraid to fight them."

Petra averted her eyes. "The only way they manipulated me was my pride. Gordon used it against me. Offered me everything I ever dreamed of. But he couldn't have predicted…"

"Predicted what?" Elaine frowned. "Robin wouldn't leave? I would come for you?"

Petra met Elaine's gaze. "I would care for you"—she turned and picked up Robin's hand—"and you."

"He beat me when I wouldn't call and beg you to come." She pulled the sheet down to display the bruises on her body—evidence of her treatment and determination to keep them safe. "I thought I was dead anyway. I couldn't stand the thought of them killing you both."

Elaine left her chair and paced the room. "I hope this proves to you how ridiculous the idea of leaving us was."

Robin turned and arched an eyebrow at Elaine. "This is how you plan on wooing her to return with us?"

Petra pulled her hand from Robin's. "I haven't changed my mind about having clients or being the head Mistress of a house." She wiped her hand over her eyes.

Robin handed her a tissue. "We know. That doesn't mean…"

Elaine spoke over Robin. "We don't give a flying fuck if you want to have clients, but I'm not leaving here without you. We love you, damn it. Isn't it enough? You said you cared for us, whatever the hell that means, you were willing to die for us, and yet you can't live with us? What kind of fucked-up reasoning is that?"

Petra snorted. "I don't know. Stop pacing, you'll wear a hole in the carpet." She swung her legs over the side of the bed and stood. She swayed and reached for the nightstand to steady herself.

Robin grabbed her arm. "Sit down a minute."

Elaine was there instantly to help. "Easy. We'll get you to the bathroom."

Petra sat down on the bed and rubbed her eyes. She picked up her water glass and drained it before she placed it on the bedside table.

"Okay. Let's try again." Petra stood with Robin and Elaine's assistance.

They walked her to the door of the bathroom. She stopped and pulled free of Robin's grip on her arm before she grabbed the frame. "I can take it from here."

Robin put her hand on her hip. "No."

Petra turned around and fixed Robin with a hard gaze. "No what?"

Robin smiled and tilted her head at Petra. "No, Mistress. You're not steady and if you don't let me help, Elaine will."

Petra rolled her eyes. "All right. If you insist."

"I insist." Elaine stepped close to Petra and cupped the back of her neck and kissed her forehead. "A trip to the local surgery if you fall and need stitches will complicate things even more. As it is, I don't think I'll be able to return to Oslo anytime soon."

"Very well." Petra raised her chin and met Elaine's gaze. "Ma'am."

"Mistress. Call me Mistress." Elaine squeezed the back of Petra's neck and kissed her cheek. "Please hurry and get cleaned up so we can get out of here. Millie has a flight booked for us tonight, but we'll have to rush to make it to the airport."

Petra's eyes were fierce as she met Elaine's gaze. "Yes. Mistress."

Chapter Twenty-One

ELAINE SIPPED HER tea. The kitchen was quiet, the hum of the refrigerator the only sound in the early morning dark. Their flight had been uneventful. Jaya's cleaners were so efficient she had not seen any notice of the deaths she had caused. She had crossed a line. A big one. One Rowan House had skirted over the years. She grimaced when she thought of how Martha would react, as well as the necessity now for added expense as they coped with the aftermath. *Was Gordon really the boss? He didn't seem smart enough to orchestrate everything. More money for Jaya and protection.* She rested her head in her hands. *How the hell did this happen? Again. And Petra. Will she stay?*

The door opened. Elaine didn't bother to raise her head. The scent of Petra's gardenia perfume wafted around her. Cool hands stroked the back of her neck, and then down over her shoulders. Elaine raised her head. "Did you sleep well?"

Petra leaned down and pressed her cheek against Elaine's. "Well enough."

She pulled a chair over and sat close to Elaine and covered her hand with her own. "I don't have words to thank you." She lifted Elaine's hand to her mouth and kissed her knuckles. "You saved me from a living hell. Gordon was going to sell me to the highest bidder." A shudder ran through her frame.

"No need to thank me. A good Mistress would have never let you leave."

"You gave me what I asked for, you respected my choice as any good Mistress should."

Elaine tugged Petra close and kissed her. "I'm not sure what I would have done if they had harmed you more than they did."

Petra's eyes darkened. "According to Robin, you were unrecognizable in your fury. Those men…"

"We are not going to speak of it. It's my responsibility. The less you know the better."

Petra met her gaze. "We are either in this together equally, or not at all"—she cupped Elaine's face with both hands—"Mistress." She kissed Elaine hard.

Elaine broke their kiss and pulled back. She brushed Petra's hair from her eyes. "Come with me." She locked her fingers around Petra's wrist and pulled her close for another kiss before turning and leading her through the door.

PETRA STOPPED AND set her feet outside the door to Elaine's suite. "Your room?"

Elaine pulled her close and wrapped her arms around her. "Yes." She stepped back. "Problem?"

Petra pulled free. "I don't know. I don't know if I'm ready for a commitment."

Elaine pursed her lips. "Come inside. We can't have this discussion without Robin."

The door opened and Robin frowned at them. "You two are ridiculous. Get in here and stop squawking like a pair of banty hens."

She turned away from them. Elaine flushed and followed her inside.

Petra closed the door, turned the deadbolt, and then flipped the bar lock in place. "We are not leaving this room until this is sorted."

Robin pointed at the bed. "I read it's harder to be angry lying down. We'll have our discussion there." Robin padded over to the bed, mounted it, and scooted to the middle of the king-size mattress.

Elaine toed off her shoes before she stretched out next to Robin. "Fine with me."

Petra rolled her eyes and huffed out a breath before she slipped off her pumps. She lay on her side on the opposite side of Robin.

Robin took each of their hands. "'Better." She curled her arms up to her chin, drawing them closer. "We are each in love with the other and to deny it would be a lie. We need to decide for ourselves what our relationship will be."

Elaine pursed her lips. "I don't even know what I want other than I know I want to be with you both."

Petra's lip trembled. "I want to be with you both. But I'm afraid of not having the freedom to be with clients. I crave the thrill. I need it. To deny it would be a lie."

Elaine's heart squeezed. "I know. And I understand the difference between clients and partners."

Robin lifted Petra's hand and kissed the back of it. "I know the difference too. I'm not willing to give you up. Elaine and I have agreed to be only with each other and you. We wouldn't demand or expect it of you."

Petra snuggled closer next to Robin. "I don't know if it's right to ask that of you."

Elaine held on to Robin's hand and raised herself. She took Petra's hand and laced their fingers together. "Right or not, we want you to be with us. We get to choose how it works. I want you both to be mine, to pledge to me, and I want to pledge to both of you." She lifted Petra's hand to her lips and kissed her knuckles. "Petra, there is space in our lives for you. Be with us. Stay with us."

"Here? What about the head Mistress?" Petra smirked. "I heard she's a real hard ass."

Elaine nipped the skin over the back of Petra's hand making her hiss. "Oh she is, but I heard she's planning to retire. And is seeking a replacement."

"Retire completely?" Petra's put-on moue of disappointment made Elaine smile.

"Not completely." Elaine tugged Petra close and kissed her as she slid her hand up to tweak her nipple. Petra yipped and broke their kiss.

"Oh please, don't stop. I could watch the two of you forever." Robin's voice was a reverent plea.

"Could you now?" Elaine leaned down and kissed Robin, taking her time and leaving them both breathless. "Forever?"

Robin groaned. "Forever, Mistress."

Petra's hand on the back of Elaine's neck made her start. She lifted her head and searched for meaning in Petra's obsidian eyes. Their gazes locked and Petra kissed her, sucking her lower lip between her teeth, nipping her, and drawing blood. "Do you want this, forever?"

The uncertain expression on her face squeezed Elaine's heart. Elaine shook off Petra's grip on her neck, wrapped her arm around her, and tugged her down to the bed. She shifted until she lay over both women, framing them with her arms, before she kissed them both soundly. "And a day."

Epilogue

ONE YEAR LATER

The dull green water lapped against the side of the ship as they sailed between the fantastically shaped rocky islands that erupted haphazardly across Ha Long Bay. Elaine leaned on the rail and studied the chaotic scene behind them as they sailed from the overcrowded dock.

"It's amazing, isn't it?" Petra's voice in her ear was husky. She draped her arm over Elaine's shoulders.

"Amazing and insane. I didn't think we were going to ever get clear of that melee at the dock without a collision. Where's Robin?"

"She's forward taking photos with the camera Lucia gave her. I've never seen her so relaxed in public." Petra leaned back against the ship's rail.

Elaine rolled her shoulders and straightened her posture. "After seeing how packed the other tour boats are, I'm glad we chartered this one. It wouldn't have suited her to be packed in with so many other people."

"Me either."

The boat steward approached, nodded politely to Elaine, and then spoke to Petra.

Elaine listened to their exchange and was grateful she had given attention to Petra's attempt to teach her Vietnamese. They finished their conversation and he left them.

"Did you get any of that?'

"Luncheon will be on the afterdeck? And something about pirates?"

Petra laughed and pinched Elaine's hip. "Close. Dinner will be served on the afterdeck and luncheon is served on the foredeck in about three hours. Tomorrow we'll meet our guide and explore some of the caves on the islands, where various invaders, pirates, and others have hidden over the years." Petra leaned closer and nibbled Elaine's earlobe.

"Keep doing that and we might miss luncheon."

"I know. Want to collect our girl and check out our cabin?"

Elaine leaned back to look into Petra's face. "Are you in a hurry? We have the next two weeks to check out our cabin."

Petra's eyes gleamed. "You finally talk me into pledging to you two and take a holiday, and now you're making me wait to take advantage of you?"

Elaine moved close to Petra, cupped the back of her neck, and rubbed her thumb over the graceful curve of her throat as she pressed her against the rail "Who said you'd be the one taking advantage?" She glanced down at Petra's dress. Her peaked nipples were obvious as they tented the red silk.

Petra's nostrils flared. "How do you do that?"

"What?" Elaine smirked at her.

"Make me want to drop to my knees right here?" Petra raised her hands and looped them around Elaine's neck.

"Starting without me?" Robin's mock tone of offense startled them. She lifted the camera and snapped a photo of Elaine and Petra. "Come on then. I've plans for you two."

Elaine stepped back and Petra looped her arm through hers. "You do?"

Robin lifted her chin. "Oh yes." She turned away and used the flat of her hand to draw up her skirt to reveal her lack of panties and perfect ass before she shot them a saucy look over her shoulder. "I do." She scampered away from them toward their cabin.

Elaine started after her and Petra held tight to her arm impeding her progress. Elaine raised an eyebrow and glared at her.

Petra released her arm and stepped in front of her, blocking her path. "So impatient. Where's she going to go? We're on a ship in the middle of a huge bay. No one here but us and a very discreet crew." She inched up the hem of her dress before she pulled it over her head to reveal a red sheer bra and matching thong. She tossed the dress at Elaine before she turned and ran in the direction Robin had taken.

Elaine caught the dress in her hand before she bolted after the two women she would follow anywhere.

About the Author

Brenda Murphy writes short stories and novels. She is a member of Romance Writers of America and the Golden Crown Literary Society. When she is not loitering at her local library and writing, she wrangles one dog and an unrepentant parrot. She writes about life, books, photography, and writing on her blog, writingwhiledistracted.com.

I hope you enjoyed reading this book as much as I enjoyed writing it. For information on book signings, appearances, work in progress snippets, previews and sneak-peeks, sign up for my email list at:

Website: www.brendalmurphy.com

Join my private readers group on Facebook:
www.facebook.com/Writing-While-Distracted

Twitter: @bmurphysideshow

Other books by this author

Dominique and Other Stories

One

The Rowan House series
Sum of the Whole
Both Ends of the Whip
Knotted Legacy
Complex Dimensions

Also Available from NineStar Press

Connect with NineStar Press

www.ninestarpress.com

www.facebook.com/ninestarpress

www.facebook.com/groups/NineStarNiche

www.twitter.com/ninestarpress

www.tumblr.com/blog/ninestarpress

www.ingramcontent.com/pod-product-compliance
Lightning Source LLC
Chambersburg PA
CBHW062019190726

48284CB00012B/708

9 781951 057848